SECOND CHANCE

Book Surge ISBN: 1-4611-1756-9

www.bluespikepublishing.com

Printed in the United States of America

To Vion DeCew

Author's Notes

One of the reason I write, is to challenge myself. With *The Quarter Boys*, the challenge was simply to prove that I could actually write a complete novel. With *Echoes*, the challenge was to prove that the first book hadn't just been a fluke, and to write something with more emotional depth that focused on character development. With this book, the challenge I set was to write a more complex mystery.

Not that the first two books weren't without some twists and turns, but I felt that the central mysteries were fairly straight-forward. So this time, I wanted to see if I could create something more intricate, without it becoming convoluted.

Things were sailing along until I got to a key plot point at the halfway mark, and suddenly realized that my entire logic was flawed because the motivation of one of the characters made no sense whatsoever. At that point, I went back and did what I should have done in the first place, and figured out what was driving each character's actions. It was a valuable, though painful, lesson: figure out the emotional and intellectual logic before rigging the plot details.

As alway, I'm indebted to my friends, my family, and my husband, Brian, for sharing me with the invisible people who live in my head for a few months (again), and to Esme McTighe for proofreading.

D.L.

OTHER BOOKS FROM DAVID LENNON

The Quarter Boys

Echoes

Blue's Bayou
(Available October 2011)

Reckoning
(Available April 2012)

SECOND CHANCE

A Novel

DAVID LENNON

Prologue

Chance surveyed the crowd gathered around his father's grave in the bright morning sun, as the minister intoned about the life of a man who hadn't passed through the doors of a church in over forty years. Chance had expected his best friend, Joel, and Joel's grandparents, Pappy and Mammau Gaulthier, to be there, and perhaps a few of his father's drinking cronies if they'd been able to get out of bed in time, but there were at least three dozen people at the funeral. About half looked to be his father's age, the rest quite a bit older.

I guess that's life in a small town, he thought. People may avoid you and talk shit behind your back for your whole life, but when you die, everyone turns out to pay their respects. He didn't feel any bitterness at the thought. In fact he found it oddly comforting. It was proof of the connection between all these people whose lives were rooted in the local soil.

He looked at Pappy and Mammau and saw genuine sadness on their faces. He wondered if it was sadness for his father or for him. He suspected it was both. Even though his father's life had been one long downward spiral, he knew from firsthand experience that Joel's grandparents had an unwavering belief in the value of every person. They always saw the potential rather than dwelling on the mistakes. Regardless of his own many mistakes, they'd never lost faith in him.

A movement behind Pappy's right shoulder caught his attention and Chance shifted his gaze. Although he hadn't seen her in fifteen years, he recognized his mother immediately.

1

Luanne LeDuc hadn't changed much. She was still small and trim, though her once-girlish features had grown somewhat harder. It wasn't the hardness of alcohol and anger that had ravaged the face of his father, Chance Sr., however, but rather a hardness that spoke of maturity and resolve. Though he hated to admit it, Chance thought it suited her. She looked more capable.

She was dressed in a simple, knee-length, black dress with cap sleeves and a high scoop neck that looked as though its sole purpose might be for attending funerals. Her blond hair was pulled back and knotted in a bun. Again, Chance had to admit that the warm honey color suited his mother far better than the peroxide blond she'd had the last time he'd seen her.

He quickly averted his eyes, afraid that Luanne might look up at him.

He felt a sudden swell of anxiety. Although he'd never expected his father to live past fifty, the end had been a shock. He'd always imagined a long, slow decline, with his father hanging on for years, making life miserable for everyone around him—especially Chance—for as long as possible. That his father had died peacefully in his sleep of a heart attack had come as a surprise and a blessing. It was the first thing he could ever remember his father having done with grace. Still, it had stirred up an unexpected mix of feelings—anger, regret, relief, guilt—that had already taken a heavy toll on him emotionally. Now to see his mother again after so many years was overwhelming him.

Luanne had left one night when Chance was seven, while his father was passed out on the sofa. She'd never come back. There'd never been any calls or letters. It was as if she'd simply vanished.

For the first few months Chance's father had continued to insist she'd be back, at first optimistically, then angrily, saying that "the bitch has no place else to go." Then he'd stopped talking about her altogether. But Chance had kept hoping.

Every morning he'd wake up and run to his parents' bedroom on the chance that she might have reappeared during the night as mysteriously as she'd disappeared.

Eventually he'd realized that she wouldn't be back, but he kept hoping that someday she'd send for him. Finally, by the time he'd turned thirteen, even that hope was gone, and if he thought about his mother at all—which wasn't often—it was with resentment and anger.

To see her now brought all his old feelings to the surface, heightening his already raw emotional state. He literally wanted to scream to release the pressure.

Suddenly he became aware that the minister had stopped speaking and looked up. The other mourners were all staring at him expectantly, and he realized they were waiting for him to place the first flower on his father's casket.

He took a deep breath and forced himself to step forward, then gently placed the red carnation on the polished pine surface.

*****

"People will be coming back to the house," Mammau said. "Do you want to walk back with us?"

Chance shook his head distractedly.

"No, I just need a few minutes. Go on ahead and I'll meet you there."

"Okay," Mammau said with an understanding look.

Chance walked back to the grave and stared at the carnation-strewn coffin. He could hear distant voices, and then tires receding down the gravel road behind him. So this is it, he thought.

A shadow appeared alongside his own on the side of the casket.

"So did you come to dance on his grave, Luanne?" Chance asked coldly without looking up.

"No," Luanne LeDuc replied in a soft voice. "I couldn't stay with him, but I never hated him."

Although it had been a long time since he'd heard it, his mother's voice was instantly familiar. The soft drawl and lilting cadence seemed like they had always been with him. He felt a momentary, reflexive sense of comfort, but pushed the feeling away and turned to face his mother.

"And what about me?" he asked, his eyes flashing with anger. "Could you just not stay with me, too?"

Luanne flinched but didn't reply.

"Because if you loved me, I don't understand how you could have left me behind with him," Chance continued, his voice breaking with emotion. "Didn't you know he'd take it out on me? That he'd punish me for you leaving?"

"I'm sorry, Chance," Luanne replied quietly. "I'm so sorry."

"Well, gee, that just makes it all better," Chance replied acidly. "Why don't we just hug now and things will all be better. No harm, no foul."

"Stop it," Luanne said, her voice suddenly more forceful. "I did what I had to do. If I'd stayed, eventually he would have killed me."

"Oh, but you weren't afraid he'd kill me?" Chance asked sarcastically.

"No," Luanne replied flatly. "You were his flesh and blood. He couldn't kill you. He loved you."

Chance snorted derisively.

"Is that what you call that? Love?" he asked. "Beating me, ignoring me, acting like he could barely stand to look at me?"

Luanne was quiet for a moment. She stared at the ground as though trying to collect her thoughts. Finally she looked up at Chance and her pale blue eyes—his eyes—were kind and maternal.

"Can we sit down?" she asked, gesturing toward a granite bench in the shade of a nearby oak tree. "There are some things I think you need to understand about your daddy."

Chance hesitated before responding. A part of him wanted to tell his mother to just fuck off and leave. At the same time, another part of him was glad to see her, and still another part was curious about why she'd come back and what she had to say.

"Okay," he replied grudgingly.

They settled on the bench and Luanne took a deep breath before speaking.

"He wasn't always the way he was when you knew him," she began. "In fact, he used to be a lot like you."

Chance felt a surge of anger that his mother would presume to know anything about him, but decided to hold his tongue.

"I remember when my family moved here," Luanne continued. "I was fourteen. All the other girls told me to stay away from Chance LeDuc. They said he was crazy, that his family was no good, and that associating with his kind could only lead to trouble. But I saw something different. No doubt he had a wild streak a mile wide, but mostly what I saw was hurt. He was like a wounded animal that was lashing out, and I thought that maybe if someone showed him some kindness he'd be different.

"So after a few weeks, I passed him a note in science class asking him to meet me at Miller's Pond after school."

Luanne's eyes became focused on the middle distance and her voice grew softer, as though she were reliving a dream.

"I remember I was so nervous," she continued. "Chance was the most handsome boy I'd ever seen. And I was afraid he'd think I was one of *those* kind of girls for being so forward. But when he showed up, he was shy and sweet and funny, and I think I fell in love with him that very afternoon."

Chance tried to imagine the person his mother was describing.

"We started going steady a few days later," Luanne continued. "Everyone told me I was going to get hurt, but I didn't care because I was convinced that Chance was a good man. With other people he was mostly sullen or just plain mean, but I knew that was just his way of protecting himself so he wouldn't get his feelings hurt. When we were alone together he was kind and gentle, and he loved to talk about his dreams."

"Wait a second," Chance interrupted. "He had dreams?"

"Of course he had dreams," Luanne snapped, breaking out of her reverie. "He was a young man."

Chance nodded, acknowledging her reproach.

"He always said that someday we'd get out of Natchez and that he'd get a job in a city and we'd have a nice house in the suburbs and a Cadillac," Luanne continued. "Maybe they weren't grand dreams, but they were dreams.

"But there was a darker side to your daddy, too, even then. Sometimes after he'd had a few drinks and was feeling melancholy, he'd talk about 'the family curse.' He was convinced that somewhere in the past, someone had done something terrible that had brought a curse on the family. He said that's why they'd lost their money and become outcasts. He was always afraid that some day the curse would touch him, too."

She sighed and shook her headly sadly before continuing.

"You have to understand, your daddy hated his life here. He hated his daddy for the way he treated him, and he hated that he had to live in a run-down old house, and mostly he hated that people treated him like he was damaged because he was another one of 'those crazy LeDucs.'"

"I know the feeling," Chance said.

Luanne smiled sympathetically.

"The worst thing your daddy could imagine was being stuck here and ending up like his own daddy," Luanne continued. "He wanted to go somewhere where no one knew his family, where he could make a fresh start. Just like you."

Instead of anger, this time Chance felt surprise that his mother did seem to know some things about him. He considered asking her how, but decided to wait.

"So why didn't you both leave?" he asked instead.

"We did," Luanne responded. "The summer before our senior year, on your daddy's 17th birthday, we packed up his truck and moved to Woodville where he'd gotten a job working in a lumber mill. Oh, the trouble that caused. My parents told me if I left they'd disown me. And they pretty much did for a long time."

She gave Chance a small, wistful smile, then the smile suddenly warmed.

"And about a month later I found out I was pregnant with you so we got married," she said.

Chance blinked his eyes in wonderment as he tried to reconcile the image of his parents that Luanne was describing with the people he'd known. He felt as though he'd just discovered he was adopted.

"Do you know why he wanted to name you after himself?" Luanne asked suddenly, staring meaningfully into Chance's eyes.

Chance shook his head.

"Because he said you'd be his second chance," Luanne said. "He wanted to give you all the things he never had so that your life could be different."

Chance was stunned. The father he'd known had always seemed intent on belittling him and tearing him down.

"For about a year things were good," Luanne continued. "We rented a small house and your daddy fixed up a room for you, and we even bought a new car. But that's when things started to go bad. Just after you were born, your daddy hurt his back in an accident at the mill and was out of work for about a month, and then when he went back they told him they didn't need him anymore.

"We tried to make do for a while and your daddy was able to pick up some odd jobs here and there, but no steady work, and after a few months the money was gone and we had to move back here."

Again she sighed.

"After he lost the job at the mill, your daddy had started to change," she said. "It was like the light was gone from his eyes and he got moody sometimes. But when we moved back in with his daddy, it got much worse.

"I thought he was stronger than that, but I guess when you live with a fear for that long and then it seems to be coming true, it takes a hard toll. It also didn't help that his daddy rubbed it in his face, ragging on him for thinking he was something special and that he could escape his family's past. If it'd been anyone else who'd said those things, your daddy might have killed him, but your daddy was scared of his daddy. His daddy had a power over him. It was a terrible thing to see."

For the first time he could remember, Chance felt sympathy for his father.

"I think your daddy was sort of a tortured soul," Luanne continued. "He had a struggle between doing what was good and doing what came naturally, what he'd learned from his daddy and granddaddy. He'd tried hard to overcome his worst self, but when things went bad he seemed to lose the will. I think he decided that if he was cursed he might as well just become exactly what everyone expected of him.

"He stopped trying to find work, and every day his mood grew darker and he was drinking more. He started getting into fights in town, and he began..." Luanne trailed off.

"Beating you?" Chance asked softly.

Luanne nodded with a look of embarrassment.

"But there was no place for me to go. I didn't have any money, and as I said, my folks had disowned me and I didn't even know where they were because they'd moved while we were in Woodville."

There was a moment of thoughtful silence, then suddenly Luanne brightened.

"So now do you understand what I meant about your daddy loving you?"

"Huh?" Chance replied.

He felt as though he'd fallen asleep during a movie and missed a crucial plot point.

"Weren't you paying attention?" Luanne asked with a look that suggested she'd just discovered he was simple.

"I guess not," Chance stammered.

Luanne gave an exasperated sigh and fixed Chance with her eyes.

"He treated you the way he did because he was trying to protect you," she explained slowly. "He didn't want you to go through what he did, so he figured that if you didn't have any grand expectations you wouldn't be hurt when your life didn't amount to much."

"That's it?" Chance asked incredulously.

"What do you mean?" Luanne asked, giving him a perplexed look.

Chance fought a sudden urge to laugh at Luanne's perverse logic. He realized that despite her attempts at insightfulness, she was still just a simple country girl whose greatest ambition had probably been to run off and marry her high school sweetheart, and then later to escape him. Then he realized that she had inadvertently provided some plausible reasons for the way his father had treated him—resentment, a projection of self-loathing, bitterness about his own failure—though she'd missed the point herself. Still, he couldn't keep a small smirk from crossing his lips.

"What?" Luanne asked with a hint of testiness.

"Nothing," Chance replied, forcing himself to look serious. "I get it now. Makes perfect sense."

Luanne studied him for a moment, as though trying to discern whether he was telling the truth.

"Good," she said, apparently satisfied.

Again they were quiet for a moment before Luanne broke the silence again.

"So I imagine you're wondering where I've been?"

"The thought had crossed my mind," Chance replied dryly. "That and why you didn't take me with you."

"Because I knew he'd come after us," Luanne replied. "I knew he'd be angry if I left, but after a while he'd let it go. But he'd never have let me take you. Besides, I was only twenty-two when I left. I didn't have any money. I didn't have a job or a home for you. I figured you'd be better off with your daddy for a while because at least you'd have a roof over your head.

"I kept thinking that once I had enough money saved I'd get a two-bedroom apartment and find a lawyer and get custody of you legally. But then I got married again and had your baby sister, Daisy, but that marriage didn't work out and it wasn't legal anyway because your daddy and I were still married. So then I was on my own again and raising the baby to boot. I kept thinking I'd get you soon, but the years kept passing and after a while I figured that maybe it was best if I stayed away because I was sure by then you'd hate me."

Chance felt as though he were watching an episode of Jerry Springer. It amazed him that both of his parents had chosen to hurt him, believing it would be in his best interest.

"But I kept checking up on you," Luanne continued breathlessly. "I used to call Mrs. Gaulthier every few months."

"Mammau?" Chance asked, surprised that his mother knew Joel's grandmother.

"Yeah, I ran into her in Fayette one day and she recognized me and told me that you and her grandson were best friends, so I asked her if it would be all right if I called now and again to see how you were doing. She told me about you moving to New Orleans and how you got stabbed. I went to the hospital to visit you once, but your daddy was there so I didn't go in the room, and then another time..."

"Okay, okay," Chance said impatiently, holding up his right hand. "So why are you here now?"

Luanne gave him a slightly hurt look at having been interrupted so abruptly.

"Because I have to fulfill a promise I made to your great granddaddy," she replied.

She reached into her purse, took out a thick yellowed envelope, and held it out toward Chance.

"What is it?" he asked, eyeing the envelope suspiciously.

"It's your inheritance," Luanne replied.

"Inheritance?" Chance laughed. "There hasn't been any money in our family for over a hundred years."

"That's not true," Luanne replied. "Your great granddaddy had some money. You'd never have known it to look at him, but he had money that'd been passed down to him."

Chance reached out slowly and took the envelope.

"But why would he leave it to me?" he asked.

"Because your great granddaddy knew that your granddaddy and your daddy would waste it," Luanne replied. "They were both big disappointments to him, and he didn't want to see what was left of the family fortune squandered.

"A few months before I left—about a year before he died—he gave me that envelope and told me to give it to when your daddy passed. He said that he hoped you'd be able to use it to make something of yourself so you could break the cycle."

Chance opened the envelope and pulled out the folded sheaves of paper. He straightened them on his lap and began reading.

It was a trust document in his name, dated September 5, 1990. The principal amount at the time it was executed had been $175,000.

He looked up at Luanne, fighting back sudden tears.

"The Gaulthiers are having people back to the house," he said quietly. "Do you want to go with me...momma?"

Chapter 1

"You realize that seniority means nothing now," Michel said, without looking up from the box he was unpacking.

"What do you *mean* it means nothing?" Sassy asked, eyeing him dubiously.

She was kneeling next to a book shelf with a copy of "The SAGE Directory of Criminology"—one of the many reference books Michel was convinced they'd need—in her right hand.

"Well, I have no experience as a private investigator and you have no experience as a private investigator," Michel replied, "so we're starting off level."

"Fine," Sassy replied breezily, "but Jones & Doucette sounds *so* much better."

It had been almost nine months since Alexandra "Sassy" Jones and Michel Doucette had left the New Orleans Police Department's Homicide Division—Sassy by choice, Michel by necessity. Sassy had taken the opportunity to go on a month-long vacation to Spain and Portugal, while Michel had puttered around his house and spent time with his on-again-off-again-maybe-on-again boyfriend, Joel.

When Sassy returned, they'd leased an empty two-story brick building halfway between Cemetery #1 and Louis Armstrong Park on N. Rampart Street, bordering the French Quarter. The owner was an elderly man who'd nearly forgotten he owned the building, and he was willing to rent it for seven hundred dollars a month so long as Sassy and Michel paid for any necessary renovations. The necessary renovations had been substantial. They'd spent most of June, July, and August replacing water-damaged dry wall, sanding and refinishing the floors, putting in new windows, painting, and patching the roof. Their goal had been to open their agency in early September, but then the hurricane had hit, the levees were breached, and flood waters covered eighty percent of the city. Although the area around the building hadn't flooded, there had been substantial water damage through the still-leaking roof. For the next few months, they'd alternated between helping with the city's clean up and getting the building ready again. Now, in mid-January, they were finally open for business.

"Says who?" Michel asked, looking back at her. "Besides, alphabetically Doucette comes before Jones. We don't want our clients to have to search through an extra twenty pages of the phone book before they find us."

"Okay, then let's call it Aardvark Detective Agency," Sassy replied sarcastically, as she stood and brushed the knees of her loose-fitting jeans. "Besides, who uses a phone book anymore? What are you, eighty? Ooh, and maybe we can give our clients S&H Green Stamps and toasters, too."

"Are you *sure* you're not a lesbian?" Michel replied as he made a show of surveying Sassy's clothes from her Birkenstock sandals to her pale yellow t-shirt.

In all the years he'd known her, he'd never seen Sassy in anything other than stylish business attire until they'd begun work on the building. Michel was certain that she'd had to make a special trip to buy the assortment of jeans and t-shirts she'd been wearing since. He was equally certain that Sassy was counting down the days until she could drop them at a homeless shelter.

"Wow, way to stereotype," Sassy replied, shaking her head with feigned offense. "Glad to see that sensitivity training the department paid for didn't go to waste."

Michel gave her a satisfied grin as Joel walked into the room carrying a large cardboard box. Sweat ran down his face from his matted hair and his white t-shirt was plastered to his slim torso.

"I'm sure this is a really important high-level discussion," he said, placing the box on top of a desk with a theatrical grunt, "but maybe when you're done one of you could give the peon a hand carrying in some of *your* shit?"

"You're just lucky we're letting you hang out with the cool kids," Michel replied.

"Oh, is that what you are?" Joel laughed. "The cool kids? Do the other folks at the retirement home know that?"

Michel responded by miming an exaggerated laugh.

There was a thudding sound from the hallway and Michel and Sassy exchanged curious looks. Suddenly Chance stumbled through the door carrying a large box with a dented corner on the bottom right side.

"Sorry about that," he said, with an embarrassed smile. "Nothing a little plaster and paint can't fix...I hope."

"Chance," Sassy exclaimed in surprise. "Last time I saw you, you were almost dead."

Sixteen months earlier Chance had been stabbed while trying to rescue Joel from a serial killer. When Michel and Sassy found him, his pulse had been barely detectable.

"Yeah, fortunately I got over that," Chance replied. "So where do you guys want this heavy fucker?"

*****

After his father's death, Chance had met with the investment advisor in Jackson who'd been managing his trust for the past twenty-three years. At his great grandfather's request, the investments had been relatively conservative, but the trust had still managed a solid five percent average annual return rate, growing from $175,000 to just over $550,000.

Chance realized that he could live on the money for at least ten years so long as he didn't go too crazy, but he knew that that hadn't been his great grandfather's intention. His great grandfather had wanted him to use the money to make something of himself, not go into temporary retirement at the ripe old age of twenty-three.

To pass the time while he decided what to do, he'd begun fixing up his father's house. He'd hired a few local tradesmen and set about renovating it from the foundation up. While he was fairly hopeless with a hammer himself, he discovered he was very good at other aspects of the project. He found it easy to envision how the space could be changed, and had a knack for calculating the time and amount of materials it would take to complete each task. He was also very good at managing the crew, and they seemed to enjoy working with him.

Most importantly, and much to his surprise, he'd found that he actually enjoyed the work. It engaged his mind in a way he couldn't remember anything else having done, and as each phase of the project was completed it gave him great satisfaction to see the fruits of his work. It also gave him pleasure to see the once-dilapidated house returned to a glory he'd never witnessed. On some level he felt as though he were giving something back to his family, perhaps restoring their dignity.

As the renovation was nearing completion, he began noticing how many other buildings in the town had fallen into similar disrepair, and realized there might be a business opportunity in rehabbing and renting them. It wasn't that he thought he could make a lot of money—the median household income in the town was about half the national average, with a quarter of the residents living below the poverty line—but he thought he'd be able to make enough to recoup his initial investment, keep the properties properly maintained, and earn a comfortable living. It would also give him a chance to keep doing something he enjoyed and for which he demonstrated an aptitude.

The name for his venture had come to him one morning as he drifted in that space between sleep and waking, and as he heard it in his mind he'd snapped awake. Second Chance Property Development. Immediately he'd known it was right. It perfectly embodied everything he hoped to achieve: a second chance for the buildings; a second chance for the people who rented apartments in them, living in well-maintained, safe homes with modern amenities; a second chance for the town through jobs and revitalized neighborhoods; a second chance to prove himself; and perhaps most importantly, a second chance to rehabilitate the name LeDuc in the town's eyes. He also relished the irony that it was the nickname his father had given him before deciding Chance had no chance of succeeding in life.

He'd started by buying a ten-unit brick apartment building and a motel with fifteen efficiency units surrounding a courtyard and pool. He'd dubbed them "227" and "Melrose Place" respectively. "227" was completed in early June and "Melrose Place" at the end of July. The total cost for the buildings and renovation was $450,000. All twenty-five units were rented by the time they'd opened, for an average of $500/month. He'd hired the father of one of his crew members to manage and maintain the properties for $3,000/month, and set aside another $2,000/month for insurance and maintenance costs. Assuming there were no unforeseen expenses, he'd recoup his initial investment in exactly five years.

His plan had been to mortgage the two properties—something he hadn't been able to do when he bought them given the speculative nature of his business and his own poor credit history—and use the money for his next project. When the hurricane hit in late August, he knew that next project would be in New Orleans.

*****

"So after the hurricane, I started thinking maybe it was time for me to give New Orleans a second chance," Chance said.

He was seated on one of the room's two desks, with Joel beside him. Michel and Sassy were in chairs facing them.

"To be honest, I'd been kind of afraid to come back because I didn't know if I'd fall back into my old life," he continued, "but I figured that with a project to work on that wouldn't be a problem.

"My first thought was to do what I'd been doing back home, but at most I could do maybe two or three projects a year, which would just be a drop in the bucket. So then I started thinking about finding something bigger that could be the cornerstone of revitalizing an entire area."

"Sounds pretty ambitious," Sassy offered.

"I know," Chance replied, "which is why I knew I'd have to partner with someone with a lot more experience.

"I was envisioning something that combined both commercial and residential. The residential would be high-end and mid-level condos, plus low-income rentals. That way it would actually benefit a whole community. Then there'd be shops and restaurants and stuff to draw tourists and people from outside the neighborhood, which would help subsidize the rentals and turn a profit for the developers."

Despite his initial skepticism when Chance told them he'd entered the property development business, Michel had to admit to himself that he was impressed.

"So I started doing some research into similar projects that had been done in the area," Chance continued, "and two names kept coming up: Henry Patterson and James Cornell."

"Why do those names sound so familiar?" Sassy asked.

"I'll get to that in a minute," Chance replied, sounding a little uncomfortable.

"So, anyway, after about a week of trying, I got in touch with Patterson and Cornell and told them my idea. At first they thought I was nuts, but as I explained the concept and what I thought it could do for the city, they seemed interested and agreed to meet with me."

"You were here and you didn't call me?" Joel asked with a hurt look.

Chance gave him a guilty smile.

"I'm sorry, but I just didn't want to talk about what I was doing until I was sure it was going to happen. What can I say? I'm kind of a drama queen. I wanted the big 'ta da' moment when I'd reveal everything."

Joel shrugged a grudging acceptance of Chance's explanation, but still looked hurt.

"So I came down here in October and Patterson and Cornell took me to some buildings they owned down by the Louisa Street Wharf. Originally I'd been thinking of doing something in the 9th Ward, but they said it was a lost cause for now because of the infrastructure damage. And when I saw their buildings I realized that it was perfect location for kicking off a renaissance in Bywater."

"Wait a second," Sassy said quickly, holding both hands out in front of her. "These buildings wouldn't happen to have been the old Bluehawk Terminal buildings, would they?"

Chance averted his eyes and chewed his lower lip for a few seconds.

"Uh, yeah," he replied in a small voice.

"Jesus Christ, Chance," Sassy exclaimed. "You got yourself involved with some of Priest Lee's boys? What the hell were you thinking?"

"Hey, sorry if I'm not familiar with your local gangsters," Chance replied defensively. "Besides, they've worked on a lot of legit projects."

"What's going on?" Michel asked, suddenly confused. "I'm missing something."

"You *do* know who Priest Lee is, don't you?" Sassy asked.

Michel nodded.

"Yeah, of course. Owner of Jacard-Lee Development Corporation, society bigwig...oh, and he happens to be the head of one of the largest crime families in the city."

"Exactly," Sassy replied. "And you heard about the fire two weeks ago at the Bluehawk Terminal?"

Michel looked embarrassed.

"I'm afraid I missed that one."

Sassy gave him a dumbfounded look.

"Really? A huge fire less than a mile from your house and you missed it? Seriously, Michel, sometimes I wonder about you."

"Hey, don't be getting mad at me," Michel replied. "I didn't do anything wrong."

Sassy fixed her eyes back on Chance.

"So what happened?" she asked forcefully.

Chance shifted uncomfortably on the desk.

"I told Patterson and Cornell..."

"You mean 'Bulldog' and 'Double-J'," Sassy corrected reproachfully, having remembered the street names more commonly used by Patterson and Cornell.

"Uh yeah, 'Bulldog' and 'Double-J'," Chance replied sheepishly. "I told them that I wanted to be a full partner in the project."

"And what did they say?" Sassy asked, her tone making it clear she was an experienced interrogator.

"They said they'd give me a 15% stake if I paid all the upfront costs to put together a prospectus for investors," Chance replied. "Since they already had the equity of the building, I'd have to buy my way in by covering the costs for the architect, structural engineer, a designer to create an identity for the project, a feasibility study, environmental impact study, traffic study, etc... They said it would cost around half a million."

"And that seemed like a good idea to you?" Sassy asked, raising one eyebrow questioningly.

Chance nodded.

"Look, they may be gangsters, but they're also business men. Everything seemed on the up and up. We signed a contract. I kept control of my money and just paid the bills as they came in."

"And where'd you get the money?" Michel asked.

"They arranged a loan for me using my property as collateral,"

"From a loan shark?"

"No, from a bank. They even co-signed the loan."

Everyone was silent for a moment.

"So how big of a project are we talking here?" Michel asked finally.

"About 90,000 square feet of retail space," Chance replied. "Almost half the size of the RiverWalk."

"Well, no one can accuse you of thinking small," Michel said, shaking his head.

"And how much would it cost to build?" Sassy asked.

"About $400,000,000," Chance replied, trying to sound casual, as though he threw around those kinds of numbers every day.

"Sorry, but I'm just a dumb country girl," Joel said. "Are you saying you'd own 15% of $400,000,000?"

Chance smiled appreciatively. He'd had the same question three months earlier.

"No, we'd have to sell shares to investors to raise the money for construction, so I'd just own whatever percentage I didn't sell," he said. "But even if I only kept one percent, it would be worth a shitload."

"Okay," Sassy interrupted, "if we're done with Real Estate and Development 101, can we get back to why you were doing risky business with gangsters?"

"It wasn't risky. I covered all my bases," Chance said, his tone almost pleading. "The only way I could lose was..."

"If the project fell through," Sassy finished. "Which it did when the building burned."

Chance nodded slowly. Sassy thought he suddenly looked very young and vulnerable.

"Okay," she said, her voice softening. "How much did you lose?"

"About $300,000," Chance replied.

"And you're sure the project is dead?" Sassy asked.

"I spoke to Patterson a few days ago," Chance replied with a dejected nod. "He said they just weren't interested anymore. They could make more money selling the property."

"I'm sorry, Chance," Sassy said sympathetically, "but what do you want *us* to do about it? It seems like you just got into an unfortunate business situation."

"It wasn't an unfortunate business situation," Chance replied, his voice suddenly angry. "I think they set me up. They took my money and burned down the building."

"Arson?" Sassy questioned. "I didn't read anything about arson. Besides, the police and insurance company would be investigating if they thought it was arson."

"Not if Patterson and Cornell paid off the cops and there was no insurance claim," Chance replied.

Sassy knew better than to argue against the possibility that there'd been a payoff to the police, and even if there hadn't been one, she suspected that investigating the fire would have been a low priority given the department's reduced man power since the hurricane, the building's owners, and that no one had been injured or killed. But the lack of an insurance claim made no sense.

"Why wouldn't there be an insurance claim?" she asked.

"Because the buildings weren't insured for replacement," Chance replied. "Patterson told me that after the hurricane the premiums were too high, so they only insured them for injury or death in case some wino fell through the floor. He told me a few weeks ago that they'd get full insurance again once the project started."

"I don't know, Chance," Michel said doubtfully, "it seems like an awful lot of work for them to go through to rip you off. No offense, but for men like that, $300,000 is chump change.

Besides, you had to have seen the architect's plans and some of the research documentation, right? I mean, wouldn't that prove that they really intended to go through with the project?"

Chance shook his head.

"You didn't see *anything*? How's that possible when you already paid $300,000 in bills?" Sassy asked.

Chance sighed.

"Patterson and Cornell told me up front that we wouldn't be seeing anything for the first three months. They said everyone would be gathering information and doing tests, then they'd start producing documents. The way they explained it made sense, so as the bills came in I just paid them."

"And that's why you think they were scamming you," Sassy said, nodding with understanding. "Because just at the point when you would have started seeing some tangible evidence, the buildings mysteriously burned."

"That and the convenient lack of insurance," Chance replied with a mixture of sadness and anger. "Look, I know it was stupid to be so trusting, but I didn't have a choice. I didn't have the experience for a project like this on my own."

"What about your buildings back in Natchez?" Michel asked. "Are you going to lose them because of this?"

"No," Chance replied. "I wasn't *that* stupid. I take in enough in rent to cover the loan payment and still get by, but my business is dead. I won't be able to get another loan, which means I won't be able to do any more projects."

"But can't you use the $200,000 that wasn't spent for that?" Michel asked.

"Commercial loans don't work that way," Chance replied. "You can't get the loan for one thing and then spend it on another. That money's gone."

"I hate to say this, Chance," Sassy said, "but I think you might be better off just taking your lumps and letting this one go. At least you haven't lost everything. And Patterson and Cornell are *not* the sort of men you want to mess with."

Chance stood up and took a deep breath.

"I realize this will sound funny coming from a former hustler," he said, "but it's the principle of the thing. They're not just hurting me. They're hurting all of the people who could have benefitted from the projects I would have done.

"All my life I've been a fuckup. For the first time, I tried to do something good for other people, and now they've taken that away. It's just not right."

Michel and Sassy looked at one another for a long moment, then Michel nodded almost imperceptibly.

"All right," he said. "What exactly do you want us to do?"

Chance's whole body relaxed visibly, as though he'd been holding his breath for a long time and had finally been able to exhale.

"I just need you to find some evidence that they never intended to do the project," he said. "That's all. If you find something, I'll confront them with it myself."

"Are you out of your mind?" Sassy exclaimed.

"Maybe," Chance replied, "but I don't want to put you guys in any more danger than I probably already am."

"No," Michel said vehemently. "The only way this happens is if you promise we'll decide what to do together...assuming we find anything. I'm not going to do this and then have you go get yourself killed. I don't need that on my conscience."

Chance considered it for a moment, then shrugged.

"It's a deal," he said.

"Let me hear you say it," Michel pressed.

Chance held up his right hand and placed his left on an imaginary Bible.

"I swear to God that in no way will I confront Bulldog Patterson and/or Double-J Cornell on my own."

Michel and Sassy both instinctively repeated the words in their minds to see if there were any potential loopholes in the promise. Satisfied, they nodded simultaneously.

"There's just one other thing," Chance said.

"Of course there is," Michel replied suspiciously. "What?"

"Obviously I don't have any money to pay you right now," Chance replied, "but if I get the money back, I'll pay you 5% of it."

"Awesome," Michel said. "Not only do you want us to investigate gangsters, but you want us to do it for free."

"Technically, it's not actually for free," Joel piped in.

"Come again?" Michel asked.

"Well, how much do you guys charge an hour?"

Sassy and Michel quickly exchanged questioning looks.

"Oh my God, you guys are so pathetic," Joel said, shaking his head. "Do you even know how much you have to make each month to stay afloat?"

"Of course we do," Michel replied with false confidence. "And we charge $50 an hour, plus expenses."

"Like hell we do, Jim Rockford," Sassy blurted out. "It's not 1974 anymore. We're going to be lucky to work forty hours a week between us. That would mean $2,000 a week, or $8,000 a month. After rent, taxes, insurance, and utilities, we'd have about $10 to split between us. We charge $150 an hour," she finished assertively.

Joel smirked as Michel shot daggers at Sassy with his eyes.

"That's fine," he said, "because I happen to charge $150 an hour for moving. So by my calculation, you owe me $4,500, which you can work out in trade by helping Chance."

"What?" Michel asked incredulously. "You never said anything about charging."

"You never asked," Joel replied matter-of-factly. "You should always ask the cost before engaging someone's services. That's the first rule of business. Well, after knowing how much it costs to run your business and how much to charge, that is.

"Besides, you guys could use the practice. You haven't done anything remotely resembling detective work in almost a year. What else are you going to do with your time? Keep arguing about the company's name?"

"Fine," Michel said, "but we'll do it for the potential 5% fee. We'll figure out some *other* way to work off your fees in trade."

He gave Joel an impish smile.

"Jones & Doucette Investigations," Chance interjected suddenly.

"What?" Michel asked.

"The name of the agency," Chance clarified. "You should call it Jones & Doucette Investigations."

"Thank you," Sassy said, jabbing her finger in the air victoriously.

"And why is that?" Michel asked. "Alphabetically D comes before J."

"Yeah, but there are already like five other Doucette Investigations down here," Chance replied. "The name Doucette is as common around here as...well, Jones every place else. Besides, Jones & Doucette has a better flow to it."

"Thank you again," Sassy said, nodding her head fervently.

"And how exactly do you know there are five other Doucette investigations?" Michel asked.

"I saw them in the phone book," Chance replied with a playful smile. "You don't think you guys were my first choice, do you?"

*****

"This whole thing doesn't feel right," Sassy said as she leaned back in her chair with her hands clasped behind her head and her feet on her desk. "Going after some kid for 300 grand isn't Lee's style. That's small time."

Joel and Chance had left a few minutes earlier.

"Maybe his guys did it on their own just for fun or a little spending cash," Michel replied from a similar position across the room.

Sassy shook her head.

"No. Nothing happens without Lee's approval. This is the sort of thing that could bring unwanted attention. I think something's going on, but I'm not sure it has anything to do with Chance."

"So you think he might have just been a casualty of war?"

"Something like that."

They were quiet for a minute.

"I have to admit I'm having a hard time buying this new Mother Theresa model of Chance," Michel said finally. "It seems out of character."

"You think the whole property development thing is a scam?"

"I don't know."

"I just don't see any angle," Sassy said. "He's been putting all the money up. He's providing homes and jobs. He's helping communities. I don't see where it benefits him."

"I know," Michel replied, "which is why it bothers me. I didn't know him very well, but from what I saw and what Joel's told me, Chance was always looking out for number one. He didn't do anything if it wasn't in his own self-interest."

Sassy stared at the ceiling thoughtfully for a moment, then looked back at Michel.

"Maybe his self-interest is redemption."

Michel thought about it for a few moments.

"Stranger things have happened," he said.

Chapter 2

Sassy and Michel sat at their desks the next morning, each with a large ceramic mug of chicory coffee emblazoned with the Cafe du Monde logo beside them.

"So where do we start?" Michel asked.

"I've been giving it some thought," Sassy replied, "and I think the first step is to let Priest Lee know what's going on."

"And we would do that *why*?"

"Because if he finds out we're checking into some of his boys and he doesn't know anything about it, we're likely to end up in a landfill somewhere," Sassy replied. "Besides, he might be willing to intercede on our behalf and save us a lot of time and trouble."

"And *he* would do that *why*?" Michel asked in a sing-song voice.

Sassy rolled her eyes like a mother on the verge of losing her patience.

"Because if something's going on," she explained slowly, "it might be worth it to him to not have that something discovered. He might just be willing to pay to make us go away."

"And" she continued after a brief pause, "he might do it as a personal favor."

She tried to keep her tone as casual as possible, but Michel immediately leaned forward in his seat, his interest piqued.

"At the risk of repeating myself," he said, "and he would do that *why*?"

Sassy let out small sigh.

"Because we know each other," she said, bracing herself for Michel's onslaught of questions.

"You *know* each other?" he asked, blinking in disbelief. "Since when do you hang with gangsters?"

"I don't *hang* with him, but we have met on a few occasions."

"Like when? You never go out. At least not that you tell me about."

"You know, just because I don't hang out in bars doesn't mean I'm a shut-in." Sassy replied. "I do manage to make it out in public every so often."

"But where would you have met Priest Lee?"

"At some charity events," Sassy replied briskly. "I used to do some volunteer work for the Children's Advocacy Center and he was on the board. I met him at a few events they threw."

"And that's it?" Michel asked, narrowing his eyes suspiciously.

"What?" Sassy asked defensively.

"The way you said you *know* each other, it just felt like more than that. Like you two were friends," Michel replied.

Sassy closed her eyes and pursed her lips for a moment.

"Fine, if you must know, we did socialize together on occasion, years ago," she said, fixing Michel with a look that suggested he shouldn't push too far.

"Whoa, whoa, whoa," Michel said, ignoring her warning. "You what?"

"We socialized. We both frequented the same music clubs and occasionally we'd have a drink together," Sassy replied. "It was no big deal. He was just a small-time hood in those days."

"Okay, you're kind of blowing my mind here," Michel replied, holding up his right hand. "I'm trying to picture this. You and Priest Lee out having drinks and hanging together."

"Jesus Christ, Michel!" Sassy exclaimed with more than a little irritation. "You know I was young once. And that's what

28

we did. We hung out in music clubs and had drinks. And sometimes we even danced.

"And there were all sorts of people there. Some of them were doctors, some of them were lawyers, some of them were cops, and some of them were crooks. That's just the way it was. It was no big deal. Back off."

"Okay, okay, I'm sorry," Michel said quickly, realizing he'd gone too far. "I just wasn't expecting that. One of these days you're going to have to fill me in on all the sordid details of your past."

"Buy the book," Sassy replied with barbed sarcasm.

Michel was silent for a moment as he tried to figure how to steer the conversation back to calmer waters.

"Okay," he said finally in his best professional tone, "so the first thing we do is talk to Priest Lee."

Sassy looked him up and down like he was a cheap suit.

"Ain't no *we* about it," she said emphatically. "*I'll* go talk to him. If I show up with your cracker ass we won't even get through the door. At least he probably won't kill *me* right away. Besides, you've got work to do."

Michel suddenly understood what it must be like to have a bossy big sister.

"What work?" he asked, sounding like a child who'd just been told he couldn't go to the circus because he had homework.

"Did you forget about the Marchand case?" Sassy replied, her tone more playful again.

Two days earlier, they'd been hired by Severin Marchand, the scion of a wealthy New Orleans family, to find out who'd broken into his studio and destroyed the costume he'd been working on for Mardi Gras.

"Yeah, that seems fair," Michel grumbled. "You get to meet with a gangster kingpin while I get stuck investigating some old queen's parade costume."

"Hey, Marchand is one of your people," Sassy teased.

"Oh, so is that the way it's going to be? I get all the gay cases and you get all the black cases?" Michel asked, feigning indignity.

"Who said anything about gay?" Sassy asked with exaggerated innocence. "I meant patrician white folks."

"Patrician, huh?" Michel asked, one eyebrow curved up.

"Don't even try to pretend with me," Sassy replied. "I know you've got some rich relatives stashed somewhere."

Michel didn't respond, but a small enigmatic smile crossed his lips for a split second.

"You really do, don't you?" Sassy asked excitedly, suddenly intrigued.

"If only you knew the half of it," Michel replied.

"Who?" Sassy asked. "Where are they?"

"You tell me your sordid details and I'll tell you mine," Michel replied with a benign smile.

"You know I'm going to take you up on that, don't you?" Sassy said. "One night I'm going to get you drunk and you're going to spill all the dirt."

Chapter 3

The family of Severin Davis Marchand IV had come to New Orleans in 1720, two years after the city was founded by the French Mississippi Company. They'd made their fortune in shipping and trade—including, it was rumored, the Atlantic slave trade—and had become one of the city's most prominent families. Ten generations of Marchands had been born in New Orleans. An only child, Severin IV would be the last of the line.

Michel had never met Marchand, though he was well aware of him. On any given night, Marchand could be found holding court in one of several gay bars in the French Quarter, sitting in a corner surrounded by a collection of other wealthy, older "gentlemen" and their younger "companions," with Marchand the center of attention. The group had always reminded Michel of a high school clique, with Marchand as the team quarterback—albeit an extremely effeminate quarterback who'd never actually touched a football.

Marchand was the sort of older gay man Michel found repulsive: arch, self-satisfied, status-conscious, and predatory; the kind of man who routinely toyed with other, less fortunate people just to amuse himself and his friends, and who could get away with it because of his wealth and status. Still, Michel knew that wealth and status could be very useful as they tried to get Jones & Doucette Investigations off the ground. Marchand could open a lot of doors for them.

Although Michel knew his primary residence was a large townhouse on Royal Street, only a few blocks from the office,

Marchand had asked Michel to meet him at his family's ancestral home in the Garden District. Michel assumed it was meant to impress him.

Marchand House, as the black iron plate affixed next to the front gate identified it, occupied an entire square block on the south side of Prytania Street, the district's most prestigious address. The house was a white Greek Revival building set back from the street behind a high brick wall. As he made his way up the driveway past lush lawns and carefully manicured gardens, Michel had to admit that he was impressed—not by the obvious wealth that the estate represented, but by how lovingly it had all been maintained.

He was greeted at the door by an elderly black man in a crisp black suit who introduced himself as Joseph, and led into a parlor to the right of the foyer to wait. As the echo of Joseph's heels clicking on the marble floors receded down some unseen hallway, Michel took in the room.

It was large, spanning the full depth of the house, with twelve-foot-high windows in the front and three sets of French doors across the back. The wall opposite the entry was covered by bookshelves rising ten rows high. The wall adjacent to the foyer had a white marble fireplace over which hung a portrait of a bearded older man in a Confederate army captain's uniform. Michel guessed it was the father of Severin Davis Marchand I, who'd probably chosen the middle name "Davis" for his son in tribute to Jefferson Davis. He also guessed that the portrait had been painted years after the war ended. It was not an uncommon practice for aristocratic southern families who still clung longingly to a memory of life before the war.

There were two couches bracketing the fireplace, and another surrounded by four chairs facing a black grand piano by the front windows. All the furniture was ornate and obviously antique, but immaculately maintained.

Michel walked over to the piano and studied the silver-framed photos neatly arranged on top around a large cut-crystal bowl of jasmine. The men, women, and children in the photos were clearly family. They all shared the wide-set eyes and small hooked nose that gave Marchand the appearance of an owl.

"Do you play?" a high-pitched, nasal voice asked.

Michel turned and saw Severin Marchand standing in the doorway.

"I'm afraid not," Michel replied. "I was just looking at the photos."

"Ah, yes, the rogue's gallery," Marchand replied with a bit too much geniality. "Welcome, Mr. Doucette."

He walked toward Michel and extended his right hand limply with the palm facing slightly downward. For a brief moment, Michel wondered if he was supposed to kiss it.

"Mr. Marchand," Michel replied, opting for a handshake.

As he'd expected, Marchand's handshake was weak, and his palm was cool but clammy. Michel fought the urge to shudder. He noticed that while the hand was soft and appeared never to have done any manual labor, the nails had been chewed to their quicks. Marchand was obviously a nervous person.

"Please, call me Severin," Marchand replied as though bestowing a gift.

"Michel," Michel replied with a nod.

"Shall we have iced tea on the veranda, Michel?" Marchand asked, gesturing toward the open French doors.

Two wicker chairs were arranged at a wrought iron table in the shade on the right side of the wide flagstone patio. As they took their seats, Michel noticed a leather binder with the gold-stamped initials SDM lying on the table to Marchand's right.

"So why haven't we met before, Michel?" Marchand asked after taking an elaborate sip of iced tea through a straw. "I thought I knew everyone of interest in this city."

Michel shrugged and smiled politely.

"I guess I must not be of that much interest," he replied.

Marchand looked puzzled for a moment, as though trying to figure out if Michel was playing games with him.

"Oh, I doubt that very much," he gushed after a moment with a smile that Michel thought was probably meant to be charming, but which came off as patronizing instead. "A former homicide detective turned private eye? That sounds *very* interesting to me."

Michel just smiled noncommittally in response.

"I'm sure we probably just move in *different* circles," Marchand said, patting Michel's right forearm lightly with his left hand.

The way Marchand had emphasized the word "different" and touched his arm felt pointedly condescending to Michel. He half expected Marchand to follow it by saying, "There, there, we can't all be wealthy, now can we?" Michel began to wonder if Marchand had requested meeting at the house not to impress him, but to emphasize the difference in their social status. He wondered if Marchand was trying to make it clear that Michel shouldn't consider himself anything more than a hired hand: no different from Joseph or a gardener or a maid. He pushed the thought away.

"So why don't you tell me what happened?" he said.

*****

"It was just heartbreaking," Marchand said with exaggerated self-pity as he finished telling Michel about the break-in at his studio and the damage to his costume. "It was completely shredded. And I was going for my fourth consecutive 'Best in Show' at the Bourbon Street Awards, which would have surpassed Torchy Laine's record."

The Bourbon Street Awards had been started in 1963 by Arthur Jacobs, the then-owner of the Clover Grill on Bourbon Street. The section of the street where the grill was located was seen as seedy and unsafe in those days, and Jacobs thought the awards would help attract tourists to his restaurant and other area businesses during Mardi Gras. What had originally been planned as a one-time event continued to grow over the years, becoming one of the highlights of Mardi Gras that now attracted thousands. Awards were given every year for Best Drag, Best Leather, and Best in Show.

Michel stared at Marchand blankly.

"You *do* know who Torchy Laine is, don't you?" Marchand asked, one eyebrow arched critically.

"I'm afraid not," Michel replied.

"Are you sure you're gay?" Marchand asked, shaking his head with a combination of annoyance and disbelief. "Torchy Laine won 'Best in Show' from 1977 to 1979. Of course he did the same 'Parade of Cleopatra' all three years and just kept adding more slave boys and even a tiger one year. Me, I'm a purist. I think that sort of thing is a little vulgar. I think a costume should be judged on its own merits."

Michel had a sudden recollection of standing in a crowd with his mother, watching a beautiful woman dressed all in gold lying on a gilded chaise as it was carried down the street by a group of well-muscled men wearing only loin cloths. He had probably been only five- or six-years-old at the time, but he remembered that even then he'd been fascinated by the men and the way their muscles rippled in the sun as they walked. Reluctantly he pushed the memory away.

"And I take it it's too late to recreate your costume?" he asked.

Marchand looked at him like he was daft.

"Of course it is," he exclaimed with exasperation. "It takes almost a full year to create an award-winning costume. It's not just something you can buy the pieces at the Party Store. I start planning for the next year three weeks after Mardi Gras. Then I have to do drawings and find materials. And it takes months to put together. I sew everything by hand. And this year it had to be something particularly extraordinary given that it's the 150th anniversary of Mardi Gras."

He let out a dramatic sigh.

"And even if I did have the time, I just don't think I'd have the heart for it after what happened."

Michel gave what he hoped would pass for a sympathetic look.

"So when can I take a look at your studio?" he asked after what felt like a respectable pause.

"My studio?" Marchand asked. "Why would you want to see my studio?"

"Because it was the crime scene," Michel shrugged. "There might be some clues there."

Marchand stared at him for a moment with what looked to be a hint of annoyance.

"But the police already did all that," he said finally. "They took their photos and dusted for fingerprints and whatever else they do and they said they didn't find anything."

Michel nodded in acknowledgment but not agreement.

"Speaking of the police," he said, "why aren't you just letting them handle the investigation? Why hire us?"

Marchand's face reddened a bit and his eyes grew agitated.

"Because the police couldn't care less," he spat. "As far as they're concerned, this was just some inconsequential act of vandalism. They said they'd keep investigating, but I haven't heard anything from them in over a week."

"Well, these things do take time," Michel offered.

"I know when I'm being stonewalled," Marchand replied.

Michel wondered whether Marchand had meant by the police or by him.

"Look, I'm not stupid, Michel," Marchand continued. "I know that in the grand scheme of things some rich old queen's Mardi Gras costume isn't that important. It doesn't warrant that much attention from the police and it's certainly not going to garner much sympathy from anyone else. But it's important to me, and fortunately I have the resources to do something about it."

Michel was taken off guard by Marchand's candor and

apparent self-awareness. He wondered if perhaps there was more to Marchand than he'd thought.

"Please, Michel," Marchand said, "I want you to find out who did this to me."

Michel cocked his head, surprised that Marchand was so certain the vandalism had been intentionally directed at him.

"What makes you so sure it wasn't random?" he asked. "Maybe someone broke into the studio looking for something to steal, saw your costume, and just shredded it for kicks."

"Because my costume was the only thing that was touched," Marchand responded. "I've got literally hundreds of thousands of dollars of antiques stored in my studio, but none of them were taken or destroyed."

Michel thought that did seem like pretty compelling evidence.

"Okay," he said. "Then I really think it's critical that I take a look at the studio first."

Marchand sighed.

"You won't find anything."

"How can you be so sure?" Michel asked.

"Because it's already been cleaned," Marchand replied. "I just couldn't stand to look at all that beautiful silk and taffeta on the floor any more, so I had my staff clean it a few days ago. I also had the window repaired so no one else could get in."

"Oh," Michel responded dully.

"But I have pictures," Marchand said as he picked up the leather binder and handed it to Michel.

Michel thumbed through the photos for a moment, then closed the binder on the table in front of him.

"Great, but I'd still like to see the studio for myself."

Marchand sighed again, but this time in surrender.

"You certainly are persistent," he said. "But then again, I suppose that's a good thing in your line of work. Columbo was nothing if not persistent. Fine, I can meet you there tomorrow afternoon. How about 1:30?"

Michel nodded.

"That will be fine. It shouldn't take long," he said. "So do you have any idea who might have done this?"

Marchand threw up his hands and shrugged.

"I have no idea," he said. "So far as I know, I don't have an enemy in the world."

Michel knew that Marchand was being disingenuous. Everyone knew they had enemies, and usually exactly who they were.

"But I've arranged a series of interviews for you with some of my friends," Marchand continued. "Maybe they can give you some ideas."

"Interviews?" Michel questioned. "I don't think that will be necessary."

"Oh," Marchand replied, clearly disappointed. "And why's that?"

Michel realized that it hadn't really been a question. Marchand was making it clear that he expected Michel to conduct the interviews as part of his job responsibilities. Still, Michel decided to push back a bit.

"I'm not sure what they could tell me that you can't," he said.

Marchand's eyes narrowed for a moment as though he were trying to figure out a puzzle, then a small smile came to his thin lips.

"Well, they may know of some people I don't who...dislike me," he ventured in a tentative voice that suggested he was feeling his way along through unfamiliar territory.

"You think they may know of some enemies you're not aware of?" Michel asked with more than a hint of doubt.

"Perhaps," Marchand replied. "Perhaps they just never told me to spare my feelings. But I'm sure they'd tell you since you'd be performing an official investigation."

Michel thought it sounded unlikely, but knew he'd have to conduct the interviews anyway to keep Marchand happy.

"Fine," he said after pretending to consider the situation for a minute. "But first you show me your studio."

Chapter 4

At seventy-two, Priest Lee was still tall, trim, and elegant. He was dressed in an impeccably tailored charcoal suit that Sassy guessed must have cost at least $5,000, a white silk shirt, and red silk tie. His face was deeply creased, yet didn't seem old because of his intense, light brown eyes.

"Welcome, Detective Jones," he said as he crossed his office with a wide smile and took both of Sassy's hands. "How are you?"

"I'm fine, thanks," Sassy replied, "but I'm no longer on the force, in case you hadn't heard.

Lee's crocodile smile indicated that he had indeed heard.

"But you are still in the detecting business, are you not?" Lee asked, his accent and phrasing still echoing his childhood in Barbados.

Sassy nodded.

"Then the title is still appropriate, n'est ce pas?"

"Or you could just call me Sassy...like in the old days," Sassy replied with a playful smile.

"Then Sassy it shall be," Lee replied as he let go of her hands and took a step back. "Please make yourself comfortable."

He indicated two black leather chairs to the left of an imposingly large mahogany desk. As he sat, Lee ran both hands along the sides of his cocoa-brown scalp, as though smoothing no-longer-existent hair.

"I have to admit I was surprised to hear from you," he said.

"Yes, it's been a while. This is certainly a step up from that place you had on North Peters," Sassy replied as she looked admiringly around the room.

Jacard-Lee Development Corporation occupied the top three floors of a high rise overlooking Lafayette Square in the Central Business District. Lee's office was in a corner on the top floor, with views toward the French Quarter and the Mississippi River. The room was large and handsome, with paneled walls the color of dark chocolate and a black marble floor. On the far side of the room were three black leather sofas clustered around a square mahogany coffee table. It was an unmistakably masculine place, and also a place that was designed to convey success and power.

"Yes," Lee replied, looking around for a moment before turning his attention back to Sassy.

"But we had much better parties at that old place," he said conspiratorially.

"Yes, you certainly did," Sassy replied.

They were both quiet for a moment.

"So what brings you here?" Lee said finally. "I'm sure it wasn't just to reminisce."

"No," Sassy agreed. "I wanted to let you know that my partner and I have been asked to look into some business involving two of your associates."

"I see," Lee replied without blinking. "And which associates might those be?"

"Henry Patterson and James Cornell," Sassy replied.

She studied Lee's face closely for a reaction but saw none.

"May I inquire about the details of this investigation, or is that confidential?" Lee asked, studying Sassy equally closely.

"Under normal circumstances it would be," Sassy replied with a small smile, "but since I'm asking for your help..."

*****

"I see," Lee said soberly after Sassy finished recounting Chance's story and his suspicions. "And you would like me to intervene with my business associates on your client's behalf."

The lack of a questioning tone caught Sassy's ear. Lee was stating the facts as though outlining the components of a business agreement.

"If you wouldn't mind," she replied to the non-question.

"Well, I generally make it a rule not to interfere in the dealings of my business associates," Lee said.

"But?" Sassy asked expectantly, sensing that there was more.

Lee leaned forward and rested his elbows on his knees, clasping his hands in front of him. He seemed to be deliberating.

"But," he said after a moment, "I might be able to look into it if you were able to help me with a problem."

"What kind of problem?" Sassy asked cautiously.

"Let me ask you first," Lee said, his tone suddenly more serious, "if I were to engage your services, could I be assured of your discretion?"

"Of course," Sassy replied, "I think that would be in my best interest both professionally and personally, don't you?"

Lee gave her a small, joyless smile.

"Yes, I suppose it would be," he said. "Well then let us assume for purposes of discussion that I am engaging you and your partner."

"To do what exactly?" Sassy asked.

Up to that point, Lee had maintained his usual composure and business-like demeanor, but now he sighed deeply, and as he exhaled Sassy saw him change before her eyes. Lee had always seemed indestructible to her, but now he suddenly looked frail and entirely human.

"My son, Deacon, is missing," he replied solemnly.

Although she'd actually seen him only once, when he'd been brought into the station for questioning, Sassy knew Deacon Lee's reputation well. Deacon had been his father's chief lieutenant and enforcer for two decades. He'd been a primary suspect in dozens of murders over the years, but none of the cases had ever made it to trial. Witnesses had a habit of disappearing or forgetting facts when he was involved.

From what she'd seen and heard, Deacon was the exact opposite of his father. He was short and thickly built, with rough, flat features. Rather than cultivated and savvy, he was thuggish and savage. Deacon was the vicious pit bull to his father's cunning fox. That a man as prudent and deliberate as Priest Lee had allowed someone so volatile to rise to prominence in his organization had always struck Sassy as odd. Then again, nothing about the relationship between Priest and Deacon Lee had ever made much sense to her.

It was rumored that Priest had fathered Deacon with a mistress, then paid her well to take the boy away and raise him in the country. When the boy's mother died while he was in his teens, Deacon had found his father's name on his birth certificate and come to the city to find Priest.

Though Priest could easily have denied paternity in those days before DNA testing had become prevalent, or simply paid the boy off to disappear again, he'd instead publicly embraced Deacon as his son, moving him into his house and introducing him to New Orleans' society.

"How long has he been missing?" Sassy asked.

"Almost three weeks," Lee replied.

"And you're sure he's not just on an extended vacation somewhere?" Sassy asked hopefully.

"That was my original thought, as well," Lee responded. "It was not unusual for Deacon to disappear for periods of time. He enjoyed gambling and often went to Las Vegas or Atlantic City. But he would always take some of his people or a lady friend with him. Not this time."

Sassy nodded for him to continue.

"After a few days I became concerned and went to his house," Lee said. "It was clear that no trip had been planned.

The mail was piled in front of his door and all of his belongings were in place."

Sassy found the idea that Deacon had a house fascinating. She'd always thought of men like him as sharks, perpetually in motion. She fought the urge to ask for details about the house.

"And no one's heard from him?" she asked instead.

"No," Lee responded with a certainty that made it clear he'd already conducted a thorough internal investigation.

Sassy nodded again, both in acknowledgment and encouragement to continue.

"Obviously people began to ask questions after a few days," Lee said, "so I told them that I'd sent Deacon to deal with a special situation and that he'd be gone for a few weeks. I hoped it would give me enough time to find out what had happened to him, but..."

He trailed off and stared at the floor.

"And what do you think happened to him?" Sassy asked.

"I believe he's been killed," Lee said softly.

While Sassy had assumed as much from Lee's use of the past tense when talking about Deacon, to hear it said still sent a shiver down her spine.

"You don't think he's just been kidnapped?" she asked.

"No," Lee replied, shaking his head sadly. "If he'd been kidnapped I would certainly have received a demand for ransom by now. And no one in their proper mind would believe they could take Deacon and later release him without paying a dear price."

Sassy had heard enough stories about Deacon's scorched-earth style of vengeance to know that was true.

"One of the other families?" she asked.

The Mafia had established operations in New Orleans in the late 1800s. The original "family" controlled by Charles and Tony Matranga was believed to be one of the first organized crime groups in the country. Over time, the city had been divided into sections, with five "families" controlling the majority of all activities. Priest Lee's group was the only one not still controlled by the Mafia.

Lee seemed lost in thought for a moment, then his eyes cleared and he regained some of his composure.

"I don't think so," he replied. "Not now. Perhaps ten years ago such a thing would have been conceivable, but not now."

"Why?" Sassy asked.

Lee paused before responding. Again his eyes grew distant for a moment.

"Because my friends and I are old men now," he said in a reflective tone, referring to the heads of the other four families. "We don't have a taste for war any longer. It's better to just live out our time in peace."

He gave Sassy a wistful smile.

Sassy found the use of the term "friends" both surprising and a little touching. While she knew that circumspection and euphemism had always been part of the criminal vocabulary, in this case she felt Lee was being sincere. She imagined that after decades of conflict, a certain level of respect and possibly even kinship would have developed between the men.

"Perhaps it wasn't sanctioned," she suggested. "Maybe someone settling a personal vendetta without permission from their family?"

Lee shrugged noncommittally.

"It's true Deacon had many enemies," he agreed.

"But you don't think that's the case?" Sassy asked.

"No," Lee replied. "If someone from within one of the families had done it, I would have heard. I have many ears."

Sassy assumed that "ears" referred to members of other families on Lee's payroll.

"Then who?" she asked. "And why?"

"I don't think this was simple vengeance. I think it was...an act of provocation," Lee said, choosing his words carefully. "I believe that someone is hoping to destabilize the current balance."

Sassy understood that Lee was referring to the balance of power between the families that had allowed them to maintain a relative peace for the past five years.

"Any idea who might want to do that?" she asked.

Lee shook his head slowly.

"If I knew, the matter would be settled by now," he said gravely.

Sassy was silent for a moment.

"But anyone who knows you would realize that you wouldn't just lash out blindly without knowing who was responsible," she said finally. "So how does killing Deacon provoke a war?"

Lee studied his hands for a moment before responding.

"If it were known that Deacon was gone, my position might be jeopardized," he replied.

"How so?" Sassy asked.

"Even an old lion will pounce when it sees a wounded antelope," Lee replied. "If I'm perceived to be vulnerable, there are some who might choose to take advantage of the situation. While I don't believe any of my old friends would try to provoke a war, I have little doubt that they would take the opportunity to strike if it were presented."

"So you think someone killed Deacon in hopes that the other families would move against you?"

Lee nodded.

Sassy considered the logic. It seemed plausible, but only if the other families were aware that Deacon was gone.

"Then why hasn't this person made it known that Deacon is gone?" she asked.

"Because that would be dangerous," Lee replied. "Despite any animosity, the old families share a common interest in maintaining the status quo. If anyone were to make an overt attack on one family, they would be perceived as a threat to us all. I have no doubt that when all is said and done the other families would be only too happy to pick over my bones, but first they would band together with me against our common enemy."

"So this person is pulling the strings behind the scenes and waiting patiently for it all to play out," Sassy said.

"That's what I believe," Lee replied.

It sounded like a far more subtle and sophisticated plan than Sassy would have expected. In her experience, those in organized crime usually relied on blunt force or intimidation to achieve their goals. Still, it sounded logical.

"And what would they have to gain from that?" she asked.

"The spoils," Lee replied flatly.

"But wouldn't the spoils just be divided among the remaining families?" Sassy asked.

"I'm afraid that we are all in a very precarious situation," Lee replied, "and that a war would be in the best interest of none of us."

"Less obtuse, please," Sassy said.

Lee smiled appreciatively at her.

"In the business world they would call it lack of succession planning," he explained. "I call it the hubris of old men. We all believed we would live forever. We've made no plans for who will take over when we're gone. In the days before us, if you cut off the head of any snake, a new head would grow in its place. Now if one were to cut off the heads, each snake would wither and die. When we're gone, the families will splinter. Someone new could move in and take what he pleases."

"And with Deacon gone you'd be particularly vulnerable to that," Sassy added.

Lee gave her a rueful look.

"I had no illusions about my son's shortcomings," Lee replied. "I loved him, but Deacon's abilities were limited. He would never have been capable of taking my place. I accepted that long ago. And unfortunately, the same is true for all of us. There is no one capable of taking over. I fear that when we're gone, things will be very different. There will be chaos."

Sassy gave Lee a small, amused smile.

"But isn't that the lament of every generation?" she asked. "That succeeding generations will be incapable of caring for the world left behind?"

"It's not a question of capability," Lee replied indignantly. "It's a question of philosophy. This younger generation has no concern for community. They are short-sighted and stupid. All they care about is money."

"No disrespect, Priest," Sassy said curtly, "but how can you say you and your friends were concerned about community? You sold drugs and guns. You ran rackets and pimped prostitutes. How does that show concern for the community?"

"People who want those things are always going to find them," Lee replied, his eyes flashing with barely restrained anger. "Do you think that would change if we were gone? No, it wouldn't. But men like us keep order. We make sure violence stays contained so that children can play on the streets without their parents having to fear that they'll be killed. We're not saints, but we're better than those waiting to take our places. They don't care about the people. They will take and take until there's nothing left and then neighborhoods will crumble."

He was quiet for a moment, seemingly trying to calm himself.

"Do you imagine that my entrance into property development was a whim, or that all of my charitable work is just for show?" he asked suddenly. "So that I can pretend to be an upstanding citizen or to ease a guilty conscience?"

Sassy knew the questions were rhetorical and didn't respond.

"And do you think that the boards of all these foundations don't know who I am and what I do?" Lee continued. "Of course they do. But they accept me as a necessary evil because I have money and influence, and because I can help the people they serve."

Sassy was surprised that Lee seemed to feel the need to justify himself to her. It seemed out of character, and she wondered if it was a ploy to gain her sympathy by painting himself as a misunderstood champion of the people.

"Maybe I'm a foolish old man," he said defiantly, "but I believe my legacy will be that I helped this city, that I gave back and made people's lives better."

They were both quiet for a minute. As she considered the situation, Sassy suddenly realized she'd been maneuvered into an untenable position. If she identified the person responsible for Deacon's killing, she'd certainly be signing that person's death warrant. But if she declined to help Lee now, he would undoubtedly see to it that Chance never got his money back.

"You know, Priest," she said, "if I find any evidence of who killed Deacon, I'm going to have to turn it over to the police. I took a vow to uphold the law, and just because I'm no longer on the force doesn't mean that's ended."

"Of course," Lee replied simply.

Sassy studied his face carefully. He seemed to be sincere.

"Just like that?" she asked skeptically.

"Just like that," Lee replied. "I understood that when I asked you to help me. I would never ask you to betray your moral code."

"Then I have your word that if I find Deacon's killer you'll let the judicial system determine and apply punishment?" Sassy asked, to clarify their agreement.

Lee nodded.

"There is no need to even inform me of your findings until the killer has been taken into custody," he said. "I ask only one thing."

Oh shit, Sassy thought, here it comes.

"If you find that any of my other people or I are in imminent danger, you'll inform me so we can take proper steps to protect ourselves," Lee said.

Sassy was surprised. The request sounded more than reasonable. Still she felt that Lee had to have some other agenda.

"I realize that this may seem uncharacteristic to you," Lee said, as though he'd read her thoughts, "but as I said, I'm an old man now and I'd rather live out my life in peace. Deacon is gone. Of that I'm certain. And nothing I do will change that. I also accept that when the other families learn he is gone I will be forced to step aside. Again, that is inevitable. So my primary concern at this point is to avoid a war that will cause unnecessary damage."

"Then why not just call the heads of the other families together, tell them Deacon was killed, and that you're ready to turn over your territory?" Sassy asked. "It seems like that would be the easiest way to avoid the war."

"Indeed," Lee replied with an arch of his eyebrows. "If only it were so easy."

"And why isn't it?" Sassy asked.

"If I were to do as you propose before you've identified Deacon's killer, the families would each suspect one another," Lee explained. "There would be no trust. I fear that things would revert to the way they were a few years ago."

"And that's the only reason?" Sassy asked.

Lee gave her a gentle smile.

"There is also the matter of pride, of course," he admitted. "If I were to go to them now, I would be perceived as acting out of fear. I would have no leverage with which to negotiate."

"Negotiate what?"

"To receive a small percentage of the earnings on the businesses I divest," Lee replied. "If I have proof of a plot against us all, however, perhaps I can use that information as leverage."

Sassy thought Lee's explanations sounded weak at best. She still felt certain that he had another agenda. She realized, however, that she didn't really have a choice if she wanted to help Chance. She just hoped that she could manage the situation to ensure that Deacon's killer was brought to justice without Lee taking his vengeance.

"All right," she said finally. "So what exactly do you think I can do to help you?"

Lee smiled. It wasn't the crocodile smile that he'd shown earlier, but still conveyed self-satisfaction in a way that made Sassy feel uneasy.

"I'm hoping you might gain access to information I cannot," Lee replied.

"What kind of information?" Sassy asked.

"As I said, I have many ears," Lee replied, "but they listen only to those who are known. Perhaps the authorities have information on those who are unknown."

Sassy understood what Lee meant and began thinking of friends she had in various law enforcement agencies.

"But whomever you speak with must be someone you can trust without question," Lee continued. "As we both know, there are many in the local police department who have reciprocal relationships with those in my world."

"Of course," Sassy replied. "And after I have the information, then what?"

Lee turned the palms of his hands up and gave her a curious look.

"Then you do what you do, of course," he said. "Find the evidence that will be needed to convict Deacon's killer."

"Okay," Sassy replied. "But I'd also like to check out Deacon's house for evidence."

"Certainly," Lee replied.

He stood and crossed the room to his desk. He took a key from the middle drawer, then wrote something on a sheet of paper.

"Here," he said, as he walked back and handed the paper and key to Sassy. "That is his address and the alarm code. The key will open both the gate and the door."

"Okay," Sassy said. "I'll be in touch."

"Thank you, Sassy," Lee said as he clasped her right hand with both hands.

Sassy considered telling him she hoped he wasn't lying to her, but decided to let it be for the moment.

"You're welcome," she said instead.

*****

"You want to go first or should I?" Michel asked as Sassy walked into the office.

"You go," Sassy replied wearily. "I need to take my shoes off. I'm out of practice in these things."

"Well, you just cannot *possibly* imagine how thrilling it was to meet with Severin Marchand," Michel began sarcastically, as Sassy sat at her desk and kicked off her dark brown slingbacks with a grimace.

"Do tell," Sassy replied dryly.

"I don't know what it is about the guy, but he just rubs me the wrong way," Michel continued. "He's just got this patronizing air about him that..."

"Thanks for the character analysis," Sassy interrupted. "What about the case?"

Michel gave her a hurt look but continued.

"I'm meeting him at his studio tomorrow afternoon," he said. "For some reason he seemed reluctant to let me see it. He's also already had the place cleaned, so I'm not sure if I'll be able to find anything."

"That's odd," Sassy said, her interest suddenly piqued. "Why would he do that?"

"He said it was too heartbreaking to look at all his beautiful silk and taffeta shredded on the floor," Michel replied.

"Wow, this guy really is a queen," Sassy said.

"You're telling me," Michel replied.

"Anything else?"

"He wants me to interview some of his friends," Michel replied. "He thinks they might be able to tell me about any enemies he has that he doesn't know about."

"That sounds pretty odd, too," Sassy said. "Is this guy all there mentally?"

"Yeah, I think so," Michel replied. "I'm not sure what the hell is going on yet, but at least we'll get paid."

"That's true," Sassy replied.

"So how'd it go with Lee?" Michel asked.

"I think we're going to need to get a bottle of something before I tell you about that one," Sassy replied.

"Already got it covered," Michel said.

He reached into the bottom right drawer of his desk and took out a bottle of Jack Daniels and two small juice glasses.

"Sorry there's no ice," he said.

"You've got to be shitting me," Sassy said, shaking her head and smiling in disbelief. "Suddenly you're all Sam Spade on me with your whiskey in your desk drawer? What's next, a fedora?"

"Ha ha," Michel replied. "You want a drink, or what?"

"Oh yeah," Sassy replied.

Michel poured an inch of Jack into each glass and pushed one across the desk to Sassy. He raised his own intending to make a toast, but before he could speak, Sassy grabbed her glass and drained it in one quick swallow.

"Ah, that's better," she said, pushing the glass back toward Michel for a refill. "Now let me tell you about Lee."

Over the next half hour and two more Jacks, she recounted her meeting in as much detail as she could remember.

"I'm going to need your help," she said at the conclusion. "That is if you're not too busy working on the big costume caper."

"I think I can probably fit it in," Michel replied with a sneering smile. "What do you want me to do?"

"Just to be safe," she said, "I think you should keep investigating Patterson and Cornell. See if they were really scamming Chance. That way if Priest doesn't come through, we may still have enough evidence for Chance to take them to court. "

"Well, it's definitely a step up from Mardi Gras costumes," Michel replied, "though your case is still sexier."

"True," Sassy replied, "but look at the bright side. At least this time your case has some black folks in it."

Chapter 5

"So how does it feel to be back?" Joel asked, as he and Chance watched the sparse Thursday night crowd milling about on Bourbon Street from the balcony of Parade.

"Weird, but good," Chance replied. "I've missed it here."

"So how are things with you and your mom?" Joel asked.

"Okay," Chance replied with a shrug. "We talk about once a week. She seems to be doing okay...for her."

"Meaning?"

"I don't know. It just seems like her whole life has been one bad decision after another." Chance said. "First my dad, then she hooked up with some guy she worked for who was married, then she had Daisy but Daisy's father dumped her, and now she's seeing some guy who lives in her apartment building who's been married like five times. The more I learn about her, the more I worry."

"About her?" Joel asked, sensing that Chance was talking about something more.

"Yeah, her too," Chance said, then drained his beer. "It's just that...I mean...my dad's whole life was fucked up, and my mom is pretty much a mess, and I've been a fuckup my whole life. And then when I finally get a chance to do something good, I get mixed up with gangsters. It just scares me. What if my dad was right? What if the whole family really is cursed?"

Joel shook his head.

"Sorry, dude. You're not getting out of it that easily."

Chance gave him a perplexed look.

"'Oh, no, my whole family is cursed and there's nothing I can do about it so I might as well just give up now'," Joel said in a high, mocking voice.

Chance stared at him with open shock.

"Seriously, Chance," Joel continued in his normal voice, "you're *not* your father. You're so much smarter. Yeah, no doubt sometimes you're the dumbest smart person I know. And yeah, you fucked up by getting involved with Bulldog and what-his-name, but what you had planned was amazing. And the stuff you've done in Natchez? No way in hell your dad could ever have even thought of something like that."

Chance felt a lump form in his throat. Joel's naked honesty had taken him completely off-guard. He put his left arm around Joel's neck and pulled him closer until their foreheads were touching.

"You know, I really love you sometimes," he said softly.

"Just sometimes?" Joel asked, as he poked Chance in the ribs.

Chance smiled tolerantly and shook his head.

"You know, you really know how to ruin a moment," he said as he let his arm drop from Joel's neck and took a step back.

"Well, you don't want to be getting all maudlin in front of all these people, do you?" Joel asked, gesturing to the few dozen people below them.

Chance watched the small crowd for a moment, then frowned.

"Do you think it'll ever be what it was?" he asked.

"I don't know," Joel replied. "Every month it gets a little bit better, but I don't know if it'll ever be the same again."

They were quiet for a moment as they stared out at the city.

"So what's going on with you and Michel?" Chance asked suddenly.

"Your guess is as good as mine."

Chance put his right hand on his hip and shimmied his head from side to side.

"What's up with this guy?" he asked in his best black girl voice. "Do you really like him that much?"

"You did *not* just Janet Jackson me," Joel said with a mock baleful look.

"Oh yes I did," Chance replied, shifting his weight and swinging his narrow hips to the left.

"You're just not right," Joel said, unable to keep from laughing.

"Seriously," Chance said. "Are you dating? Not dating? Fucking? Not fucking? What's going on?"

"None of the above," Joel replied immediately, then reconsidered. "Actually we're definitely not fucking. But as far as dating, I don't know. We spend a lot of time together, but we haven't really talked about where it's going."

"Why not?" Chance asked.

Joel started to answer, then stopped himself.

"Wow," he said. "I never thought about that. That's a really good question."

"And do you have a really good answer?" Chance replied.

Joel considered it before responding.

"Well, I'm not sure how he feels," he said, "but honestly, I'm not sure if it's what I want."

"Really?" Chance replied, blinking his eyes with exaggerated surprise. "I thought you were mad in love with him."

"I am," Joel replied, "but I don't know if he can give me what I need."

"See, I told you he was old," Chance said, reverting to his black girl persona. "You need to find yourself a nice young stud to give you the good stuff. You know what I'm saying?."

Joel stared at him with a deadpan expression.

"Are you done, Lil Kim?" he asked. "I'm not talking about sex. I mean emotionally. I'm just not sure that I'm ever going to feel like he really needs me."

"I'm not following you," Chance said.

"The thing that I loved about Michel from the moment I met him was that he already seemed complete," Joel replied. "It was like he already knew who he was and had this whole life. And the fact that he wanted me to be part of it made me feel really special."

"But?" Chance asked.

"But over time I've realized that the downside of him being so complete is that I've never felt like he actually *needs* me. I think he wants me, but I feel like if I weren't around he'd be fine."

"Have you told him that?"

Joel sighed.

"No," he said wearily. "I don't want to come off like some needy chick. 'Oh, I need you to prove I'm the center of your universe. Please make me feel special.'"

Chance smiled with a combination of appreciation and sympathy. They were both quiet for a few moments.

"As you know," Chance said finally, "I'm not exactly the best person to be giving relationship advice since most of mine ended when the hour was up, but it seems to me that if you really love him you have to give him a fair chance. You can't expect him to read your mind. I think you should tell him how you feel and see what happens. Worst case, he's not able to give you what you need and you move on. But I think it would be pretty stupid to assume the worst and just walk away from it before you find out. That's like something I would do."

Joel stared into the night sky with a look of contemplation for nearly a minute, then broke into a sly smile and cut a sideways glance at Chance.

"Yeah, that really is something you'd do," he said, trying to suppress a laugh.

"Fuck you," Chance replied with mock indignation.

"Hey, you said it first," Joel said.

"Yeah, but you didn't need to agree so quickly," Chance replied with an exaggerated scowl.

Joel turned and took Chance's hands. He tilted his head down and made a comically contrite face.

"I'm sorry," he said. "You know I love you."

"Yeah, yeah, I know, blah, blah, blah," Chance replied, breaking into a grudging smile.

"And thank you," Joel said. "You're right. I need to tell him how I feel and give him a fair chance."

Chapter 6

"Ken Lauer," the voice on the other end of the phone answered.

Ken Lauer had been a law student at Loyola while Sassy was getting her graduate degree at Tulane. They'd met when he briefly dated a woman in Sassy's social circle, and had hit it off over their shared interests in the law and Cajun cuisine. He'd taken a job with the Justice Department right out of school and was now a prosecutor with the FBI's Organized Crime Unit. He and Sassy had remained close over the years and gotten together whenever Lauer was in New Orleans.

"Hey, it's me," Sassy responded.

"Hey," Lauer replied cheerfully. "I was beginning to think you'd fled the city when I didn't hear back the last few times I called. Is everything all right?"

Sassy felt a pang of guilt as she realized how long it had been since she'd given him a call.

"Everything's fine," she replied. "I'm sorry I didn't call back. It's just been kind of hectic down here since the hurricane. I'll fill you in on the details over a few scotches the next time you're in town."

"Okay, that's a deal," Lauer replied, his tone unconsciously shifting into professional mode as he realized that this wasn't just a casual call. "So what's up?"

"Well, I'm working on a case involving Priest Lee," Sassy replied.

"Priest Lee?" Lauer replied with obvious concern. "I hope

whoever hired you is paying you damn well, because you really don't want to mess with Priest Lee."

"Well, actually I'm working *for* Lee," Sassy replied.

"Wow, things really have changed for you," Lauer replied.

Sassy thought she heard a hint of rebuke in his voice and felt compelled to explain quickly what she was doing.

"Are you sure you don't want to turn this over to the police?" Lauer asked when she was done.

"I can't imagine that finding Deacon Lee's killer would be a top priority," Sassy replied. "Besides, if Priest won't report Deacon missing, they can't start an investigation."

"All right," Lauer agreed reluctantly, "but be careful."

"Oh, don't worry. First sign of trouble and I'll start running fast."

"So what do you need from me?" Lauer asked.

"I'm hoping that you guys might have information on a new player in town. Someone that Priest might not know about."

Even as she said it, Sassy realized it was actually what Lee wanted, and the thought made her uneasy.

"I can't believe we'd know about anyone that Priest wouldn't," Lauer replied, "but I'll check it out. I'll also see if we've picked up anything on someone planning to make a move against Priest or any of the other families."

"Great," Sassy replied. "I appreciate it."

"No problem," Lauer replied. "I should be able to get back to you this afternoon."

"Sounds good. I'm going to check out Deacon's house, but I should be back by four."

She gave him the office number.

"Okay, I'll be in touch," Lauer replied.

Sassy felt a sudden surge of doubt and an odd need to know that Lauer approved of what she was doing.

"Ken, do you think I'm crazy for getting involved in this?" she asked.

Lauer was silent for a few seconds before responding.

"Well, I don't think it's the smartest thing you've ever done," he said, "but I understand why you're doing it. Just remember who you're dealing with."

It wasn't the complete affirmation that Sassy had been hoping for, but it was enough.

"I will," she said.

Chapter 7

Deacon sure had security on his mind when he bought this place, Sassy thought as she stepped out of her car. The building was an Italianate gray granite block, with black steel shutters and thick iron bars set into the frames of every window. It looked more like a giant mausoleum than a house, and was completely out of character with the rest of the industrial buildings on that section of St. Ferdinand Street in Bywater. It seemed to have been dropped there by a tornado.

The three-story house was set back on a large lot, surrounded on both sides and in back by five-story brick buildings with no facing windows. The only way to approach it was from the front, where it was protected by a ten-foot-high stone wall topped by spikes and dotted with security cameras.

Sassy walked to the wrought-iron gate and peered into the front yard, hoping that Priest hadn't forgotten to mention that Deacon had left behind a pack of now-ravenous guard dogs. Seeing no signs of life, she unlocked the gate and stepped inside, pulled the gate shut behind her, and quickly walked to the front door.

The first thing Sassy noticed when she stepped into the marble-floored foyer was the complete absence of smell. There were no lingering food odors, no smells of stale smoke or cologne. The air was completely neutral, like a bank or office building.

She stepped into the room to the left of the foyer. Other than a chandelier that looked to be original to the house and a security camera in the back right corner, it was empty. She crossed the foyer to the room on the opposite side. It was the mirror image of the first room: pale gray walls, white trim, chandelier, no furniture, and a security camera.

Well, if there are cameras, she thought as she walked back into the foyer, there must be a recorder somewhere.

To the right of the stairs was a short hallway. Sassy walked down it, stopping to check a closet tucked under the stairs on the left and a half bathroom on the right. Neither looked to have been used in quite a while. The bathroom didn't even have toilet paper or towels.

At the end of the hallway was the kitchen, which ran the full width of the house. Sassy imagined that the original owners must have entertained often to have built such a large kitchen. From the steel plates bolted over the French doors lining the entire back wall, she guessed that Deacon didn't entertain at all. She stepped into the room and took a look around, immediately spotting the glowing red light of the security camera mounted in the back left corner.

With its pristine white cabinets and black granite counters, the kitchen looked brand new, despite the fact that the white finishes on the appliances—rather than the currently more fashionable stainless steel—suggested they were actually a few years old. She walked to one of the Fisher&Paykel ovens and opened it. The plastic sleeve with the manufacturer's warranty was still taped to the top rack. She flipped it up and looked for a copyright date on the back of the enclosed sheet: "©2000." The oven hadn't been used in the five-plus years since it had been installed.

She began opening random cabinets and drawers. Most of them were empty, though she did find two plates, three glasses, and a small assortment of silverware. Finally she checked the refrigerator. An expired half-gallon of milk, a quart of orange juice, an unopened pack of English Muffins, and one tub of margarine were the only contents.

I guess you ate out a lot, she thought.

She took one last look around the kitchen to see if anything caught her eye, then headed back up the hallway to the foyer, her footsteps echoing loudly in the empty space.

The staircase to the second floor rose five steps to a landing, then turned to the right. Sassy stood on the landing and looked up. The space above the stairs was open all the way to the third floor. She could see that the stairs from the second to the third floor ran in the opposite direction of those she was on, starting near the front wall of the house, then turning left and ending directly above where she was standing. She could see two more cameras mounted on the walls above, their lenses trained on the stairs.

She walked up to the second floor. A wide hallway wrapped the stairwell, forming a banistered gallery in the shape of a squared horseshoe. There were four doors leading off the gallery: two in the back wall and one on either side of the stairs closer to the front of the house. She decided to start with the room to the far right and work her way clockwise around to the stairs to the third floor.

Like the rooms off the foyer, the first two rooms were bare. She walked to the third door and tried the knob. To her surprise, it was locked. She fished the key Lee had given her out of her pocket, but it didn't fit the lock.

She considered going back to her car to get the pick set from the trunk, but decided against it. Her skill at picking locks had never been particularly good, and it had been at least five years since she'd last tried. Instead, she raised her right hand and pounded hard on the center panel of the door. The sound it made was low and muffled.

Okay, no way I'm going to be able to bust that down, she thought.

She decided to search the rest of the house first, then come back if necessary. She continued to the fourth room and found it also empty.

She walked up to the third floor. Unlike the gallery on the second floor, there was just a straight hallway running the width of the house. Where the front rooms had been on the other floors, there was a patio instead, accessible through French doors on both sides of the stairs. She looked out and could see a heavy stone railing running around the edge of the building. Along the top were more cameras and four large floodlights that Sassy imagined would be capable of lighting the entire block.

Jesus, this place is like a prison, she thought.

She turned to face the only interior door off the hallway. She expected it to be locked, but when she tried the doorknob it opened. A gentle mix of bergamot, ginger, and vetiver immediately enveloped her and she smiled without realizing it. It was the smell of L'Homme by Yves Saint Laurent, one of her favorite colognes. She closed her eyes and breathed deeply for a moment. While the scent wasn't strong, after being deprived of any olfactory stimulation in the rest of the house, she found it intoxicating. Finally she opened her eyes and stepped into the room. She'd obviously found Deacon's bedroom.

Sassy hadn't known what to expect in Deacon's house. She'd thought maybe it would look like the rappers' houses she'd seen on "MTV Cribs," with gaudy furniture, video games, ridiculously large TVs, and "Scarface" posters in every room. What she found instead came as a complete surprise. She felt as though she'd wandered onto the set of a lavish period movie about French nobility, and half-expected to see a man in a long curly wig come wandering into the room at any moment.

The centerpiece of the room was a kingsize bed with an ornately carved fruitwood headboard with ivory, ebony, and tortoise shell inlays depicting two vases of flowers set inside large ovals that were surrounded by laurel leaves. The bed was covered by a thick olive-and-dark-cherry-striped quilt that matched the room's wallpaper.

Bracketing the bed were matching Regency-period side tables of light walnut, with gently curved legs and hoof feet.

Along the right wall of the room were two Regency armchairs with floral needlepoint fauteuils, and a small, round marble-topped table between them. On the wall opposite the bed was an eight-foot-high fruitwood armoire with inlays that matched those on the headboard.

From the side, Sassy noticed wires extending out of a single hole on the back of the armoire. She moved in front of it and opened the doors. Inside were a forty-two-inch flat screen TV, a DVD player, and three shelves of DVDs. She shook her head, amazed that someone who had the taste to buy such a beautiful antique would defile it by cutting a hole in the back to hook up a TV.

She perused the DVDs. They were pretty much what she'd expected—a mix of buddy comedies and action-adventure flicks—until she got to the last three on the bottom shelf.

"Well now, aren't we smooth, Mr. Lee," she said aloud. "'The Bridges of Madison County,' 'The Bodyguard,' and 'The Notebook.' My, my. You just don't give the girls a chance, do you? Melt their panties right off."

She picked up the remote control, took a step back, and hit the ON button, curious what kinds of shows Deacon might have watched. What she saw was a collage of twelve color images of the inside of the house. They were numbered 3–15. She hit the INFO button and saw that she was watching channel 1. She switched to channel 2 and twelve images of the exterior of the house came up, numbered 16 –27. She changed to channel 3 and saw a full-screen image of herself standing in Deacon's bedroom watching herself on the TV.

Kinky, she thought, as she looked up at the video camera mounted above the bedroom door.

Then she tried to find a channel showing something other than the feeds from the security cameras. All of the channels above 27 were blank.

"You certainly had very limited taste in programming," she said as she switched the TV off and closed the armoire.

She turned and walked to an open doorway on the left side of the room and flicked the light switch. It was a hallway leading to three doors: one on the right, one on the left, and one at the end. Sassy opened the door on the right and an overhead light illuminated automatically. For a moment she thought she'd passed out and reawakened in Giorgio Armani.

The entire back wall of the room was lined by a double row of suits. Even from a few feet away, Sassy could tell they were expensive. They looked to be arranged by style, and then by color within each style. The right wall had jackets on a top rack and pants below, again arranged by color. The left wall was split, with dress shirts on a rack at the top, and rows of ties on wooden dowels below. The wall backing up to the hallway was lined by shelves of sweaters in every color imaginable, organized from light to dark.

Sassy ran a finger over the top of a pale yellow sweater near the door. It was the softest cashmere she'd ever felt. Be still my heart, she thought.

She turned to the door across the hall and opened it. Again the overhead light came on automatically. It was another walk-in closet—about half the size of the first, but still larger than any closet in Sassy's house—dedicated entirely to shoes, and organized again by style and color. Sassy noted that there were no sneakers or casual shoes. She shook her head admiringly and closed the door.

She walked to the end of the hall and opened the last door. As the light snapped on, she let out an audible gasp. It was the most beautiful bathroom she'd ever seen outside of a magazine.

The room was tiled from floor to ceiling with onyx travertine marble. On the center wall, two glass bowl sinks were mounted on a gray slate counter atop a dark cherry vanity with polished chrome fixtures. In the back right corner was a shower large enough to hold six comfortably. Its front wall was floor-to-ceiling glass, and there were vertical rows of shower heads mounted in the other three walls. Next to the shower was a separate room housing the toilet. And along the entire left wall of the room was the largest Jacuzzi tub Sassy had ever seen.

"You were a man after my own heart, Mr. Lee," Sassy murmured. "Just give me a big old bed, a huge closet full of designer clothes, and the world's biggest bathroom, and I will be a happy woman."

She walked to the vanity and opened each drawer. The contents were all neatly arranged: shaving accessories in the top, various ointments and creams in the middle, and over-the-counter medications in the bottom. She opened the cabinet doors and found cleaning products—all arranged in neat rows—and a small chrome waste basket. She pulled out the waste basket and looked inside. There were only four AA batteries.

Either you were anal-compulsive or you had a very good housekeeper, Sassy thought as she put the waste basket back under the sink and closed the cabinet. In the mirror, she noticed the camera mounted above the door and decided that, with Lee's obsession with security, it had to be the former.

She walked back to the door and stared longingly at the Jacuzzi for a moment before turning to leave. Then suddenly she stopped. Something wasn't right. She looked back at the Jacuzzi and calculated the distance from the doorframe to the left wall. It looked to be a about twelve feet. She quickly walked back to the second closet and did another approximate measurement.

Isn't that odd, she thought sarcastically. Though the bathroom and closet both appeared to back up to the hall, the bathroom was actually about five feet deeper. She walked back into the bedroom and looked to her right. There was a five-foot-wide bookcase built into the wall behind the door.

Sassy closed the bedroom door, placed her hands three feet apart on the middle shelf of the bookcase, and pushed. The right side of the bookcase moved back an inch and Sassy heard a satisfying click.

"Open Sesame," she said, as she stepped back and let the bookcase swing gently away from the wall.

*****

Severin Marchand's studio was actually a brick warehouse near the river on Jackson Street, less than a mile from his family home. It was a large, open space with thirty-foot ceilings criss-crossed by ducts carrying precisely controlled air from a massive HVAC unit on the roof. The room was divided roughly in half, with one side dedicated for storage and the other for Marchand's studio space.

The storage area had a cargo door on the end wall, and was neatly arranged with furniture in the center and shelves for smaller items around the outside. The studio side had a small kitchen against the side wall, a storage closet and bathroom on the back wall, and several wireframe dress dummies, a sewing machine, and a modern red couch in the center. The only window in the room was a transom over the side entrance, next to the kitchen.

Michel had immediately been struck by the dryness of the room. Having lived all his life in New Orleans, he'd only experienced that low a level of humidity a few dozen times, usually in forensics labs and museums.

"So what's in the boxes?" he asked, gesturing at four neatly stacked palettes of boxes just outside the storage area.

"Old costumes," Marchand replied. "I need to have them delivered to the Mardi Gras Museum. They want to do an exhibition on the Bourbon Street Awards."

"So you keep all of your old costumes?"

"Of course," Marchand exclaimed as though offended by the idea that he might not. "They're works of art."

Michel nodded.

"I just thought maybe you'd recycle some of the pieces for new costumes."

Marchand fixed him with an icy stare.

"That would be like wearing the same outfit to the White Party two years in a row," he said in a clipped voice.

"Of course it would," Michel replied, attempting to sound serious, despite the fact that he was fighting the urge to laugh. "How many costumes are there?"

"Nine," Marchand replied distractedly, as though he'd already lost interest in the subject.

Michel knelt down and began placing the photos Marchand had given him on the floor. As he compared them to the actual studio, he began shifting them around until he had what amounted to a panoramic collage of the room.

"These were taken the day you discovered the break-in?" he asked.

Marchand had wandered into the storage area and was examining a small porcelain vase as though he were seeing it for the first time.

"What?" he replied, looking up. "Uh, yes...no wait, it was the next day."

Michel studied the photos. They weren't as thorough as the crime scene photos he'd grown accustomed to while working on the force, but they gave a fairly complete picture of the crime scene, with the exception of the window over the door.

"The costumes weren't here when the break-in occurred?" he asked, noticing that the boxes didn't appear in any of the photos.

Marchand put down the vase with what appeared to be annoyance and walked back toward Michel.

"Excuse me?"

"The costumes," Michel repeated. "They weren't here when the break-in occurred? I don't see the boxes in any of the photos."

"They were in the back," Marchand replied, waving his hand toward the storage area. "They were hanging on a rack. After what happened, I thought I should have them packed up

71

and taken to the museum in case the culprit should come back again and try to destroy my legacy."

Wow, dramatic much? Michel thought.

"So you called the museum and asked if they'd like them?" he asked.

"Of course not," Marchand replied too quickly. "They've been asking for them for years. I would never try to promote myself that way."

"No," Michel agreed. "That would be vulgar."

Marchand studied him for a moment, trying to decide if Michel was mocking him.

"Do you have a step ladder?" Michel asked before Marchand could decide.

"Mmmm, yes, in the closet," Marchand replied, making it clear he had no intention of getting it himself.

Michel retrieved the ladder and set it up in front of the door. He climbed up three steps and began examining the transom window.

"This is alarmed," he said after a few seconds.

"Of course," Marchand replied.

"But the alarm didn't go off?"

"No, the window wasn't opened. The glass was broken and whoever it was climbed in through the opening."

Michel stopped looking at the window and turned to face Marchand with a quizzical look.

"Was there blood?"

"Not that anyone saw," Marchand replied.

Michel raised one eyebrow skeptically.

"I find that hard to believe," he said. "Glass doesn't just fall out when it's broken. There are always fragments imbedded in the frame. Even a small adult would have a hard time getting through this window without touching the sides."

"Perhaps they picked all the glass out before they climbed through," Marchand replied with a casual shrug. "All I know is what I saw. There was no blood."

Michel doubted that anyone would take the time to pick out the glass during a break-in, but decided not to argue the point. He jumped down and walked back to look at the photos.

"I don't see any glass," he said, pointing to a photo that clearly showed the floor in front of the door. "Are you sure there was glass on the *inside?*"

"What are you suggesting?" Marchand asked suspiciously.

"What if someone let themselves in with a key, then broke the window from the inside, hoping to make it look like a break-in?"

Marchand gave Michel a puzzled look, as though trying to figure out where this line of thinking was leading.

"Who else has a key and knows the alarm code?" Michel asked.

"Well, there's a key at the house," Marchand replied uncertainly. "And any number of the staff would know the alarm code. People are bringing things here and taking things back to the house all the time. But if you're suggesting it was a member of my staff, I'm afraid you're mistaken."

"Why's that?" Michel asked. "Let's be honest, Severin. You're a very wealthy man, and I'm pretty sure your staff are not wealthy. You don't think it's possible that some of them resent you?"

Marchand let out an agitated sigh.

"Despite what you may believe, my people are treated very well," he said testily. "In fact, they are treated like family, and they are compensated very well. Loyalty is very important to me, and I believe it should be reciprocated. Most of the staff have been with me for many years, and in some cases they're the second or third generation of their families to work for my family. I trust them implicitly."

"So there's no one who might have a grudge against you? No one who was let go in the last few month?"

Marchand shook his head adamantly.

"No. The last time anyone left was over a year ago, and that was by choice. One of the gardeners got married and moved to Dallas."

Michel thought Marchand sounded convincing, but he still liked the theory that the crime had been committed by someone with access to the studio.

"Maybe it was an accident," he offered. "Maybe someone was delivering something to the studio, knocked over the costume by mistake, and when they realized it was damaged they tried to cover it up by making it look like a crime."

"It sounds like you're grasping at straws to support your theory," Marchand replied.

"Then why isn't there any glass on the floor in the photo?" Michel replied with obvious frustration.

Marchand pursed his lips for a moment.

"Perhaps because the photo was taken the next day," he replied finally. "By that point at least a half dozen people had been traipsing in and out. Maybe one of the staff thought to clean up the glass for safety reasons."

"Will you check on that?" Michel asked.

"Of course," Marchand replied with a tolerant smile. "Whatever you like."

Michel wished that Marchand weren't there so he could thoroughly search the ground outside for broken glass, but decided he could come back later if necessary.

"Fine," he said. "I think we're all done here."

"Good," Marchand replied as though he'd just been let out of detention early. "Now about the interviews. The first one is scheduled for 4 PM, and then one every twenty minutes after that. I assume that will be enough time?"

"4 PM today?"

"Of course," Marchand replied. "The more quickly we can get to the bottom of this the better."

Michel almost laughed at the use of the phrase "get to the bottom of this." It was like Marchand thought he was in some old dime store detective novel.

"That won't be a problem, will it?" Marchand asked imperiously.

"No, I suppose not," Michel replied, realizing he didn't really have a choice. "So your friends will meet me at my office?"

"Oh," Marchand replied with unconvincing guilt. "I'm afraid I didn't think of that. I asked them all to met you at Good Friends Bar. And I'm afraid it's too late to call and change plans since I know they all have appointments this afternoon."

Again, Michel realized he wasn't being given a choice.

"Okay," he replied. "Who am I meeting first?"

"Scotty McClelland," Marchand replied. "If you're not sure who he is, just ask the bartender. He'll know."

Oh, I'm sure of that, Michel thought.

Chapter 8

Behind the bookcase in Deacon's bedroom was a wide but steep set of stairs leading down one flight. Based on the age of the rough-hewn timber, Sassy guessed that they had been an original feature of the house, probably used by servants to move about without disturbing their employers. There was a light switch on the left wall. Sassy flipped it and bright fluorescent lights flickered to life.

Those obviously aren't original, she thought as she started down.

At the base of the stairs, the space widened another four feet to create a narrow hall along the right side of the stairs. Sassy stepped into it and looked around. The wall directly in front of the stairs clearly had an opening cut into it. It appeared to be the same size as the one behind the bookcase, but had been nailed shut with four horizontal two-by-fours. She turned to her right and looked at the floor under the stairs. There were newer panels of plywood there, suggesting that at one point there'd been another flight of stairs, probably down to the kitchen. There didn't appear to be any way out of the hall other than the stairs down which she'd come.

Okay, so why seal off all but one entrance? Sassy wondered. If Deacon had wanted an escape route, he'd only managed to create a box canyon to trap himself.

She turned her attention to the wall that ran the width of the space. It was definitely newer, made of drywall rather than plaster. The gaps between the three panels hadn't been seamed.

Eenie, meenie, minie, mo, she thought as she moved in front of the left-hand panel and pushed against it with both hands. Nothing happened. She took a few steps to her right and tried the center panel. Again nothing. She moved to the left panel and tried one more time. Still nothing.

Motherfucker, she thought as she stepped back and brushed off her hands. Don't even *try* to tell me there's no door here.

She leaned against the right wall and stared at the floor as she tried to decide what to do next. She knew she could go back to the car for her lock pick and try to get into the other room on the second floor, but she was convinced the tapes for the security cameras were behind the wall here. She sighed in frustration and let her head fall back. As she did, her eyes drifted up and she saw a mark on the ceiling.

"What have we here?" she asked as she walked forward to get a better look.

On a bulge near the middle of the room was a curved scrape about four inches long.

"Here you were thinking you were all tricky with your hidden door, Mr. Deacon Lee," she said triumphantly, "but you got yourself a saggy ceiling."

*****

Sassy sat on the stairs and looked at the remains of the center drywall panel on the floor. She was covered in sweat and dust, and feeling frustrated. She'd managed to pry an edge of the panel loose using a butter knife from Lee's kitchen, then had ripped large pieces off by hand. Underneath she'd found a wood frame bolted to a steel panel with a peephole in the center. There were no handles, door knobs, key holes, or hinges, but still she was sure it was a door. She took a deep breath and considered what she knew about Deacon that might help her figure out how to open it.

Clearly he had very good taste, she thought. She doubted

that fact would lead anywhere, so she set it aside. He was also compulsively neat. That might be helpful, though probably not on its own. And he was extremely concerned with his own security, possibly even paranoid. That seemed the most fruitful avenue to explore.

Okay, that would probably preclude some kind of hidden latch or button, she reasoned, because he'd be too worried that someone might find it. Which would leave a key of some sort. Obviously there's no keyhole, so that would mean an electronic key or opener. But if he were really paranoid, he wouldn't have trusted anything electronic because the batteries could die...

She stopped herself and smiled.

"Unless you change them every day," she said aloud, remembering the four batteries in the trash in Lee's bathroom.

Given his neatness, she doubted that they'd been there for more than a day. She hauled herself up from the step and walked back up to the bedroom to retrieve the remote control from the armoire.

Standing back in front of the steel wall panel, she studied the buttons on the remote. Obviously the TV button works the TV, she thought, and presumably the DVD button works the DVD player, so let's see what VCR does. She hit the button and nothing happened. Then she hit the ON button and again nothing happened.

She stared at the remote, trying to maintain her patience. All right, if I were being chased by bad guys, which button would I want to hit? Of course, she thought as her thumb moved to the On Demand button. The biggest one.

She pressed the button and heard grinding sounds followed by a heavy clank, then a whoosh like the opening of a giant can of soda. The panel moved gently forward a few inches.

Why didn't I notice that earlier? she wondered. This is a cable remote and the guy didn't even have cable.

She gripped the left edge of the door and swung it open, then stood there in amazement. Deacon Lee's safe room occupied almost the entire space under his bedroom closets and the hallway leading to his bathroom. The walls, floor, and ceiling were covered by steel plates, and there were two rows of fluorescent tube lights along the tops of the side walls.

The top half of the back wall was taken up by twenty-four video monitors, mounted in three rows of eight. In the center of the wall was a metal desk with a telephone and computer, and to the left of the desk were three portable racks of black DAT recorders, hooked by a cobweb of cables to the monitors.

In the back left corner of the room were a toilet and sink. The rest of the left wall was taken up by a comfortable-looking twin bed. The walls to the left and right of the door were shelved, and held an array of dry and canned goods and cases of bottled water. Immediately next to the shelves on the right was a full-sized refrigerator, and next to that, another door that was bolted at the top and bottom from the inside.

What really captured Sassy's attention, however, were the guns that occupied the remainder of the right wall. She estimated there had to be at least forty weapons, ranging from pistols to shotguns to semi-automatic assault rifles. They were carefully arranged by type on steel shelves, with the appropriate boxes or magazines of ammunition next to each.

She walked to a shelf and picked up a silver Walther PPK .380 handgun. She released the magazine and checked it. It was fully loaded. Deacon wasn't just storing his guns here, she thought. He was ready for a war.

She crossed to the DAT recorders and hit the Play button of the one on the top of the left rack. Nothing happened. She hit the Eject button. The cartridge holder opened, but nothing came out. It was empty.

"Son of a bitch," Sassy muttered as she tried the second recorder and found it empty, too.

She quickly opened the remaining recorders with the same results. She'd initially assumed that whatever happened to Deacon had taken place somewhere outside the house, given his extensive security system. Now the absence of the tapes made her question that assumption. Not only might he have been taken or killed in the house, but by someone he trusted who also knew about the safe room.

She took a quick look around, then turned on the computer. The screen brightened and she waited for the desktop to appear. Instead a blinking question mark popped up.

"I'm no fucking Bill Gates," she muttered with frustration, "but I'm pretty sure that's not good."

She switched off the computer, then unbolted the side door and pushed it open. On the other side was Deacon Lee's office.

*****

Sassy finished searching the drawers of Deacon's desk and turned on the computer. While she waited for it to boot up, she looked around the room. It reminded her of Priest's office with its dark-paneled walls, mahogany desk, and black leather chairs. Unlike Priest's office, however, it was dominated by the bank of video monitors on one wall.

How could someone live like that? she wondered sadly.

She looked back at the computer screen and was greeted by another blinking question mark.

Damn it, she thought, as she sat down hard in Deacon's desk chair. She knew that if she were on the force she'd have access to experts who might still be able to retrieve information from the computer, or she could call in a team to search every inch of the house, but as it was, she was out of options. The trip to Deacon's house had been a waste of time.

She sat back and stared at the gleaming top of the desk. She noticed absently that there wasn't a single mark or scratch on it. Her own desk at home bore the imprints of a thousand letters she'd written and checks she'd signed over the years. Deacon either didn't write anything, or he always used a pad.

She sat up suddenly and opened the shallow drawer in the center of the desk. There was a white note pad nestled in the right corner.

"You really are rusty at this detective shit," she said as she took out the pad and held it at an angle to the light.

There were clear indentations in the top sheet. She placed the pad on the desk and took out a pencil, then began rubbing the side of the graphite lightly over the paper. A phone number appeared.

She quickly picked up the phone on Deacon's desk and punched in the numbers. She held her breath excitedly as she heard it begin to ring. After the third ring, someone picked up.

"Hello?"

The voice was male. It was deep and heavily accented. Sassy guessed the speaker was from somewhere in the Caribbean.

"Oh, I'm sorry," she replied. "I think I dialed the wrong number."

"Okay, no problem," the voice responded.

Sassy hung up and tore the sheet of paper from the pad. Well, that's a start, she thought as she folded it and placed it in her shirt pocket.

*****

Ten minutes later Sassy was back at her car. She'd put everything in the house back as she'd found it, with the exception, of course, of the broken drywall. She'd also taken the remote control. She was about to open the car door when she sensed someone standing behind her. She turned quickly and saw a young woman standing in front of Deacon's gate.

The woman looked to be in her early twenties. She was pretty, with short black hair and light caramel skin. Her eyes were very large and anxious.

"Are you looking for Deacon?" she asked, looking around nervously as though she were afraid of being seen.

81

Sassy wasn't sure how to respond. Obviously the woman had seen her coming out of Deacon's house.

"Uh, no," she replied. "I was just dropping something off."

The woman looked more agitated.

"No, I mean are you trying to find him?"

Sassy hesitated for a second before answering.

"Why would I be trying to find him?" she asked carefully.

"Because he's been missing for three weeks," the woman replied, looking around nervously again.

"And you are?" Sassy asked, walking toward the woman.

"Kimora Tucker," the woman responded.

She stared at the ground for a moment before continuing.

"I'm Deacon's girlfriend. Or one of them, anyway."

"And you think Deacon's been missing for three weeks?"

Tucker nodded.

"I thought maybe his father had hired you to find him."

Sassy considered how to proceed.

"Let's say he did," she offered. "What do you think happened to Deacon?"

Tucker seemed to relax a little, as though she'd been waiting for an opportunity to talk with someone.

"I think he may have gotten mixed up with the wrong people."

Sassy fought the urge to laugh. When you were Deacon Lee, who exactly constituted the wrong people? she wondered.

"Any idea who?" she asked.

"I don't know," Tucker replied shaking her head woefully. "But I know something was going on. He kept going to meetings by himself, and about a month ago he said that things were going to be changing soon. I asked him what he meant, but he wouldn't tell me."

Sassy nodded.

"And you think whoever he was involved with might have done something to him?"

Tucker's lower lip quivered and her eyes filled with tears.

"He would have called me if he were all right," she said, her voice breaking as she began to sob.

Sassy reflexively put her right arm over Tucker's shoulders and pulled her close. She found it oddly touching that a man like Deacon had a woman who obviously loved him so much. She decided to drop all pretense.

"I'll do whatever I can to find him," she said. "I promise."

Tucker seemed to gain some comfort from the words, and took a few ragged breaths to pull herself back together. Sassy let her go and took a step back.

"If you hear from Deacon or need to get in touch with me, here's my number," she said, handing Tucker one of the business cards she'd printed on her home computer the night before.

"Thank you," Tucker said, in a tone that seemed genuinely grateful.

"Oh, just one thing," Sassy said as she turned back, halfway to her car. "I'd appreciate it if you kept this conversation just between us."

Tucker gave her a confused and nervous look.

"Trust me," Sassy said. "It would be better for both of us."

*****

Michel arrived at the Good Friends Bar a few minutes before 4 PM. Already about twenty men were seated around the large rectangular bar, chatting in small groups. Michel quickly perused their faces to see if he recognized any of them from Marchand's entourage. No one looked familiar, so he walked up to the bar. The bartender, a cute younger guy with spiky brown hair and very blue eyes, came walking over and gave a big smile.

"So what can I get you?" he asked in a honeyed drawl.

Even though it was the obvious question, the bartender still managed to make it sound provocative. I guess that's how they earn their tips, Michel thought.

"Actually I'm just looking for someone," he replied.

"Scotty McClelland?" the bartender asked enthusiastically.

"Uh, yeah," Michel replied, surprised. "How did you know?"

The bartender waved his right hand dismissively.

"Severin said a tall, dark, handsome man would come in looking for Scotty this afternoon."

He gestured to the crowd behind him and smiled flirtatiously.

"Obviously you're the first one of those to come through the door today."

"Uh, thanks," Michel replied, still a little flustered. "So is Scotty here yet?"

"Upstairs," the bartender replied. "Just step over the rope at the bottom of the steps."

"Okay, thanks," Michel replied.

He started to turn away, but the bartender touched his right shoulder. Michel turned back with a curious look.

"Did you want anything to drink?" the bartender asked. "It's on Severin's tab."

Michel considered it for a moment. He knew that a drink or three would make the interviews pass much more quickly, but decided it was too early.

"No, thanks," he said.

"Okay," the bartender said, "but if you change your mind, I'll be here."

Michel nodded and walked to the stairs. As he stepped over the rope, he glanced back at the bar. The bartender was whispering excitedly to two older men who simultaneously looked up at Michel.

So much for conducting a discreet investigation, he thought.

*****

The interviews with Marchand's six friends had lasted almost exactly twenty minutes each, as Marchand had planned. The script had run the same with each: first an expression of sympathy for Marchand and disbelief that anyone would do such a thing, then an assertion that they couldn't think of anyone who didn't like Marchand, and finally a "sudden" revelation that maybe there was one person who might benefit from destroying Marchand's costume—Ari "Ray" Nassir, the contest runner-up the past two years.

Michel stretched and looked at his watch. It was a few minutes before 6 PM. He was more than ready for a drink now, but dreaded going downstairs. He knew that by now every patron in the bar would have heard that some sort of meetings on Severin Marchand's behalf were taking place upstairs.

He stood up, walked out on the balcony, and lit a cigarette. The foot traffic on St. Ann and Dauphine streets was light. By now, most people had already made it home from work or stopped someplace for a drink.

He heard a sudden burst of laughter below and a chorus of goodbyes, and leaned over the balcony to see what was happening. A well-dressed man with jet black hair and tan skin stepped out onto the curb and looked down St. Ann toward the Bourbon Pub. Michel recognized him immediately. It was Ray Nassir.

Although Michel had never met Nassir, he'd seen him around in the bars on a few occasions, and had learned his name though mutual acquaintances. That seemed to be the way it was in the local gay scene: everyone knew *about* everyone else, even if they didn't know them. He'd heard that Nassir was of Pakistani descent, though he'd grown up somewhere just outside New Orleans.

Nassir looked at his watch, then crossed the street and began walking up Dauphine Street toward Esplanade.

This is too good a coincidence to pass up, Michel thought, as he headed toward the stairs. When he reached the bottom, he heard the room go suddenly quieter and felt eyes watching him. He tried to act casual, taking the time to wave goodbye to the bartender as he crossed the room, then stepped out a side door onto St. Ann. He stood there for a few seconds and made a show of trying to appear as if he were deciding where to go next. Then he slowly crossed the street, walked to the corner of Dauphine, and turned right.

Nassir was already nearing the intersection of Dumaine, the next cross street. Michel turned and looked back toward the bar. There were only a few tourists two blocks away. He began jogging after Nassir.

He was still almost a quarter block behind Nassir and already breathing heavily when Nassir turned right onto the next street. Michel forced himself to sprint to the corner, then stood there for a moment trying to catch his breath before calling out to Nassir.

"Excuse me, Mr. Nassir," he called when Nassir was about thirty feet away.

Nassir turned and looked at Michel. It was the first time Michel had seen Nassir's face without a filter of dim lights, moving heads, and smoke between them. He guessed that they were probably about the same age, though Nassir's face was more boyish, with large brown eyes and softer features. He was almost more beautiful than handsome, though there was nothing overtly feminine about him.

"Do I know you?" Nassir asked cautiously.

"No, my name is Michel Doucette," Michel replied, taking a few steps forward. "I'm a private investigator. I was hoping I might be able to speak with you in private for a few minutes."

"About what?" Nassir replied nervously.

"I'd rather not talk about it here," Michel replied, trying to sound reassuring. "But my office is only a few blocks away."

Nassir studied Michel closely, then seemed to decide that he wasn't dangerous.

"I'm on my way to meet friends for dinner right now," he

said, "but if you want to stop by my apartment around 7:30 PM, we can talk then."

"That would be fine," Michel replied. "I'll just need the address."

*****

Sassy was sitting at her desk when Michel walked back into the office.

"Where've you been?" she asked.

"At the Severin Marchand Dog and Pony Show," he replied with a tired grimace.

"What's that supposed to mean?"

"I was interviewing Marchand's friends over at the Good Friends Bar."

"You were doing interviews in a bar?" Sassy asked, her eyebrows knitting together with disbelief.

"Not my idea," Michel replied, holding his hands up defensively. "Marchand set it up. I really don't know what's going on. This whole thing feels like it's been elaborately staged. It was obvious that Marchand told his friends exactly what to say, and he's trying to point the finger at a guy named Ray Nassir, who was the runner-up at the Bourbon Street Awards the last few years."

"If he's so sure that Nassir did it, why wouldn't he just tell you? Why bother making you conduct the interviews?"

"That's what I can't figure out," Michel replied, sighing with frustration.

"Maybe he's just getting off on people knowing he's hired a private detective," Sassy offered. "Maybe he thinks it gives him an air of mystery. That would explain why he set up the interviews in a public place."

"Yeah," Michel agreed, "but it's seems like a lot of trouble to go through. Fucking drama queens."

"So what are you going to do next?"

"I'm actually meeting with Nassir at his place in about an hour."

Sassy nodded.

"What about Patterson and Cornell?" she asked. "Have you had a chance to check them out at all?"

"Yeah, I spent the morning online researching projects they've worked on, and then I checked their jackets."

Sassy knew that jackets referred to their police files. She also knew that information wasn't public.

"And how'd you manage that?" she asked, narrowing her eyes.

"I have my sources," Michel replied.

"Yeah, well you and your sources better not get caught or we're going to lose our licenses," Sassy chastised. "So did you find anything?"

"Neither one has been arrested for over nine years," Michel replied. "Not even a suspicion of anything. And Chance was right about their credentials. They're big-time players in the development game. It looks like they may have gone legit."

"Or they got much better at not being caught."

"Maybe that, too," Michel agreed.

"Anything else?"

"I was looking through the documents Chance gave us. The architecture firm on the project was called Harding & Lutz. I'll see what I can find out about them tomorrow."

"Sounds good," Sassy replied.

"So what about you?" Michel asked. "Did you find anything at Deacon's house?"

"You still got that bottle?" Sassy asked.

Chapter 9

"Sorry, but I'm in a hurry, Mr. Doucette," Ray Nassir said as he ushered Michel into his living room. "I hope you don't mind, but I just have to jump in the shower. Make yourself comfortable. I'll be right back."

Nassir disappeared into a room off the living room and a few seconds later Michel heard the faint sound of running water. He took a seat on a low, pale green sofa in front of the windows that ran one full wall of the room. Nassir had good taste, he thought as he looked around. The room was minimalist, but not sterile. The furnishings were all modern in style, but looked to be originals rather than Pottery Barn or Crate and Barrel copies. The colors were mostly muted, but there were splashes of bright color in the throw pillows and many contemporary paintings.

A few minutes later, Nassir came back into the room. He was wearing only a short white towel around his waist. His jet black hair was slicked back, and the thick hair on his chest and legs looked to still be damp.

"So can I fix you a drink?" he asked.

"I thought you were in a hurry?" Michel replied, flustered both by the unexpected question and Nassir's lack of clothes.

"I am, but there's *always* time for cocktails," Nassir replied with a slow smile. "So what can I get you?"

"A Jack on the rocks, I guess," Michel replied.

Nassir walked to a large bird's eye maple bar in the corner and began fixing the drinks with his back to Michel. Michel took the opportunity to get a better look at Nassir's body. His torso was long and slim, but tightly muscled. His legs were more muscular, like the legs of a soccer player, and he appeared to have a nicely rounded butt.

As Nassir turned back, Michel quickly looked away. Nassir walked over carrying a tumbler of Jack Daniels and what looked like a Cosmopolitan. He handed the tumbler to Michel, then sat in a chair opposite Michel and stretched out. Michel noted with surprise that Nassir's chest hair didn't appear to have been trimmed at all, something that was increasingly uncommon for gay men.

"So I assume you're the same detective who was upstairs at the Good Friends?" Nassir asked.

Michel smiled and nodded.

"You heard about that huh?"

"It was the talk of the evening," Nassir replied, then took a sip of is drink. "So what can I do for you?"

"Well, Severin Marchand hired me to find out who destroyed the Mardi Gras costume he was working on for this year," Michel replied.

"You're kidding," Nassir replied in a tone that suggested he sincerely thought Michel was making a joke.

"I'm afraid not," Michel said.

He realized that he felt slightly embarrassed to admit what he was investigating to someone outside Marchand's circle of friends. It was certainly a huge step down from homicide.

"So which Bette was the old girl planning to do this year?" Nassir asked with sudden interest.

"Excuse me?"

"Oh, he didn't tell you?" Nassir replied with a slight roll of his eyes. "Every year Severin does Bette Davis. Usually from one of her costume dramas."

Michel could imagine that with his flat face, small hooked nose, and large, wide-set eyes, Marchand would make a very believable Bette Davis.

"I take it you don't approve?" he asked, having noted Nassir's eye roll.

"Don't get me wrong. He makes a great Bette, and he's an amazing tailor. The detail on his 'Virgin Queen' costume was incredible."

"But?"

"But Charles LeMair and Mary Willis designed the original costume," Nassir replied. "Severin just copied it. Every year he just copies. I prefer something more original and creative."

"Such as?" Michel asked.

Nassir jumped up immediately and walked to a bookcase near the front door. He took down a photo album and began thumbing through it as he walked back toward Michel, then sat on the couch with his left knee almost touching Michel's right. He placed the album on the coffee table and pointed at a photo.

In it, four men dressed as oversized gargoyles were perched in squatting positions along the roofline of a small scale replica of Paris' Notre Dame Cathedral. Despite the fact that his body and face were covered in gray paint and he was sporting enormous outstretched wings, Nassir was immediately recognizable as the man on the far right.

"Wow, that's pretty cool," Michel said, genuinely impressed. "How did you get your wings to stand up like that?"

"I'm an architect," Nassir replied. "Structure is part of what we do."

Michel sat forward and looked at the other photos on the page. In one, Nassir stood with his arms outstretched as he was being spray painted gray. He was wearing only a gray thong, and his torso and legs were completely shaved. Michel felt himself flush a little.

"That was awful," Nassir said, sitting forward so that his shoulder touched Michel's and pointing at the picture. "I was sweating gray for a week, and it took two months for my body hair to grow back."

"I'll bet," Michel replied a little too quick.

He took a nervous swig of his drink.

"You don't happen to have any photos of Marchand's costumes, do you?" he asked, wanting an excuse to stop looking at the photo.

"Sure," Nassir replied. "I've got photos of all the winners and runners-up for the last ten years."

He got up and walked back to the bookcase to get another album. Michel took the opportunity to move a few inches farther to his left.

"So I'm curious why you wanted to talk to me," Nassir said as he walked back with the new photo album. "Severin and I aren't exactly close friends."

He sat back on the couch, this time with his back against the right arm rest and his left leg curled under him so that his body was turned toward Michel. He rested the album on his lap and looked at Michel expectantly.

"To tell you the truth," Michel replied uncomfortably, "I've spoken with several of Marchand's friends to find out who they thought might have a grudge against him, and your name kept coming up."

Nassir's face grew suddenly angry.

"I'm a suspect?" he asked with disbelief.

"I didn't say that," Michel replied evenly, "but I thought I should talk with you."

Nassir closed his eyes and took several deep breaths. Michel thought he saw several emotions flit across his face in the span of a few seconds. When he opened his eyes, Nassir appeared calm again.

"I didn't need to sabotage that old queen to win," he said matter-of-factly. "I just had to outlast her. Which I did."

"Meaning?"

"The only reason he won the last three years was because he paid off the sponsors to put his friends on the judging committee. But this year it's a whole new committee. His days are over."

Everything about the investigation to that point—the fact that Marchand's studio had been cleaned before he could examine it, the public interviews with Marchand's friends, the way they'd all mentioned only Nassir as a possible suspect—had felt staged. Now a thought occurred to Michel.

"Would you mind showing me Marchand's costumes for the last few years?" he asked suddenly.

Nassir gave him a confused look, but nodded and scooted forward on the couch, closer to Michel. As Nassir placed the photo album on the coffee table, Michel noticed that his towel had ridden higher up his thighs, and thought he saw the front of it twitch. He pushed the thought away and tried to concentrate as Nassir began flipping through pages.

"Here's his 'Virgin Queen' from last year," Nassir said, angling the book toward Michel. "Check out that beadwork. It really was amazing, though I still don't think he deserved to win."

He flipped two more pages.

"And here's Baby Jane Hudson from the year before. Not a very difficult costume, though he fit the part."

Another page.

"Apple Annie from 'Pocketful of Miracles.' Again, not very difficult."

Nassir continued to flip through pages and provide commentary, though Michel was only half listening as he tried to concentrate on the photos.

"And this was the first time he made runner-up," Nassir said. "In 1999, for 'Jezebel'."

It was the photo Michel had been expecting. He recognized the bright red silk and taffeta immediately.

"This has been very helpful," he said quickly. "I really appreciate your time."

"Um, okay," Nassir stammered, clearly surprised. "So that's it? I'm no longer a suspect?"

"Nope," Michel replied breezily. "I'm convinced you'd have no reason to destroy Marchand's costume."

"Great," Nassir replied, though it was obvious he was still unsure what had happened.

Michel started to stand but Nassir stopped him.

"You're not going, are you?" he asked.

"Well..."

"Please, finish your drink," Nassir said. "Let's get to know one another better."

This time Michel was certain he saw Nassir's towel move.

"Are you trying to seduce me?" he asked.

Nassir responded by making a disappointed face.

"Well, I was, but if you can't tell, I guess I wasn't doing a very good job of it," he said.

"No, I could tell," Michel replied, his eyes dropping to Nassir's towel for a second. "You were definitely giving me a clue. But I thought you were in a hurry to go somewhere."

"I am in a hurry," Nassir replied, "but who said I was going anywhere?"

He arched his eyebrows and lowered his upper eyelids simultaneously. Michel found the look both comical and effectively seductive.

"So then all of this with the shower and the towel..." he trailed off.

"Yup," Nassir replied plainly. "Can you blame me? Some hot detective shows up at my door to question me? It's like something out of a porn movie."

Michel laughed.

"Yeah, I suppose it is."

"So did you want to frisk me or cuff me first?" Nassir asked in a tone that was half-joking and fully enticing.

"I'll bet you say that to all the boys," Michel replied.

*****

"Well, thanks for...everything," Michel said as he shifted uncomfortably inside the door of Ray Nassir's apartment.

Nassir was standing a few feet away, still naked. He closed the distance between them and draped his arms around Michel's neck, then kissed Michel deeply.

As he stepped back, Nassir extended a business card between the index and middle fingers of his right hand. Michel wondered briefly where the card had come from, but took it.

"Just in case you want to get together again," Nassir said hopefully. "Or you could just stop by the Good Friends. I almost always stop in for a drink around 5:30 PM."

Michel was suddenly reminded of Severin Marchand, and wondered if Marchand had scheduled the interviews when he did in hopes that Michel would see Nassir after and approach him in the bar. It seemed likely. He was looking forward to his next conversation with Marchand, but decided he'd make Marchand wait a few days.

Michel realized Nassir was staring at him expectantly, and looked down quickly at the card.

"You work for Harding & Lutz?" he asked, surprised.

"I'm a partner," Nassir replied. "Why, have you heard of us?"

"A friend of mine was involved in a project that you were the architects on," Michel replied. "You didn't happen to work on the Bluehawk Terminal redevelopment, did you?"

"Ew, commercial work," Nassir replied, wrinkling his nose in a way that Michel found very cute. "I only do residential work. But it sounds familiar. I'm sure I've heard people talking about it at the office, but I try not to clutter my brain with details that have nothing to do with me."

Michel nodded. He was torn between wanting to be discreet and not wanting to lose a chance to gain information.

"The project was killed when the terminal burned," he said. "I was just curious how far along it was."

"Just curious?" Nassir asked, smiling in way that was both skeptical and seductive.

Michel considered how to answer.

"Let's just say it's professional curiosity," he said finally.

Nassir studied him for a moment, then broke into a sly smile.

"I'll tell you what," he said. "I'll see what I can find out—discreetly, of course—if you agree to go on a proper date with me."

*****

Sassy was loading her dinner dishes into the dishwasher when the phone rang. She looked at the clock on the stove and saw it was just after 8:30 PM.

"Hello," she answered with annoyance, prepared to tell off a telemarketer.

"Hey, calm down, tiger," Ken Lauer replied. "I didn't realize it was past your bed time."

Sassy smiled.

"Sorry about that. I just wasn't in the mood to go on a cruise or refinance my house right now."

"No problem," Lauer replied understandingly. "Sorry I didn't get back to you earlier, but I got stuck in a meeting that led to dinner, etc."

"That's okay. So did you find out anything?"

"Nothing concrete," Lauer replied. "There's no chatter about anyone making a move against Lee or the other families. But, there is a newer player in town who's been expanding his territory, though so far he hasn't tried to move into anything controlled by the big boys."

"Sounds like a possibility," Sassy replied. "Who is it?"

"His name is Granville Kingston," Lauer replied. "He's got operations in Metairie, Kenner, Algiers. Basically all the areas surrounding the city. He moved to New Orleans from Jamaica about fifteen years ago and joined up with a gang that did a lot of small-time stuff like breaking and entering and selling dope on street corners.

"Five years ago he took control of the gang and merged it with several other smaller gangs in the area. They started branching out into importing narcotics, gambling, loan sharking, and prostitution."

"How'd he manage a merger?" Sassy asked. "Kill the other gang leaders?"

"No," Lauer replied. "Apparently he convinced them to join up with him. This guy's very smooth. We know he's operating, but we haven't been able to get any of his guys for anything other than a few misdemeanors, and we've got nothing directly on him so far."

"Sounds like he'd be smart enough to plan a move against the families, but it doesn't sound like he's the type to start a war," Sassy replied thoughtfully. "But it definitely sounds like he's worth talking with."

"You're sure you want to do that?" Lauer asked with obvious concern.

"No, but I'm going to do it anyway," Sassy replied. "Do you know where I can find him?"

*****

Michel was almost home when his cell phone rang. He looked at the caller ID and saw it was Joel. For a moment he considered not answering, then decided to pick up.

"Hey," he said, trying to sound normal.

"Hey yourself, Mr. Busy Detective," Joel replied. "What are you doing right now? You want to get together?"

Michel hesitated for a second before responding.

"I'd better not," he said. "It's been a long day and I'm beat."

It wasn't a lie, but still didn't feel like the truth.

"Okay," Joel replied. "How about tomorrow night then?"

Michel knew he had to talk to Joel about what had happened with Nassir, though he wasn't looking forward to it.

"Sure," he said. "How about 7 at my place?"

Chapter 10

Michel was sitting at his desk trying not to think about what he was going to say to Joel. He'd hoped to talk to Sassy about what had happened with Nassir the previous night, but when he'd arrived at the office, he'd found a note saying she'd gone to a meeting and wouldn't be back until after noon. Since then he'd just been staring into space and feeling guilty.

He shook his head to clear his mind, then picked up the phone and dialed a familiar number.

"Detective Sergeant Ribodeau," a voice answered on the second ring.

"So how's my old desk treating you, Detective Sergeant?" Michel replied.

Al Ribodeau had been a friend and colleague for many years. He'd been a beat cop, but after Michel and Sassy left the force, he'd been promoted to the homicide division. Michel felt it had been long overdue.

"Hey, Michel," Ribodeau replied. "What can I do for you?"

Ribodeau's tone was friendly, but Michel sensed he would have to be careful not to impose on their friendship too often. He and Sassy had only been in business for a few days and this was the second time he'd called Ribodeau for information.

"I was hoping you could check on something for me," he replied, then quickly added, "I promise not to make it a habit."

"Sure, what do you need?"

Ribodeau's lack of reassurance that he didn't mind helping confirmed Michel's intuition.

"I wanted to find out if there was a police report filed for a break-in at a studio owned by Severin Marchand," he said. "It's on Jackson Street near the Irish Channel."

"Severin Marchand, huh?" Ribodeau replied as Michel heard the sound of typing in the background. "Sounds like you're traveling with a pretty chi-chi crowd these days."

"Oh yeah, you know me. Always hanging with the A-list."

Ribodeau was quiet for a moment, but Michel could still hear him typing.

"I don't see anything," Ribodeau said finally. "Are you sure Marchand owns the building? It could be filed under a different name."

"No, he definitely owns it," Michel replied. "That's all I needed to know, Al. Thanks. Now I owe you two beers."

"And you know I'm going to collect one day soon. You and Sassy can tell me all about the fabulous world of private investigation."

"You got it, Al," Michel replied. "Take care."

He hung up the phone and smiled. That was the last piece of the puzzle he needed before he spoke to Marchand. Marchand had already left three increasingly agitated messages on his cell phone since the previous afternoon, but he hadn't returned any of them. He would wait until the next morning to call and set up a meeting.

He was startled by a knock on the doorframe and looked up to see Chance standing there.

"You watching 'Golden Girl' re-runs on your computer?" Chance asked.

"Huh?" Michel replied, confused.

"Well, I saw the big smile on your face and I know how much you old people love to watch shows about other old people. 'Golden Girls,' 'Murder She Wrote,' 'Diagnosis Murder'."

"Wow, that was really funny," Michel replied dryly. "So have you been watching 'Absolutely Fabulous'?"

Chance stared at him with a blank expression.

"I don't get it."

"Because it's a show about drunken sluts."

"Oh, I see," Chance replied in a voice like he was talking to a small child. "You were implying I would watch it because I'm a drunk slut. But actually, only Patsy was a slut. Edina didn't get laid at all. And I don't really drink much anymore. But it was a nice try. I probably would have gone with 'American Gigolo' or 'Midnight Cowboy'."

Though he found it irritating, Michel had to admit that Chance was quick.

"So what are you doing here anyway?" he asked.

"Um, I'm a client. Remember?" Chance replied. "And I thought I'd come by to see if you've found out anything since you haven't bothered to call me."

Michel realized he was going to have to start behaving more professionally toward Chance. Despite the fact that they might end up working for free, he and Sassy had agreed to take on the case.

"I've been checking around and you were right about Patterson and Cornell," he said. "They've done some big projects. I can see why you'd take a risk with them."

Chance stared at Michel as though waiting for the punchline.

"No, that's it," Michel said. "No jokes, no insults. Other than their association with Priest Lee, they were a good choice. And even that association seems to be professional now. Neither one has been arrested for nine years. I don't doubt that they still have a piece of the pie, but they're not getting their hands dirty anymore."

"So what does that mean? You don't think they were scamming me?"

"I don't know yet," Michel replied. "I've got a contact at Harding & Lutz. I've asked him to check into things and see how much work was actually done."

Chance looked impressed.

As if on cue, they heard the front door open, and a few seconds later Ray Nassir appeared in the doorway.

"Hey, I was hoping I'd find you here," he said with a big smile.

He started to walk toward Michel, then noticed Chance sitting on the edge of Sassy's desk and stopped, seemingly unsure what to do.

"Hi Ray," Michel replied quickly. "Ray, this is Chance LeDuc. Chance, Ray Nassir."

"Hi," Chance said, eyeing Nassir and smiling broadly.

"Hi," Ray replied, then turned his attention back to Michel. "Sorry to just drop by, but I was hoping you might be free for lunch."

Michel pretended to look at his watch, then frowned.

"Sorry," he replied. "I wish I could but I've got a meeting in a half hour."

"Oh, okay," Nassir replied, obviously disappointed. "Well, I brought that stuff you asked me for."

He held up a thick brown pocket folder.

"Oh great," Michel replied hurriedly. "Why don't we just go up to the conference room for a minute. I'll be right back, Chance."

Michel led Nassir up the stairs to the vacant office on the second floor and closed the door behind them.

"This is a conference room?" Nassir asked, looking around the empty room. "Who's your decorator?"

"Uh, yeah. Technically it's just an empty office that we may rent out, but I figured it would do in a pinch."

"What kind of pinch?" Nassir asked with a sexy smile as he took a step closer to Michel.

Michel felt himself blush.

"Not *that* kind of pinch," he replied.

"So who was that?" Nassir asked, nodding toward the stairs.

"Just a client."

"I thought maybe he was your boyfriend."

"Why would you think that?" Michel asked.

"I made a few calls last night and found out you had a younger boyfriend," Nassir replied casually. "I thought that might be him."

"You checked me out?"

"Don't worry, I'm not a stalker," Nassir replied reassuringly. "I just like to know what I'm getting into. In case I get into it, that is."

"No, that's not him," Michel replied. "He's actually Joel's best friend...and a client."

"So you do have a boyfriend then?" Nassir asked with a disappointed look.

"No. At least not anymore. Technically. It's kind of complicated."

"I see," Nassir said, nodding uncertainly.

He seemed about to ask another question, then stopped himself. His demeanor became suddenly more professional.

"Anyway, I made copies of all the Bluehawk files," he said, handing the folder to Michel. "I included time sheets so you can see how many hours were spent on it, and printed out some small-scale versions of the drawings that had been done."

"Wow, you really went all out," Michel said.

"I try."

Michel smiled and looked directly into Nassir's eyes.

"I really appreciate it, Ray," he said.

Nassir studied Michel for a moment, then smiled back.

"So if you're not technically involved, how about showing your appreciation by going out to dinner with me tonight?"

Michel gave him a guilty look.

"I can't," he said. "Actually I'm getting together with Joel tonight to talk."

"I see," Nassir replied.

He hesitated a moment before continuing.

"Well, depending on how things go, if you want to get

together again, you know how to reach me. If not, I guess I'll see you around."

He started to turn but Michel reached out and gently touched his shoulder.

"I'm sorry," Michel said. "I didn't mean to get you involved in my mixed-up private life. Obviously I had no idea what was going to happen last night."

"That's true," Nassir replied. "But you didn't try to stop it either. Maybe you should consider why that is."

He gave Michel a wistful smile and turned away.

Fuck, Michel thought as he watched Nassir walk out the door. Now I remember why I hate dating.

*****

When Michel walked back in the office, Chance was sitting in Sassy's chair with his hands behind his head, his feet on her desk, and a big smile on his face.

"So who was *that?*" he asked.

"That's funny, he asked me the same thing about you," Michel replied.

"He did?" Chance asked excitedly.

"Yes, but he didn't have a hard-on at the time."

"I don't have a hard-on," Chance replied. "I just have a big package. So did he really ask who I was?

"He asked if you were my boyfriend."

"Oh," Chance replied, his ardor slightly dampened.

"Besides, I thought you didn't like older men," Michel said.

He almost added "unless they're paying you," but after the debacle of his "Absolutely Fabulous" joke, decided against it.

"I like *that* one," Chance replied with a lewd smile. "He's hot. I guess some old guys just age better than others."

He made a show of looking Michel up and down, then made a sour face.

"So who is he?" he asked more seriously.

"Just a friend," Michel replied, trying to make it sound as casual as possible. "In fact, he's my contact at Harding & Lutz, and he just dropped these off."

He held up the pocket folder.

"You're sleeping with him, aren't you?" Chance exclaimed suddenly.

"What?" Michel stammered. "Why would you think that?"

"You're the worst liar," Chance replied, shaking his head.

"Why do you think I'm sleeping with him?" Michel asked defensively.

"Let's see," Chance replied as though preparing to argue a court case. "First there was the whole awkward dance you went through when he came in. Then you took him upstairs even though he's your contact on *my* case. And finally, he thought I was your boyfriend even though you introduced me as Chance. If he was really a 'friend' he'd know that your boyfriend's name is Joel."

Michel realized that Chance had the makings of an excellent detective. He considered how to refute Chance's evidence, then stopped himself. Although he wasn't used to sharing his personal life with anyone but Sassy and Joel, he suddenly felt the need to be honest with Chance.

"Yes," he said. "I slept with him. Once. Last night."

Chance stared at Michel as if waiting for him to continue.

"I was interviewing him for another case and it just happened," Michel finished with a guilty sigh.

"And did you just happen to forget about Joel at the time?" Chance asked.

Michel had expected Chance to be angry, but Chance's tone was even, almost sympathetic.

"Of course not," Michel replied. "But I'm not even sure where things stand with Joel these days, and something just clicked with Ray."

Chance nodded.

"You've got to tell Joel."

"I know," Michel replied. "We're getting together tonight."

"Just do me a favor and tell him as soon as you see him," Chance said. "Don't wait."

"Why?" Michel asked, suddenly apprehensive .

"Just trust me," Chance said. "It'll be better that way."

Chapter 11

Sassy turned off the Airport Highway and headed north. She'd encountered intermittent showers since she'd left the city a half hour earlier, but now it began to rain more steadily.

Ken Lauer had told her that Granville Kingston lived just outside LaPlace, a farming community twenty-five miles northwest of New Orleans. Sassy had never been to the area before, and as she continued north she was surprised to see large stands of trees begin to appear along the sides the road. By the time she'd gone another mile, the stands had grown together into a dense forest, though she could see occasional glimpses of open fields beyond the trees.

She looked at her odometer and slowed down. According to Yahoo, a left turn was coming up. She saw a gap in the trees and turned onto a narrow strip of asphalt. The trees were closer to the road now and formed a canopy overhead. She turned on her headlights.

At first she'd debated whether it was really wise to approach Kingston given that she'd promised Priest Lee she'd be discreet. Lauer had told her, however, that Kingston had no apparent ties with any of the New Orleans families. Finally she'd decided that it wouldn't do any harm for Kingston to know that Deacon was missing. Plus, if Kingston were involved, he already knew.

Sassy saw a mailbox on her left and stopped. She'd expected to see guards at the end of the driveway, but there was no one in sight. She studied the trees looking for security cameras, but didn't see any.

This guy is sure a lot different from Deacon, she thought as she turned onto the dirt drive.

A quarter mile up the trees began to recede away from the edges of the driveway, and in the distance Sassy could see a white farmhouse. There were several cars parked in front.

Twenty yards from the house, she saw an old woman sitting on a wood crate next to the driveway. The woman was dressed in the traditional Jamaican style of a long skirt, short-sleeved top, and head scarf, all made from bright yellow and red calico. She was sitting under a striped beach umbrella and staring intently into a stand of trees inside an enormous cage that was set back a few feet from the drive.

Sassy stopped the car and got out. The woman didn't seem to notice her.

"Excuse me," Sassy said. "I'm looking for Granville Kingston."

"He be in the house," the woman replied in a thick Jamaican accent, without looking away from the cage.

Sassy noticed a burlap sack of sweet potatoes lying by the woman's feet, then looked into the cage. She didn't see anything but the trees, which she realized were loaded with mangos.

"What's in there?" she asked.

"Monkeys," the woman replied.

Sassy searched the trees but didn't see any movement.

"Where are they?" she asked.

"It's raining," the woman replied.

"Monkeys don't come out in the rain?" Sassy asked.

The woman turned her head slowly and regarded Sassy curiously.

"They only got but one suit of clothes," she replied.

"So what do they do?" Sassy asked. "Sleep?"

The woman's eyebrows raised and she tilted her head slightly. Her expression suggested that she'd decided Sassy was simple-minded.

"I ain't never seen a sleeping monkey," she said.

Then she turned her gaze back on the cage.

Sassy got back in her car and continued toward the house. As she got closer, she could see several men milling about on the front porch. To her relief, they didn't seem concerned by her approach. They just watched her lazily for a moment, then went back to their conversations. In her experience, Jamaican men were usually respectful of older women. She hoped it would be enough to get her in to see Kingston, or at least enough to keep her from getting killed.

*****

Ten minutes later Sassy was ushered into the kitchen at the back of the house. Granville Kingston was at the stove cooking scrambled eggs in a large cast iron skillet. He was dressed in blue and gray plaid pajama pants and a ribbed gray tank top. His face was obscured by a cascade of long, fine dread locks, but Sassy could see that his body was lean and muscular like a gymnast, though much taller.

"Would you like some, Miss Jones?" he asked, looking up and giving Sassy a charming smile.

For a moment Sassy had trouble responding. Kingston was one of the sexiest men she'd ever seen. He was unquestionably handsome, with pale green eyes, high cheekbones, and full sensual lips, but it was something in his expression that made her heart flutter. He exuded the confidence of someone who knew exactly what he wanted and how to get it.

"No thank you," Sassy forced herself to respond. "I already had breakfast."

Kingston chuckled softly.

"Yes, of course you did," he said in a deep, melodious voice that still carried strong traces of his native country. "I'm afraid you caught me still sleeping."

Damn, if that's what he looks like when he first wakes up, I can only imagine how he looks after a few hours, Sassy thought.

"I apologize for the intrusion," she said, "but I wasn't sure how to contact you to make an appointment."

She watched Kingston as he spooned the eggs onto a plate.

"It's quite all right. I hope you don't mind if I eat while we talk," he said, gesturing toward the kitchen table.

"Of course not," Sassy replied as she took a seat. "I have to admit I was a little surprised that you even agreed to see me."

"Why is that?" Kingston asked as he carried his plate to the table and settled into the chair next to Sassy.

"A strange woman comes to your house wanting to ask you questions?" Sassy replied. "Most folks in your line of work wouldn't have been so accommodating."

Kingston just smiled benignly in response.

"So how can I help you, Miss Jones?" he asked as he lifted the first forkful of eggs to his mouth.

Sassy waited while Kingston chewed. Even his chewing was sexy, she decided. It was slow and purposeful, and she liked the way his thin mustache danced playfully over his expressive lips.

"I wanted to ask you some questions about Deacon Lee," she replied when he'd finished swallowing.

"Deacon Lee?" Kingston asked.

Sassy realized she was still staring at his lips and quickly shifted her gaze to his eyes.

"Yes," she replied. "You know who he is?"

"Of course. He's the son of Mr. Priest Lee."

"He's been missing for three weeks," Sassy said.

Kingston looked surprised.

"And what does this have to do with me?" he asked.

His demeanor didn't change at all, but he pushed the unfinished plate of eggs to the side.

"I don't know that it has *anything* to do with you," Sassy replied. "That's what I'm hoping to find out. Priest Lee believes that Deacon was taken by someone planning to make a move into his territory. From what I've heard, you're the only person who might have the organization to pull that off."

It wasn't an accurate assessment, but Sassy felt it was sufficient to explain her being there.

"You flatter and insult me at the same time," Kingston replied with a sly smile.

"How so?"

"You flatter me that I would be capable of making such a move, but insult me that I would be foolish enough to try it. My operation is sufficient for now. Why would I jeopardize it by incurring the anger of Mr. Lee?"

Sassy considered the reasoning.

"Maybe because with Deacon out of the picture, Priest's anger wouldn't be nearly as dangerous," she replied.

Kingston chuckled again.

"You underestimate Mr. Lee, I think," he said. "Maybe Deacon was the blunt instrument, but Priest Lee wielded him."

"You talk as though you know them," Sassy said.

"No," Kingston replied, shaking his head. "I have met them, but I do not know them. I know what I hear and observe."

"When did you meet them?" Sassy asked, her curiosity piqued.

"Several years ago," Kingston replied. "I went to the heads of all five families and made offerings to them. And in exchange, they gave me their blessing to grow my operation so long as I didn't encroach on their own businesses."

Sassy wondered why Priest hadn't mention Kingston as a possible suspect.

"That was very smart," she said.

"Does that surprises you?" Kingston asked. "Do you think that most people in my business are stupid?"

"No," Sassy replied, "it doesn't surprise me at all. In fact, in my experience, the people in your 'business' are generally quite smart. At least the ones who survive. So Deacon was there when you met with Priest?"

Kingston nodded.

"And you never met with him again?"

"No," Kingston replied. "I keep to my own business."

"A business which has been growing and which now encircles the city," Sassy noted.

"Yes, that's true," Kingston agreed. "And someday I hope it will extend into the city. But that time is not now."

"Why not?"

"Because I have respect for what Mr. Lee and the heads of the other families have built," Kingston replied. "When they are gone, then it will be my time, but for now I will wait."

"And the idea of expediting their departures has never occurred to you?" Sassy asked.

Kingston fixed Sassy's gaze with his shimmering green eyes.

"Miss Jones, you have made inquiries about me, yes?" he asked.

Sassy nodded.

"Then you know that I prefer pursuasion to violence," Kingston continued. "I built my organization by convincing the leaders of many groups that it would benefit us all to work together. The older families, they wasted so much time and so many lives settling their differences. And why? Because of ego. There is enough to go around for everyone. All that is required is to set egos aside and work toward the common good. Killing Deacon Lee would not serve that common good."

"Who said Deacon was dead?" Sassy asked. "I just said he was missing."

Kingston chuckled once more.

"You couldn't take a man like Deacon Lee as a prisoner and keep him alive. It's not something he would ever forgive."

Sassy realized that Priest Lee had said almost the same thing when she'd asked him why he was certain Deacon was dead.

Suddenly there was a muffled ringing very close by.

"Excuse me for a moment please, Miss Jones," Kingston said as he stood and took a cell phone from the right pocket of his pajama pants.

He flipped it open and began speaking in hushed tones as he walked to the far side of the kitchen. It was the opportunity for which Sassy had been hoping. She slipped her cell phone out of her left jacket pocket and dialed the number she'd found in Deacon Lee's office. She put her left index finger on the SEND button and slipped the phone back into her pocket just as Kingston finished his conversation.

"I'm sorry, Miss Jones," he said, walking back toward her with his cell phone still in his left hand, "but I have some business to which I must attend."

"Of course," Sassy said as she stood. "I just have one more question."

Kingston nodded for her to continue.

"Who do you think would kill Deacon?" she asked.

Kingston shrugged and shook his head solemnly.

"Killing the son of your enemy is old school," he said. "I'm certain both Priest and Deacon Lee had many enemies and many old scores. Perhaps someone decided to settle some of them before it was too late."

"Perhaps," Sassy replied thoughtfully. "Anyway, thanks again for your time. I'll see myself out."

They shook hands and Sassy began walking toward the door. When she was halfway across the room she pressed the SEND button on her phone. Kingston's phone didn't ring.

Sassy stepped outside and lifted the phone to her ear. She could hear a man's voice with a thick Caribbean accent.

"Hello? Hello? Is anybody there?"

"Oh sorry," Sassy said. "Wrong number again."

Chapter 12

Michel and Chance finished looking through the documents. It was clear that Harding & Lutz had legitimately been working on the Bluehawk Terminal project. Michel wished he could think of something comforting to say.

"Oh well, I guess that's the way it goes in business,," Chance said suddenly. "Sometimes you win, sometimes you lose. This time I lost."

Michel had expected Chance to be angry or upset, but his tone sounded resigned, even accepting.

"Are you okay?" Michel asked.

Chance gave him a weak smile.

"I guess I'll have to be," he said. "I don't really have much choice, right? Besides, it's not like any puppies died. It was just money."

"But still..."

"Thanks," Chance interrupted abruptly, "but I think I'm just going to take a walk."

Michel frowned slightly.

"Are you sure?" he asked. "Do you want to go get a drink?"

"No, thanks," Chance replied. "That was my father's way of dealing with his problems. I'll be okay. I just need a little time to absorb it. Besides, you have your own issues to think about."

"Okay," Michel replied, realizing Chance was right.

"I appreciate you trying to help, though," Chance said with unusual sincerity. "It means a lot to me, and some day I'll pay you back for your time. I promise."

"Don't worry about it," Michel replied.

"No," Chance replied with finality. "I'm going to pay you back."

*****

Michel spent the next hour alternately feeling sorry for Chance and wondering what he was going to say to Joel. He'd just made it back to thinking about Chance for the fifth time when Sassy walked into the office.

"Wow," she said when she saw the brooding look on his face. "Looks like someone's having a bad day."

"Hmmm?" Michel replied, looking up at her distractedly.

"What's the matter? No luck with Nassir last night?" Sassy asked.

"Oh, I wouldn't say that," Michel replied with a mordant smile, "but it definitely wasn't him."

"So then more interviews with Marchand's friends?" Sassy tried.

"No," Michel replied. "Actually the case is done. Marchand did it."

"What?" Sassy replied with surprise. "Are you sure?"

"Yeah."

"But why?"

"I'm still not sure about that," Michel replied without much interest. "I haven't spoken with him yet. I thought I'd let him stew for a day. I'll talk to him tomorrow."

Sassy studied him for a moment.

"So then no luck with Chance's case?" she asked, wondering why he seemed so distant and melancholy.

"No, that's done, too," Michel replied. "I got the records from Harding & Lutz. It was legit. Patterson and Cornell really intended to go ahead with the project. So unless we find out they changed their minds and burned the building, Chance is out of luck."

114

Sassy stared at Michel in disbelief.

"So wait a second. Are you telling me you solved both Marchand's and Chance's cases since I saw you last night?"

"Yeah, I guess so," Michel replied without enthusiasm.

"You do realize we get paid by the hour, don't you?" Sassy asked, hoping to lighten his mood. "You're supposed to try to stretch things out."

She watched Michel for a reaction but didn't see any.

"All right, Michel," she said. "What's up with the long face? Talk to me."

Michel looked up at her. He'd been working with her long enough to know that the set expression on her face meant she wouldn't let him go until he'd given her a satisfactory answer.

"It's about Joel," he said finally.

"Oh," Sassy replied. "What did he do?"

"Not what he did. What I did. I had sex with Nassir."

"What? You had sex with a suspect?" Sassy asked incredulously.

"Well, not until after I was sure he was innocent," Michel replied guiltily.

"Okay, you know what?" Sassy said. "This sounds like we're going to need drinks again. Where's that bottle?"

Michel opened the bottom drawer of the desk and took out the Jack Daniels and one glass.

"You go ahead. I need to keep a clear head," he said as he placed them on his desk.

Sassy looked at them for a moment, then shook her head.

"No, forget it," she said. "Sounds like we've got a lot of ground to cover and I should keep a clear head, too. So why don't you tell me about Chance's case first, then Marchand, then I'll tell you where I've been today, and *then* we can talk about Joel. Okay?"

She hoped that by getting Michel to focus on work first she could get him out of his somber mood.

"Okay," he replied with a nod.

115

*****

"Everything Kingston said seemed logical and was consistent with what Lauer told me about him," Sassy finished.

"So where does that leave us?" Michel asked.

His focus and energy had gradually returned over the last hour, and now he was fully engaged in the discussion.

"I don't know," Sassy replied. "I suppose we need to find out if this was targeted at Priest or if someone was just settling a score with Deacon. Either way, I think that Priest's theory about someone trying to start a war is looking dubious."

"Maybe Priest is just becoming paranoid in his old age," Michel offered in agreement. "Living your entire life looking over your shoulder has got to take a toll on you. I'm sure he sees enemies and conspiracies everywhere."

"You're probably right," Sassy replied. "Still, I'm not willing to entirely rule out the possibility that he's right. I just think we need to broaden the scope of the investigation to include other possibilities."

"I agree," Michel replied. "So what do you want me to do?"

Sassy smiled.

"What?" Michel asked.

"Nothing," Sassy replied, with an embarrassed shrug.

"*What?*" Michel persisted.

"I'm just touched that you asked me what you should do," Sassy replied, almost apologetically. "I just appreciate the respect that shows."

"Are you getting menopausal on me or something?" Michel asked, cocking his head and giving Sassy a quizzical look.

"No," Sassy replied, "It's just that...well...when we were on the force, I was the senior officer, so it was just sort of natural that you'd look to me for guidance sometimes. It's just nice that things are still the same now. That's all."

Michel smiled.

"Well, that's just because this is a black people case," he said. "If this were a white people case or a gay people case, then I'd expect you to come to me for guidance."

"Smart ass," Sassy replied, narrowing her eyes at him.

Michel stood up and walked over to her. He grabbed her by the upper arms and gave them a gentle squeeze.

"Sas, I'm always going to look to you for guidance," he said. "You're one of the smartest people I know."

"Just one them?" she asked with a mock challenging look.

"Well, Stan Lecher is pretty damn smart," Michel replied, referring to the former chief investigator for the Orleans Parish Coroner's Office with whom he and Sassy had worked on several cases.

"Okay, I'll give you that one," Sassy replied with a warm smile. "So enough of this touchy-feely stuff. Back to work."

Michel let go of Sassy's arms and walked back to his desk, taking a seat on the edge.

"I think the first thing you should do is talk to Marchand," Sassy said, "so we can get that one out of the way. In the meantime, I'll call Lauer again and see if he has info on anyone specific who might want to kill Deacon."

"I'm betting that's a long list," Michel said.

"Well, we can start with the most recent and work our way backward," Sassy replied. "So until we have some leads, I guess we're in a holding pattern."

"Okay," Michel replied.

"All right," Sassy said, settling onto the edge of her desk, "now let's talk about Joel."

"I'm getting together with him in a little while and I'm going to tell him about Nassir," he said. "I just haven't figured out what I'm going to say yet."

"What *is* there to say?" Sassy asked. "Just tell him the truth."

"But I don't want to hurt him."

Sassy gave Michel a hard look.

"Michel, nothing you say is going to keep him from being hurt, and frankly, you have no right to try to control his reaction."

"Meaning what?" Michel asked with a hurt look.

"Meaning that it's not fair for you to try to manipulate how he's going to feel, because that's just about you trying to make yourself feel better. If he doesn't seem so upset, then you won't feel so guilty. Right?"

Michel thought about it for a few seconds then nodded.

"I mean obviously you don't want to say, 'Hey, guess what? I fucked around with some other guy last night. Ha ha ha,' but you need to allow him to feel what he's going to feel. Don't try to couch it in any of that 'It had nothing to do with you or my feelings about you' bullshit. Just tell him the truth."

Michel realized she was right. If he were in Joel's position, he'd just want to know what happened. He wouldn't be interested in excuses or justifications, and he certainly wouldn't want to hear any "kind" sentiments designed to make him feel better about the situation.

"Okay," he said. "I'll just tell him what happened and take it like a man."

"I think that's what got you into trouble in the first place," Sassy replied with a self-amused smirk.

Chapter 13

At first, Joel's reaction had been surprisingly benign. He'd said that Michel didn't owe him any explanation, and that they'd made no commitment and were both free to see other people and have sex with whomever they wanted. Michel had begun to believe that everything would be fine, and that they'd be able to work past what he'd done.

Then Joel had fallen silent. For almost five minutes he'd been sitting on the edge of the fountain in Michel's garden, staring down at the patio stones while Michel watched him from a lounge chair. The usually soothing burble of the fountain had grown increasingly louder and more irritating to Michel with each passing minute. He tried to block it out, and for what seemed like the hundredth time, fought the impulse to say he was sorry.

"It's okay," Joel said suddenly, as though reading his thoughts.

He looked into Michel's eyes and gave a resigned smile.

"I really am sorry," Michel replied, feeling that it was finally appropriate.

"I know you are," Joel replied, "And it's okay."

"Are you sure?" Michel asked.

Joel nodded.

"I think it was good this happened, because it helped clarify some things for me," Joel replied.

Michel felt a knot of anxiety forming in his stomach.

"What kinds of things?" he asked cautiously.

"Basically that I don't think we can ever be more than friends," Joel replied simply.

"But what happened with Nassir didn't mean anything, and it had nothing to do with how I feel about you."

The words had come tumbling out despite the promise he'd made to Sassy, only Michel realized he wasn't saying them to try to make Joel feel better. He was saying them because they felt true, and because he suddenly realized he was on the verge of losing something very important.

"Maybe not consciously," Joel replied.

"Meaning what?" Michel asked.

Joel studied the ground for a moment, then looked directly into Michel's eyes.

"Think about it, Michel," he said. "We've been going through this dance for a long time now. We're sort of together, then we're not, then we're friends, then we're sort of boyfriends, and it just keeps going on and on. Why do you think that is? Why don't we ever get to the point where it feels like we're really together?"

Michel shrugged.

"I guess because we've been taking it carefully after the way things started."

"*We* have or *you* have?" Joel asked pointedly. "Because I'm sure how I feel about you, and I've always been sure what I wanted. The only thing I've ever questioned is how you feel about me."

"I love you," Michel replied.

"I know you do," Joel replied, then hesitated.

"But?"

"But you love me on your terms," Joel replied.

Michel gave him a perplexed look.

"You always keep me at a safe distance," Joel said. "You never let me get too close. *You* control the relationship. We get together when *you* want to get together. We have sex when *you* want to have sex. You show affection when *you* feel like it."

Michel shrugged.

"How else would it be?" he asked. "Why would you have sex if you didn't feel like it? Or show affection unless you were feeling it in that moment?"

"*You* wouldn't," Joel replied matter-of-factly, "and I guess that's the problem. I want you to want me all the time. I want you to want to show me affection all the time."

"But that's unrealistic," Michel replied.

"Maybe, but I want you all the time. I always want to show you that I care about you," Joel said, "but if I do and you're not in the mood, you just freeze me out. It's subtle, but I feel it anyway. And that's what really hurts. In case you haven't noticed, I'm a pretty hot little piece of ass."

"I know you are," Michel replied, "and I hope you know that I didn't have sex with Nassir because I don't find you attractive, or you're not enough for me. It was just a stupid mistake."

"Look, the fact that you had sex with another guy is really inconsequential," Joel replied. "Does it hurt? Yeah. But I'm over it. Sometimes we all do stupid shit. That's really not the issue here."

"Then what is?" Michel asked, confused.

"I think there's a part of you that doesn't really want to be in a relationship," Joel replied. "That's why you keep me at a distance, and that's why you slept with Nassir. It's like you were unconsciously sabotaging things because we were on the verge of getting back together again."

Michel started to protest but stopped himself, wondering if maybe Joel was right.

"I guess I always sensed it," Joel continued, "but I hoped that over time you'd be able to open yourself up more and give yourself to me fully. But you haven't, and what happened with Nassir makes it clear you probably never will."

They were quiet for a minute as Michel thought about what Joel had said.

"I'm not sure what you mean about giving myself fully to you," he said finally.

"That's the problem," Joel replied with a rueful laugh. "You can't even conceive of it."

"No, seriously," Michel said. "Explain what you mean."

Joel sighed, then made a gesture of acquiescence.

"If you were to ask me whether I'll love you forever," he explained, "I would say yes without hesitating. Would it be true? I don't know. There's no way I could know. But I'd say it because I'd want it to be true. If I were to ask you the same question, you'd just give me a charming smile and try to dodge answering, and if I pressed, you'd say there was no way you could know. That's the difference between giving yourself over to someone and holding yourself back."

"But I can't help that," Michel replied. "To say I'll love you forever knowing that it might not be true would feel like a lie."

"I know that," Joel replied. "You're not a hopeless romantic. You're practical and you're moral and could never lie like that. But knowing that doesn't make it any easier. I want to feel like you really need me, and that if you could, you'd choose to spend the rest of your life with me. I know you love me, and you choose to have me in your life, but I don't feel like you *need* me there. I always feel that if I weren't here you'd get along fine. And I think you know that, too, on some level. That's why you keep me at a distance. I'm like *a* part of your life, but not *really* part of it."

"I don't really know what to say," Michel replied softly. "I'm sorry. I didn't mean to make you feel like I don't need you."

"I know you weren't doing it on purpose," Joel replied. "I don't think you can help yourself. It's just who you are. I think the only person you feel really comfortable letting close is Sassy."

Michel knew it was true. Sassy was the closest friend he'd ever had, and the only one with whom he'd ever shared all aspects of his life.

"So now what?" he asked.

"I'm going to go," Joel replied, standing up.

He walked over to Michel and leaned down, then softly kissed Michel on the right cheek. Michel wanted to wrap his arms around Joel's neck and hold him tightly, but he was afraid he might start crying if he did.

"Give me a call if you want to talk some more," Joel said, then walked into the house and left.

Chapter 14

Michel arrived at Severin Marchand's townhouse on Royal just before noon. He hadn't slept well and was feeling emotionally raw. Still, he was looking forward to his conversation with Marchand. He knew it would give him a chance to take out some of the frustration he was feeling about Joel. He rang the bell and waited. After what seemed like minutes, he heard Marchand's unmistakable voice come out of the intercom.

"Yes?"

"It's Michel Doucette."

There was a long pause, then the buzzer sounded. Michel opened the wrought iron gate and walked into an arched brick passageway that lead to a courtyard in the center of the building. He was only halfway down the short passageway when Marchand appeared at the end, silhouetted by the bright sun filling the courtyard.

"I expect people who work for me to return my phone calls immediately," he said imperiously, "and I certainly don't expect them to stop by my house uninvited."

Michel walked past Marchand without acknowledging that he'd said anything, and stepped into the courtyard. He took a look around and nodded.

"Nice place," he said. "You have any iced tea?"

He looked at Marchand and smiled casually. Marchand's mouth began working like a goldfish struggling to breathe outside of its bowl, but no sound came out. A quick succession of emotions flitted across his eyes: anger, indignation, confusion, and finally worry. Then he closed his mouth and walked quickly to a doorway on the far side of the courtyard, and disappeared into the house.

A minute later he returned carrying a glass of iced tea and set it down hard on the small round wrought iron table next to Michel, who had taken a seat under a wide umbrella. Marchand took the seat facing him.

"So why haven't you spoken to Ray Nassir?" he asked immediately. "I spoke with my friends after you interviewed them, and they all said that they told you they thought Nassir might have been responsible for destroying my costume."

Michel took a long, slow sip of the iced tea, then smiled.

"I have," he replied.

Marchand's eyes narrowed.

"When?" he asked. "I was told he was in the bar that night and you didn't speak to him."

Michel nodded.

"That's true," he said. "But I did speak with him later that night at his place."

"At *his* place?" Marchand replied, obviously not happy.

Michel took another long sip of iced tea. Then he placed the glass back on the table and leaned forward so that his elbows rested on his knees.

"Oh, I'm sorry," he said with feigned innocence. "Was I supposed to talk to him in the bar so that everyone would see it?"

Marchand's owlish eyes blinked rapidly four times and his small mouth grew even smaller.

"I know what happened, Severin," Michel said. "I know that was your 'Jezebel' costume in the pictures."

Marchand blinked again, and now his eyes conveyed fear.

"Clearly I underestimated you," he said.

"Clearly," Michel replied. "Did you think I'd been fired from the police department because I was incompetent?"

The look on Marchand's face made it obvious that was exactly what he'd thought.

"The fact is, I was a very good detective," Michel continued. "The problem was that I'm not very good at following orders. Especially when my instincts tell me to do something else. Maybe you should have checked that out before you decided to hire me."

Marchand continued to stare at Michel for a few seconds, then his eyes dropped to the ground.

"So now what?" he asked.

"Now I want to know *why* you did it."

Marchand closed his eyes and sighed.

"Because I was out of ideas," he said in a self-pitying voice. "I'd done all the Bettes that were worth doing, and I couldn't come up with anything else."

"So why not just do nothing?" Michel asked. "Why not just retire with your dignity, say that you'd decided it was time to give someone else a chance?"

Marchand opened his eyes. They were glassy and red.

"Because I'd already told everyone that my costume this year was going to be the most fabulous ever," he replied, his voice quavering. "I kept hoping that something would come to me but it didn't, and I couldn't face the humiliation of admitting that I'd lied."

Michel felt sorry for Marchand—not for the situation he'd been in, but because he was so desperate for validation from people who probably didn't even like him.

"So you figured if you made it look like a crime, you'd be able to elicit sympathy rather than being embarrassed," he said.

Marchand nodded with exaggerated misery.

"Okay, but why try to point the finger at Ray Nassir?" Michel asked. "Obviously you wanted people to see me talking with him in the bar that night, and since he isn't a friend of yours, it would be natural that they'd all assume he was a suspect. So why Ray?"

"Because he's young and he's talented," Marchand spit out, as though accusing Nassir of committing a horrific crime.

Michel let out a short hard laugh and shook his head.

"And that's a reason to try to destroy his reputation?" he asked. "Isn't that the way it's supposed to be? We make our mark on the world, then someone younger and more talented comes along, and we step aside and let them have their moment in the sun?"

Marchand stared at Michel for a moment. Michel couldn't read his expression.

"Not someone like him," Marchand said finally.

"Meaning?"

"He's not from here," Marchand said, enunciating each word slowly and clearly.

"What are you talking about?" Michel asked, suddenly confused. "He was born and raised in the area."

"But his people aren't from here," Marchand replied with disgust.

Michel was momentarily stunned. While he'd observed casual racism all his life, he'd never encountered anything so overt.

"I hate to tell you this, Severin," he said, his voice tight, "but *your* people aren't from here either. No one is *from* here. New Orleans is the original melting pot."

"But without my people this whole country would still be uncivilized," Marchand replied defiantly. "Look at those people in the Middle East. They're nothing more than savages, killing their children and blowing one another up on the streets. They don't deserve to even be in this country."

Michel felt true rage for one of the few times in his life.

"First of all," he said, struggling to control himself, "Pakistan is part of South Asia. Second of all, if you think we're any different in this country, you're deluded. People kill one another here every day, and for reasons that are no better or worse than in the rest of the world."

Marchand opened his mouth, but Michel cut him off.

"Tell me, Severin," he said, "how many people did you help out after the hurricane? Did you open your homes to anyone? Donate any money or time?"

Marchand didn't reply. He just glared at Michel.

"And you think you're more civilized," Michel continued, shaking his head. "You have everything, and still you want to hold someone else down because they're different from you. You're pathetic. You're an ignorant, petty, frightened old queen."

For a moment Marchand's whole body trembled, and Michel thought Marchand might physically attack him. Then Marchand's eyes focused on something behind Michel, and he became suddenly still. Michel looked over his shoulder but saw only a brick wall. When he turned back, Marchand was smiling calmly at him.

"I trust we're done here," Marchand said brightly, as though the previous minute had never happened.

Michel wondered if that was how Marchand coped, by simply blocking out anything he found unpleasant or difficult.

"Yes, we're done," Michel replied, studying Marchand's face carefully.

"And how much do I owe you for your time?" Marchand asked. "And, of course, your discretion."

"I'll send you a bill for the time," Michel replied. "The discretion is free."

"Are you sure?" Marchand asked, raising his eyebrows.

Michel realized it wasn't a challenge to his integrity. Marchand was simply accustomed to paying to protect his privacy.

"I'm sure," Michel replied.

*****

Michel walked back to his car on Esplanade, drove up one block, then turned right on Chartres Street toward Bywater.

Although the documents he'd gotten from Ray Nassir were pretty conclusive proof that Henry Patterson and James Cornell had intended to move ahead with the Bluehawk Terminal project, he was curious to see the buildings for himself.

As he approached the block between Clouet and Louisa Streets, he could see the terminal a block farther toward the river on his right, just beyond the railroad tracks. The three buildings were surrounded by a large parking lot, which had been enclosed with a high chain link fence. Michel could see a black Mercedes and a silver Lexus parked close to the center building. He drove two more blocks and parked on Chartres, then walked down to the railroad tracks and headed back toward the terminal.

The three buildings were identical flat-topped granite and glass rectangles. The two end buildings were neglected but largely intact, with just a few broken window panes here and there dotting their surfaces on the upper two floors. The windows on the first floor had been covered with plywood. The center building, too, looked to be in relatively good shape on the first two floors. The top floor, however, bore clear evidence of the fire. The eight windows in the middle looked at though they'd been blown out by a bomb. All that remained were twisted shards of steel along the edges of the frames that now held plywood panels. The walls to the sides and tops of the windows were scarred with tendrils of soot.

Michel began walking along the side of the tracks in front of the terminal, trying to appear casual, as though he were a just a tourist who'd decided to take a stroll to less-traveled parts of the city—despite the fact that he was dressed in a jacket and tie. He kept his head facing straight ahead, but studied the buildings and watched for the owners of the two cars out of the corner of his eye.

At the end of the terminal's parking lot, the fence turned left along a narrow road that connected the terminal directly to Chartres Street. Michel could see a gate in the side fence, about sixty feet from the corner. It was slightly ajar. He continued to the corner, then crossed the road and turned left toward the river.

When he was nearly even with the gate, he stooped down and pretended to tie his shoe. He knew he'd have to risk being seen crossing to the gate, but realized he might never have an opportunity to get inside the buildings again. He took a long look at the terminal, then back up the street. There was no one in sight. He stood, quickly crossed the street to the gate, and slipped inside.

He ran to the shadows along the side of the first building and began making his way quickly toward the center building. He could see a door directly behind the Mercedes, and broke into a jog. When he reached the door, he ducked down behind the car's hood and surveyed the buildings and streets surrounding the terminal. Satisfied that he hadn't been seen, he stood and gently tried the handle to the door. It was unlocked.

He pulled the door open a half inch and peered inside. The room was dim, but he could see that it was large and open, taking up almost the entire first floor, with a very high ceiling. He watched for any movement for a moment, then pulled the door open another foot and stepped inside. He closed the door quietly and listened. He could hear distant voices.

He surveyed the room. At the far end were two elevators, with a wide marble staircase in between. The wall facing the river had been boarded up, though some light still filtered in around the ragged edges of the plywood. Michel guessed it was mostly windows, like the wall facing the railroad tracks.

On the far right of the room was a booth with a sign that read "Tickets," some ancient vending machines, and another staircase that mirrored the one at the far end. Michel walked to the base of the stairs and listened again. The voices seemed to be farther away now so he started up.

The second floor was almost identical to the first, though the windows hadn't been boarded, and in the bright light

Michel could see the detail more clearly. The ceiling was divided into three square sections, each one vaulted and supported at the corners by thick, round, pink-and-gray marble columns with richly carved bases and caps. The floor was also marble, and through a thick layer of dust Michel could see fine, geometric inlays. He imagined that in its day the terminal had probably been quite elegant.

Behind him was another set of stairs leading to the top floor. He took another quick look at the room, then headed up to the top floor. As he reached the first landing the air turned suddenly acrid and he almost let out a cough. He pulled the right lapel of his jacket over his nose and mouth, and continued up.

When he reached the top landing he stopped. The room looked like a painting of the other two floors, but rendered only in tones of gray and black. The walls and ceiling were coated with soot, and the floor was covered by a fine dusting of ash. He took a few tentative steps forward. The floor still seemed structurally solid.

Because of the plywood covering the center windows on both sides, it was difficult to see much at first, but as his eyes began to adjust he could make out more of the details in the room. The walls facing the river and Chartres Street were lined with large, semi-circular booths, and in the far back corner were stacks of tables and chairs. He realized that at one point the room had been a restaurant.

He walked carefully to the center of the room, listening for any creaking that would indicate the substructure of the floor had been damaged, then stopped and turned in a slow circle, studying the pattern of the fire. The booths near the corners were largely untouched, but as he turned toward the middle of the room the damage grew increasing more pronounced, with the booths under the plywood-covered windows having been almost entirely incinerated. The damage to the rest of the room appeared to be primarily superficial: just smoke damage to the ceiling, smoke and water damage on the side walls, and some charring directly above the middle booths.

Although he'd had only introductory training in arson detection at the police academy, he could clearly see that the fire had been set. The chance of fire erupting simultaneously on both sides of the room was incalculably small, and there was no evidence that the fire had traveled from one side to the other. The heavy damage to the booths only in the center also indicated the use of an accelerant in those areas.

Someone got a big pay day not to report this, he thought, shaking his head.

He was about to head back downstairs when he noticed two swinging doors with circular windows just to the left of the stairs. He walked to them and ran the index finger of his left hand horizontally across one of the windows. He looked through the narrow slash he'd made in the dirt and soot, and saw a steel-framed glass walkway connecting to the adjacent building. There was another set of swinging doors at the far end. He guessed they led to the restaurant's kitchen. He considered checking it out but decided against it. The frame looked far too rusted and unstable.

He turned away and started quietly down the stairs. He thought he heard the faint sound of a car engine starting.

Chapter 15

Sassy hung up the phone and stretched in her chair. Ken Lauer had agreed to send her the Justice Department's files on Deacon Lee. Until then, she had nothing to do. She wondered what was taking Michel so long at Marchand's house and hoped he'd be back soon so they could grab a late lunch. In addition to hearing about his meeting with Marchand, she was curious how things had gone with Joel. She got up and walked to the window, and looked out between the wide slats of the dark green plantation shutters. The streets were nearly empty.

She turned around and gave a start. Kimora Tucker was standing in the doorway.

We have *got* to put a buzzer on that outer door, Sassy thought.

"Sorry," Tucker said with an anxious smile. "I didn't mean to scare you."

She seemed as nervous as she'd been the last time Sassy saw her, but now she also looked as though she hadn't slept in days. Her skin was sallow and slack, and she had dark circles under her large eyes.

"That's okay," Sassy replied gently. "We really ought to keep that outer door locked. We're likely to end up with a crack head living in here."

Tucker attempted a smile in reply.

"Please," Sassy said, indicating a chair in front of her desk. "Can I get you something to drink? Some coffee or water?"

Tucker shook her head distractedly.

"No, thank you."

They both sat.

"So how are you doing, Kimora?" Sassy asked.

Tucker looked down at the floor and shrugged.

"Not so good," she replied.

Sassy nodded sympathetically.

"So how can I help you?" she asked, leaning forward and folding her hands on her desk.

Tucker hesitated. She looked as though she suddenly regretted having come.

"It's okay," Sassy urged with a kind smile. "Whatever you say stays between us."

Tucker stared at her own hands for a moment, then looked up at Sassy.

"I've been thinking about who might have wanted to hurt Deacon," she said.

Sassy nodded encouragingly.

"A few weeks before he disappeared, we were at Harrahs," Tucker continued. "Deacon loved to play blackjack, so we used to go about once a week. Usually he broke even, but he'd been on a bad streak for about a month, and that night when he went to get his chips the woman made a call and the casino manager, Mr. Hollander, came down and started talking with Deacon."

"About what?" Sassy asked.

Tucker shrugged.

"I couldn't hear because they were too far away, but Deacon started getting angry, and then the security people came and escorted him to Mr. Hollander's office."

"So what do you *think* it was about?" Sassy asked.

"Money," Tucker replied. "He'd been losing a lot. And when he came back from Mr. Hollander's office we left and we didn't go back the next week."

"Any idea how much he might have owed?" Sassy asked.

"He always played with $5,000 chips," Tucker replied, "and

like I said, he'd been losing a lot. It could have been a few hundred thousand dollars."

"So then you think his disappearance might have to do with the money he owed?" Sassy asked.

Tucker shrugged again and gave Sassy a helpless look.

Sassy knew a reputable casino like Harrahs wouldn't have had Deacon killed, but it was possible he might have borrowed the money to pay off his gambling debt and then been unable to repay the loan.

"How long before he disappeared did you say this happened?" she asked.

"About two weeks," Tucker replied.

It sounded like too short a period of time for someone to decide to kill Deacon for not making loan payments, but at least it was a lead.

"All right," Sassy said. "I'll check it out. And if you think of anything else, you know where to find me."

"Thank you," Tucker replied.

She suddenly looked to be on the verge of tears.

Sassy stood up and walked to the other side of her desk. She knelt down and put her right hand on Tucker's left forearm.

"I know this is hard on you," she said gently, "but you need to get some sleep. Whatever happened to Deacon, you running yourself ragged isn't going to help. I'm sure he wouldn't want it that way."

Tucker looked into Sassy's eyes and the tears began to come.

"I know," she said through ragged breaths, "but I miss him."

"I know you do," Sassy said.

Tucker wiped her eyes with the back of her right hand and took a deep breath.

"I know what people thought about Deacon, but he wasn't like that with me," she said. "He was sweet, and kind, and thoughtful. He made me feel like I was the most important person in the world when I was with him. And I felt safe."

Sassy tried to reconcile the different aspects of Deacon in her mind: his volatility, his paranoia, his compulsive neatness, his chronic gambling, and now his apparent gentleness with those close to him. She recalled several studies she'd read on comorbidity between impulse-control and obsessive-compulsive disorders. While there were correlations between some behaviors Deacon exhibited, such as pathological gambling with high levels of anxiety, and violent outbursts with obsessive-compulsive disorder, she couldn't remember any case studies that tied them all together. She imagined it would have been fascinating to study Deacon in a clinical setting.

"I understand," she said in a soothing voice, "but you've got to take care of yourself."

Tucker looked at Sassy with pleading eyes.

"Do you think he's still alive?" she asked.

Sassy considered how to respond. She was torn between telling the truth and comforting the distraught young woman.

"I'm sure he's fine," she lied.

*****

Michel hurried down to the second floor and stopped. He was sure he could hear a car engine now, and it seemed to be moving farther away. Shit, he thought, as he turned and raced down the stairs to the first floor. He didn't relish the idea of being locked in the building without any tools to pry the plywood off the windows.

He was almost to the door when it suddenly opened. A tall, broad man in a dark blue suit was silhouetted in the doorway, with his back to Michel.

"Yeah, that motherfucker's going to make an offer all right," the man said in a booming voice. "He's gonna offer to bend us over and fuck us up the ass."

Michel heard a high-pitched cackle, followed by another voice.

"Hey, the dude's obviously got some money. You check out that suit and that ride? Maybe he'll make a fair offer."

Michel considered running back to the stairs, but realized he was much closer to the door, and the man might turn at any second. He decided to stay and see what happened.

"You're tripping," the tall man said. "Cake boy be down here thinking he's gonna be able to buy the whole city for a goddamned nickel."

"Maybe so, maybe so," the other voice replied, getting closer.

The tall man took a step into the room and turned his right shoulder toward Michel, but continued to look into the parking lot. Suddenly another man appeared outside the door. He was smaller and stockier than the first, and dressed in a black and silver pinstriped suit. His head was shaved. When he saw Michel standing behind his companion he stopped.

"Who's the white man in our building?" he asked nonchalantly, as though it happened every day.

The tall man turned and looked at Michel without expression. Michel took a step forward and offered his right hand.

"Hi. Sorry to just let myself in," he said. "I saw the cars but didn't see anybody. I'm..."

"Michel Doucette," the tall man finished.

Michel nodded with surprise.

"Yeah, you must be Henry Patterson and James Cornell."

"I'm Cornell," the tall man replied. "This is Mr. Patterson. Mr. Lee told us you might have some questions for us, though we thought you'd stop by our office."

Michel gave an embarrassed smile.

"So did you see what you came here to see?" Patterson asked.

Michel thought about saying that he'd just arrived, but knew that his footprints would be too easy to follow in the dust and ashes.

"Yeah," he said. "I was just hoping I could ask you a few questions."

"Sure," Cornell replied. "Why don't we step outside. I want a cigarette, and I wouldn't want to start a fire."

Patterson responded with another high-pitched cackle and slapped his friend on the left shoulder heartily.

Outside in the sunlight, Michel could get a better look at the two men. Cornell looked to be in his early fifties. His hair was close-cropped and graying at the temples, with just a few flecks of white in the front and in his thin mustache. His skin was several shades darker than Patterson's and showed his age. Shallow creases had formed by the sides of his mouth, and the skin along his jaw line had started to sag. Patterson's face, by contrast, was smooth and full. Michel guessed that he and Cornell were around the same age, but Patterson could easily have passed for a decade younger.

Michel and Cornell lit their cigarettes simultaneously.

"So what can we do for you, Mr. Doucette?" Patterson asked, leaning against the trunk of the Mercedes and folding his arms across his barrel chest.

"From what I just overheard, I take it that you were showing the property to a potential buyer," Michel replied, not answering the question.

"The only thing that cracker...no offense...is gonna be buying down here is a hangover and a couple of twenty-dollar hustlers," Cornell said derisively. "He's not serious. He's just playing games."

"Mr. Cornell, your lack of faith astounds me sometimes," Patterson said, followed by another of his joyful cackles.

Michel decided he liked the two men. Their easy rapport and obvious affection for one another reminded him of his relationship with Sassy.

"So why do you want to sell?" he asked. "Seems like you could go ahead with Chance's plan. The fire damage doesn't look too bad."

He purposely avoided saying anything about the arson.

"It's not," Patterson replied, "and under normal circumstances we probably would, but these aren't normal circumstances."

"Because of the hurricane?" Michel asked.

Both men nodded emphatically.

"Getting financing for a project that big is always tough," Patterson said, "but there are always people looking to make some money. Since the hurricane, though, the money's dried up. People are nervous. They want to see what happens with the levees. Truth is, this is probably the best time to invest down here, but until we make it through another big storm without flooding, people are going to hold back."

"But you knew that when Chance approached you," Michel interjected.

"Yeah, which is why we told him it might take a few years," Cornell replied, "but he seemed to be all right with that."

Michel realized Chance had glossed over that detail. He wondered if had been intentional in order to make his financial problem seem more immediate.

"But now that there's been a fire, there ain't no way we're gonna be able to get any investors," Patterson said.

"Why?" Michel asked.

"Because fires make people nervous," Cornell replied. "Once a building has a fire, no one wants to touch it. They think it's jinxed, like if you have one fire there are gonna be fires breaking out all the time."

"And no matter what they can see with their own eyes," Patterson added, "they're always convinced there's hidden damage. You have a fire in a building, you may as well just burn it to the ground and start from scratch."

Michel thought it sounded plausible.

"So why not just hold onto it and wait for the market to rebound?" he asked. "If you sell now you're obviously not going to get what you might in a few years."

"Believe me, if we could we would," Patterson replied, "but now the insurance company is threatening to pull the coverage we have if we don't get flood and fire insurance. You have any idea how much that costs for a place this big located right on the river?"

Michel gave Patterson a curious look.

"Why's the insurance company getting involved?" he asked. "Chance told me you didn't make a claim."

"We didn't," Cornell replied. "We didn't even call and tell them about the fire. But somehow they found out. Now they want ten grand a month. We tried shopping around, but everyone's telling us the same thing."

"And right now we just don't have that kind of cash," Patterson said. "We've got everything tied up in some projects in the Ninth Ward. It's not our usual thing to do strictly residential projects, but you gotta do what you can to help out, you know what I'm saying?"

Michel nodded though he wasn't convinced they were being completely honest. He guessed that even during lean times Patterson and Cornell could scrape together ten thousand dollars from their sock drawers. He decided it was time to play his trump card.

"So how does the arson figure into all this?" he asked abruptly.

The two men's faces suddenly lost all expression.

"What arson?" Cornell asked, making it sound more like a threat than a question.

Both men stared hard at Michel, and he was suddenly very glad they were outside where passers-by might see them. Despite the fact that he was significantly younger, he was certain that either man could kick his ass without a problem.

"Come on," he said, trying to sound both relaxed and authoritative, "I was a cop. I know arson when I see it."

"So what are you saying?" Patterson asked, sounding equally as threatening as his partner.

"I'm not saying anything," Michel replied, "but look at it from Chance's perspective. He invests $300,000 into the project, then just before he's going to see some results, the building mysteriously catches on fire. Then you guys pull the plug despite the fact that the damage isn't very bad. What would you think if you were in his situation?"

Patterson and Cornell stared a him for almost a minute without saying anything, then Patterson nodded his head grudgingly.

"I'd think someone was trying to rip me off," he said. "But if you think we'd set our own building on fire for a few hundred thousand, you're whacked. We could have made a hundred times that if we'd gone ahead with the project."

He shook his head in dismay.

"If you could find the investors," Michel said. "You just admitted that wouldn't be easy."

"No, it wouldn't," Patterson agreed, "but it would have been worth it to try. Not just for the money we could have made, but for what the project could have brought to the area."

Michel knew from the numbers Chance had mentioned that Patterson and Cornell had, in fact, stood to profit far more by completing the project, and also from the records Ray Nassir had given him that the planning had been well underway. Still, the evidence of arson was clear.

"Okay, so you didn't start the fire," he said. "Who did?"

Patterson and Cornell gave him their hard, blank stares again.

"Mr. Doucette," Patterson said flatly. "As far as we're concerned, our building caught on fire, and now for practical reasons it's in our best interests to tear it down and sell the land. Beyond that, anything you think is speculation. Now if you'll excuse us, we have other business."

Michel watched as Patterson walked to the passenger side of the car and got in. Cornell walked to the driver's side and opened the door, then looked back at Michel.

"If you need to speak with us again," he said menacingly, "try stopping by our office."

Michel nodded in reply. Cornell started to get into the car then stopped and looked back at Michel again.

"Oh, and I'm about to lock the gate," he said, "so unless you feel like climbing, you best get your ass out of here."

Chapter 16

"So how'd things go with Marchand?" Sassy asked around a mouthful of food as soon as Michel walked back into the office.

She'd given up waiting for him a half hour earlier and walked to a corner market to get a chicken salad sandwich, which she was in the process of devouring.

"Fine," Michel said as he plucked a potato chip from Sassy's paper plate. "He admitted he did it."

He popped the chip into his mouth and savored the artificial barbecue flavor for a moment. He hadn't had any appetite after his conversation with Joel, nor that morning when he'd woken up, and had been too busy with Marchand, then Patterson and Cornell to have lunch. He suddenly realized that he was ravenous.

"Did he tell you why?" Sassy asked.

"Because he was out of ideas and didn't want to be embarrassed," Michel replied with a snorting laugh.

"So he set up the whole charade and paid us good money just to keep from being embarrassed?" Sassy asked incredulously.

Michel nodded.

"Sometimes you people are just crazy," Sassy said, shaking her head.

"Way to lump all the white people together," Michel replied. "Nice."

"Oh, I meant gay this time," Sassy clarified. "You all can be such drama queens."

Michel gave her a withering look as she took another bite of her sandwich.

"So did he pay you?" she asked, after she'd finished swallowing.

"I told him I'd send him a bill," Michel replied. "But he did try to bribe me to be discreet."

"And what did you say?"

"No, of course."

Sassy sat back in her chair and gave Michel a critical look.

"You do know we're not bound by the same ethical guidelines now that we're not cops, don't you?" she asked sarcastically.

"Speak for yourself," Michel replied. "Once a cop, always a cop."

"A poor cop," Sassy added.

She finished the last bite of her sandwich, dropped the paper plate in the trash, and brushed off her hands.

"So what happened with Joel?" she asked.

"Let's talk about that later," Michel replied.

He wasn't trying to avoid the subject, but to his surprise realized he simply didn't feel like talking about it. He was more interested in talking about their cases. And in eating.

"Good, we can go out to dinner," Sassy said, and for a second Michel wondered if he'd said he was hungry out loud. "Then you can take me to Harrahs."

"Harrahs? Why Harrahs?" Michel replied, confused.

"Because I have a lead on Deacon," Sassy replied.

"You mean you're going to let me help you with your case, mom?" Michel asked with exaggerated enthusiasm.

"I didn't say you could help," Sassy replied, narrowing her eyes at him, "but you can come with me."

"Cool," Michel replied. "How about eight? I'm starving and really need to get some food now, so I probably won't be ready for dinner until then."

"You haven't eaten lunch yet?" Sassy asked.

Michel shook his head.

"So then where have you been all this time?"

"Oh, I was talking with Bulldog and Double-J," Michel replied nonchalantly.

"You were talking with Bulldog and Double-J?" Sassy repeated with disbelief. "And how did that happen?"

"After my meeting with Marchand, I decided to check out the Bluehawk Terminal," Michel replied, "and they kind of caught me inside."

"And they didn't kill you?"

"Actually they were very nice...until the end," Michel replied.

"Why, what happened at the end?" Sassy asked.

"I asked them who set the fire," Michel replied as though it were no big deal.

"Whoa," Sassy exclaimed. "Are you saying it was arson?"

"Yeah," Michel replied. "It was set on the third floor of the middle building, just in front of the windows. I'm sure it looked a lot more spectacular from the outside than it really was. From what I could see, the damage was all pretty superficial."

"And you're *absolutely* certain it was arson?" Sassy pressed.

"No question," Michel replied.

"Then we should call the cops."

"With what evidence?" Michel asked. "I wasn't exactly on the property legally. Besides, I'm not sure Patterson and Cornell were responsible."

"Why not?"

"They had way more to gain by completing the project."

"So then who?" Sassy asked.

"Maybe the same person who killed Deacon," Michel replied, "and maybe Priest was right about someone trying to start a war. Think about it. If you were trying to provoke a war, would you concentrate all your energy in just one place, or would you attack on multiple fronts?"

"So you think whoever it is might be going after Priest's associates now, too?" Sassy replied.

"It's a possibility," Michel shrugged. "The fact that the damage was so superficial makes it seem like it was intended more as a warning."

Sassy remembered her promise to Priest to inform him if it looked like he or any of his people were in imminent danger. She decided that at this point all they had was speculation. There wasn't any clear proof.

"So how are you going to follow up?" she asked.

Michel thought about it for a moment.

"Right now I'm going to follow up by having some lunch," he replied. "After that, I'm not sure. If Patterson and Cornell aren't willing to cooperate, I'm not sure there's anything we *can* do."

Chapter 17

"This is a nice surprise," Ray Nassir said as he and Michel settled into their seats by a window looking out onto Dauphine Street.

A month before the hurricane, a new owner had taken over the venerated Quarter Scene Restaurant and reopened it as Eat. Michel had been meaning to try it since, but hadn't had a chance. On the spur of the moment, he'd decided to call Nassir to see if he was free to meet for a late lunch.

"Sorry for the last minute," he said. "Hopefully you weren't too busy."

"That's one of the advantages of being a partner," Nassir replied with a charming smile. "You can always find someone else to do your work."

The way he said it somehow didn't come off as bragging.

"Have you been here before?" Michel asked as he perused the menu.

"Not since it was the QSR," Nassir replied. "You?"

"No, but the menu looks good."

They were quiet for a minute as they decided what to get, then the waitress brought them iced teas and took their orders.

"So to what do I owe the honor, detective?" Nassir asked finally.

"Well, I did promise to take you out for a thank you dinner," Michel replied, "but since it looks like I'm going to be busy with work for the next few nights, I figured this would be sort of an interim thank you. Plus I just felt like seeing you."

147

It was true. As he'd left the Bluehawk Terminal, he'd found himself suddenly thinking about Nassir. He'd felt guilty at first, that he was betraying Joel, but the more he'd thought about Nassir, the more excited he'd become at the prospect of seeing him again. He'd begun to wonder if maybe Joel was right, that they weren't meant to be more than just friends.

Nassir seemed surprised.

"That's nice to hear," he replied. "I was afraid that we were going to end up with one of those awkward we-hooked-up-once kind of things, where we'd see each other in the bars and just kind of nod and then get away from each other as fast as possible."

Michel smiled, knowing exactly what Nassir meant.

"No," Michel replied. "I think we can avoid that."

"So how did things go with Joel?" Nassir asked. "If you don't mind me asking."

"I don't mind," Michel replied.

He considered what to say. It didn't seem appropriate to go into the details when he was on what was arguably a date.

"I guess I'd say not well."

"Not well for him or for me?" Nassir replied flirtatiously.

Michel admired Nassir's directness, but still it felt premature and somewhat callous to be discussing the possibility of any sort of relationship yet.

"Look, Ray," he said, "I like you, or what I've seen of you so far, but I'm really not in a place to start any sort of relationship right now."

"Who said anything about a relationship?" Nassir replied with a suggestive smile. "I'm just talking about going back to my place for cheap, meaningless, mind-blowing sex."

Michel studied him for a moment, trying to determine if he was serious, then raised his hand to get the waitress' attention.

"Can we get that to go?" he asked.

*****

Michel picked up his watch from the nightstand. It was just before five. He and Nassir had been in bed for almost three hours, and he still hadn't had lunch.

"Time for the walk of shame, I guess," he said, sitting up and reaching for his boxer shorts.

"You could always stay a while longer," Nassir offered, lying back against the pillows with his hands folded behind his head. "Then we could go out for that dinner."

Michel leaned back across the bed and kissed him.

"I can't," he said. "My partner and I are having dinner, then we're doing a little field work on a case."

"Oh shit, I almost forgot," Nassir said, sitting up suddenly. "I saw your friend as I was leaving to meet you."

"Which friend? Chance?"

"Yeah," Nassir replied. "He was in our office with another guy. They were saying goodbye to one of the other partners as I was coming down the hall. They walked out just ahead of me."

"What did the other guy look like?" Michel asked, wondering if it was Joel.

"Older guy, very nicely dressed. Short gray hair, about your height," Nassir replied. "He was like politician handsome. Good looking, but also kind of nondescript. They got into a silver Lexus."

Michel immediately thought of the other car parked at the Bluehawk Terminal. He also suddenly remembered that Cornell had referred to the owner as "cake boy," a slang term for gay, and had said the only things the man would be buying were a hangover and a couple of hustlers. It was too improbable to be a coincidence. Chance was up to something.

"I'm sorry, Ray," he said as he began to dress quickly. "I've got to jet."

"Uh, okay," Nassir replied, confused by the sudden change in Michel's demeanor.

He wondered if Michel was just trying to avoid another prolonged, awkward goodbye.

Michel finished buttoning his shirt and slipped on his shoes. He leaned across the bed and gave Nassir a long kiss, then stood up, grabbed his jacket and tie from the chair next to the nightstand, and headed for the door.

"I'll give you a call tomorrow," he said without pausing as he walked out of the room.

Nassir stared at the doorway and listened to the click of the front door shutting. He suddenly felt very empty. He wondered if this was how it would always be with Michel.

*****

Michel walked quickly toward N. Rampart and pulled out his cell phone. Chance picked up on the second ring.

"Hey, can you meet me at the office?" Michel asked, trying to sound casual.

"Why?" Chance asked suspiciously anyway.

"I was at the Bluehawk today," Michel replied. "I think you were right about the arson."

There was a brief pause before Chance replied, this time enthusiastically.

"Sure. When?"

"I'm on my way there now," Michel replied. "How about fifteen minutes?"

"Cool, I'll be there."

Michel hung up the phone and looked at his watch. He had just enough time to find out what Chance was up to, go home, and take a shower before he had to meet Sassy.

*****

Michel was sitting at his desk with his feet up when Chance bounded in. His eyes were bright and his skin was flushed, as though he'd run all the way there. It was a sharp contrast to the way he'd looked the last time Michel had seen him.

150

"So does this mean I'm going to get my money back?" he asked excitedly.

Suddenly his expression became inquisitive. He cocked his head to the right and began visibly sniffing the air.

"Damn, you don't waste any time, do you?" he asked.

"What?"

"I was a hustler," Chance said. "I know the smell of sex. Did you do it right here in the office?"

Michel suddenly wished he'd gone home to shower first. His face began to feel hot.

"Was it that Nassir guy again?" Chance continued. "Or are you just being a big slut now that Joel dumped your ass?"

"Are you done?" Michel asked, refusing to be baited.

Chance closed his eyes and took one more theatrical sniff. Then he looked at Michel and smiled like a bratty child.

"Okay, now I'm done. So tell me about my money."

Michel stared at him for a moment, then smiled back with curdled sweetness.

"How about you tell me about your friend with the silver Lexus first, then I'll tell you about your money?"

Chance's face suddenly lost its exuberance.

"How did you find out about that?" he asked.

"I was at the Bluehawk when your friend was there," Michel replied. "Then Ray saw the two of you leaving his office and getting into the Lexus. It wasn't too hard to put it together."

"I really wish you'd stop sleeping with people who work at places related to my case," Chance said.

"Don't be cute," Michel replied. "I want to know what you're up to. Who's your friend?"

Chance sighed resignedly.

"He's an old customer," he said. "He's in town from Ohio. I ran into him at Oz last night and asked him to help me out."

"To do what?"

"Initially I just wanted to see if Patterson and Cornell were serious about selling the building or if they were just waiting until I left town so they could develop the project on their own," Chance replied.

"Initially?"

"Yeah," Chance replied, "but Jervis is a developer, and when he saw the place he thought it really had potential, so we went to Harding & Lutz to talk with them."

"So you were thinking about doing an end-around and cutting Patterson and Cornell out of the deal?" Michel asked pointedly.

"Hey, they're the ones who decided they didn't want to go ahead with it," Chance replied defensively.

"I thought we had an agreement that you'd stay away from Patterson and Cornell," Michel said.

"I am staying away," Chance replied, "but there's no reason I can't try to set something else up. After all, I paid for all the research and the plans."

Michel realized that Chance was right. There was no reason he couldn't find investors and move ahead with the project on his own. Still, he had a feeling that Patterson and Cornell wouldn't see it that way.

"Okay, you're right," he said, "but I still think you're playing a dangerous game. Bulldog and Double-J are not the sort of guys you want as enemies. Just do me a favor and hold off on doing anything else until I can figure out what's going on. From what they said today, they don't expect anyone to buy the property for a while anyway."

Chance considered it for a moment, then nodded.

"But if someone else buys it, you owe me ten million."

"Deal," Michel replied with a smirk.

"So were you bullshitting about the arson just to get me here?" Chance asked.

Michel considered lying so that Chance wouldn't get his hopes up, but decided to tell the truth.

"No, I wasn't bullshitting," he replied. "It was definitely arson, but I'm not sure that Bulldog and Double-J did it."

Chance gave him a surprised look.

"Then who?"

"We think it might have something to do with another case we're working on for Priest Lee," Michel replied.

"Wait a second," Chance said. "You guys give me shit for doing a deal with Patterson and Cornell, and now you're working for their boss?"

Michel shrugged.

"What can I say?"

"Wow, first you become a slut, and now you're working for gangsters," Chance chided, shaking his head. "You are just on a fast train to hell."

"And I'm saving you a seat," Michel replied with a wry smile.

They were quiet for a moment, then Chance gave Michel an expectant look.

"So aren't you going to ask me about Joel?" he asked.

"I didn't want to put you in an uncomfortable position," Michel replied.

"Why would it be uncomfortable?" Chance replied. "He's my best friend, and you're...well, sort of a friend...I guess."

"Okay, so how's he doing?"

"Okay, I think," Chance replied. "He was pretty bummed out last night, but this morning he seemed better. I think he feels like it was the right decision."

Michel felt a sense of relief, not just because Joel was dealing well with the situation, but because he'd been feeling the same way himself.

"He even has a date," Chance added. "With someone age-appropriate."

"A date?" Michel replied, so surprised that he completely missed Chance's dig at him. "With who?"

"Some guy from school," Chance replied. "I guess the guy's been trying to get him to go out with him for a while, so this afternoon Joel called him."

It hadn't occurred to Michel that Joel might start dating someone else, and certainly not so quickly. Even if it had, he wouldn't have been prepared for the rush of conflicting emotions that suddenly hit him.

"That's great. I'm happy for him," was all he said.

"Really?" Chance asked skeptically.

"Of course," Michel replied with what he hoped would pass for convincing nonchalance. "Why wouldn't I be? I just want him to be happy."

Chapter 18

"So what did you expect him to do? Curl up in a ball and cry over you for the rest of his life?" Sassy asked, as they turned into the drive in front of Harrahs and pulled up behind another car at the valet station.

"Well, maybe not the rest of his life, but at least for a few days," Michel replied.

Sassy raised an eyebrow at him.

"Seems to me that you were getting busy with your architect this afternoon," she said. "You've apparently moved on. Why shouldn't he?"

Michel didn't answer.

"Oh, is it because you're the great Michel Doucette?" Sassy teased. "And no one should be able to get over you?"

"Something like that." Michel replied absently as he edged the car forward another fifteen feet and put it in park.

"Apparently not *that* great," Sassy said under her breath, as she opened her door and stepped out.

They walked through the lobby to the casino. A middle-aged woman with age- and gravity-defying breasts was standing just inside the entrance, waiting to greet them. She was dressed in a gold lamé evening gown, and her white-blond hair was piled high on her head.

"Welcome to Harrahs," she said cheerfully.

Her face seemed permanently fixed into an overly enthusiastic grin. Michel tried to read whether the expression was genuine or painted on. He couldn't tell.

"We're here to see Mr. Hollander," Sassy replied, trying to make it sound as though she and Michel had an appointment.

"Certainly," the woman replied with a dazzlingly white smile. "If you wait here, I'll find him. Would you like me to send over a cocktail waitress?"

"No, thank you," Sassy and Michel replied in unison.

The woman began walking across the casino. Almost immediately, she was replaced by a woman who looked like her twin, but this twin was brunette and wearing a silver evening gown. Michel had a sudden vision of a room full of greeter clones waiting to be activated.

"I guess now we know where former beauty pageant contestants go to die," Sassy whispered.

Michel suppressed the urge to laugh out loud.

"That was really easy," he said. "You wouldn't think casino managers would be so readily available."

"They're probably hoping we're a couple of high rollers," Sassy replied. "You see this crowd, or lack thereof? It's a sad day when you can't even find people who want to throw their money away."

A moment later the woman in gold came back, accompanied by a tall, slim man in an immaculate black suit. He was benignly handsome, with lacquered silver hair. The woman gestured toward Sassy and Michel, then floated away.

"I'm Mr. Hollander," the man said, smiling solicitously as he extended his right hand to Sassy.

"I'm Alexandra Jones," Sassy replied, using her given name, "and this is my partner, Michel Doucette."

When he heard the word "partner," Hollander's expression seemed to falter for a moment, then he recovered and shook Michel's hand, as well.

"So what can I do for you?" he asked in a courteous, professional tone.

"We'd like to ask you a few questions about Deacon Lee," Michel said.

This time Hollander's expression didn't just falter. It changed completely.

"If you have police business to discuss with me, I'd appreciate it if you'd schedule an appointment during the day," he said in a hushed, tight voice.

"Actually we're not cops," Sassy replied. "We're private investigators."

Hollander's expression grew more unyielding.

"Then I have nothing to say," he declared. "We don't discuss our guests...with anyone."

"We're working for Priest Lee," Sassy replied. "If you'd like, I can give him a call and you can confirm it."

She pulled out her cell phone and held it up in front of Hollander. The look on his face suggested it was a loaded gun. He stared at it for a moment, then shook his head.

"That won't be necessary," he said quickly. "But I'd prefer to discuss this in my office."

He turned and began walking across the casino without waiting. Sassy and Michel looked at one another for a second, then quickly followed.

*****

"We understand that Deacon was losing a lot of money recently," Sassy said, as soon as they were seated in front of Hollander's desk.

"Mr. Lee did seem to be going through a bad streak," Hollander replied. "But that happens occasionally with our more frequent guests."

"How bad a streak?" Michel asked.

Hollander looked annoyed but turned to his computer and began typing. After a few seconds he looked back at Sassy and Michel.

"$350,000," he said flatly.

"And that was on a credit account, I take it," Michel said.

"Of course," Hollander replied. "Mr. Lee had an account with us."

"Is that considered a lot for one of your 'more frequent guests'?" Sassy asked.

"For some," Hollander replied. "We set limits based on our guest's individual financial situations. For Mr. Lee, that was within his limit."

"So then it wouldn't have been enough to get him kicked out of the casino until he paid it down?" Sassy asked.

Hollander's expression became suddenly wary.

"No. Why?" he asked.

"Because we understand that you and Deacon had an argument a few weeks ago and he stormed out of the casino," Michel replied.

Hollander studied them both for a moment before responding.

"Yes, we did have a disagreement," he said. "We have a system in place that alerts us when guests are nearing their limits so that we can bring it to their attention. It's an automated system. When a guest comes into the casino, the alert appears when the teller brings up their account. The standard procedure is then to call the manager on duty."

"So Deacon was nearing his limit?" Sassy asked.

"Technically, yes," Hollander replied. "It's necessary to set some dollar value in the computer. For Mr. Lee that value was arbitrarily set at $400,000. But the reality is that the amount is actually at the manager's discretion. In Mr. Lee's case, I would have been more than willing to extend additional credit."

"So then what was the argument about?" Michel asked.

"How do I put this?" Hollander wondered aloud. "Mr. Lee took offense at the fact that his account had been flagged. And the truth is it should never have happened. I should have noticed the alert and manually overridden it."

"So he was pissed off because he felt you embarrassed him," Sassy said.

"Yes, that would be another way of putting it," Hollander agreed.

"So then he wasn't banned from the casino?" Michel asked.

"Of course not," Hollander replied.

"Have you seen him since?" Sassy asked.

"No," Hollander replied, "but we did receive full payment on his account..."

He turned back to his computer and began typing again.

"...two weeks ago."

Michel and Sassy exchanged quick, curious looks.

"How was the money received?" Michel asked.

"It was wired from Mr. Lee's bank, as usual," Hollander replied.

Sassy stood up suddenly.

"Well, thank your for your time, Mr. Hollander," she said. "We won't take up any more of it. You've been very helpful."

Hollander looked confused but stood up, too.

"I trust that our conversation will remain private?" he asked. "Except for the interested party, of course."

"Of course," Sassy replied. "And we trust that you won't mention it to anyone either."

"No, of course not," Hollander replied stiffly.

*****

"So either Deacon is still alive or someone is cleaning up his messes," Sassy said as they stood in front of the casino waiting for Michel's car.

"I'm betting the latter," Michel replied.

"Miss Jones? Mr. Doucette?" a gravelly voice called to them from the right edge of the concrete canopy that sheltered the entrance.

They turned and saw a man standing next to a black Lincoln Town Car stretch limousine with tinted windows. He was older, probably in his sixties, but solidly built. His dyed black hair was slicked back and he was dressed in a double-breasted blue suit.

"Mr. Villorisi would like a moment of your time, please," he said, gesturing toward the car with his left hand.

Michel and Sassy knew who was in the car immediately. Angelo Villorisi was the head of one of the city's other crime families. They took a few cautious steps forward.

"For what?" Michel asked.

"I wouldn't know," the man replied flatly, then gestured toward the car again. "If you please."

"This should be interesting," Sassy whispered as they started toward to the car.

*****

Sassy remembered seeing photos of Angelo Villorisi when he was younger. He had been robust, handsome, and extremely dapper. Now he reminded her of a withered tree dressed in a beautiful suit. He was painfully frail, and his intelligent eyes had sunken deep above his protruding cheek bones and hollow cheeks. From his ragged, wheezy breathing, she guessed he was suffering from emphysema or lung cancer.

"I take it you're looking for Deacon Lee," he said in a raspy voice once they were seated across from him in the plush back of the limousine.

"Why would you think that?" Sassy replied.

Villorisi stared at her for a moment.

"Don't treat me like I'm stupid, Miss Jones."

Though his voice was weak, it carried an undeniably threatening tone. Sassy imagined that he must have been quite fearsome in his day. Still, she wasn't ready to give in that easily.

"Why would you think that?" she repeated.

Villorisi sighed deeply, then went into a long coughing fit.

"Fine, we'll play it your way," he said when he'd recovered. "You've been seen at Priest Lee's office, Deacon's house,

Granville Kingston's house, and now Harrahs. What's the one thing they all have in common?"

"Deacon?" Sassy replied, surprised that Villorisi was implying a connection between Deacon and Kingston.

Villorisi nodded gravely.

"So don't be coy with me. I know what you're up to," he said. "I know everything that goes on in this town."

"Then why would you need to speak with us?" Michel asked, feeling emboldened by Sassy's brashness.

Villorisi leaned forward and fixed him with a cold stare.

"I put up with the smart mouth from her because she's a lady and a personal friend of Priest Lee," he hissed. "I don't put up with it from you. You disrespect me again and you'll have a tough time holding onto your pecker when you piss because you won't have any thumbs."

He leaned back against his seat with obvious effort and looked at Sassy.

"My apologies for my crude language," he said.

Sassy stole a quick look at Michel. He looked genuinely unnerved by Villorisi's threat.

"That's okay, I've heard worse," she said, looking back at Villorisi. "So how can we help you?"

"You can't," Villorisi rasped, "but I can help you."

"How?" Sassy asked. "And *why?*"

"I have my reasons," Villorisi replied cryptically. "They're none of your concern. Just accept what I'm offering with gratitude."

"With all due respect, Mr. Villorisi," Michel said, deciding to heed the old man's warning while still asserting himself, "it's difficult to accept the credibility of information without understanding the reason it's being offered."

"And what exactly do you mean by 'gratitude'?" Sassy added.

It was obvious from the frustrated look on his face that Villorisi wasn't accustomed to dealing with people who questioned his actions or motives. He looked back and forth from Sassy to Michel several times, as though trying to size them up.

"Okay," he said finally. "Perhaps I overstated when I said I know everything that goes on in this town. Sometimes, like now, I know *something* is going on, but not exactly *what*. It occurred to me that if I point you in the right direction, perhaps you might clarify the situation for me."

"Then you do need our help," Sassy said.

Michel had wanted to say the same thing, but had decided not to press his luck.

"Let's just say it would be quid pro quo," Villorisi replied with a faint smile. "I give you information, and if you find anything of interest, you share it with me."

"So that would be the 'gratitude'," Sassy clarified, wanting to make certain that Villorisi wouldn't expect anything else from them.

"Correct," Villorisi replied.

Sassy looked at Michel for a second to make sure he was in agreement, then turned back to Villorisi.

"That's fine," she said, "just so long as you understand we can't give you any information that might compromise our professional obligations to Priest."

"Understood," Villorisi replied.

"Okay, so what have you got for us?" Sassy asked. "You implied earlier that there's a connection between Granville Kingston and Deacon."

Villorisi nodded.

"Deacon was seen at Kingston's place on several occasions in the weeks leading up to his disappearance."

"Any idea what it was about?" Michel asked.

Villorisi shrugged.

"This is only speculation, of course, but I imagine they were exploring the possibilities of merging their resources," he said.

"So basically you think Deacon got tired of waiting for

Priest to hand over the reins and decided to take matters into his own hands," Sassy said.

"Again, I'm only speculating," Villorisi replied.

"So then what do you think happened to Deacon?" Michel asked.

Villorisi turned the palms of his hands up.

"Perhaps Kingston decided that Deacon was too much trouble," he said. "Or perhaps Priest got wind of it and decided to take preemptive measures. Or perhaps Deacon is in hiding until they're ready to make their move. As I said, I'm hoping you might be able to clarify the situation."

"And what makes you think we can find out more than you can?" Sassy asked. "Seems to me you've got things pretty well covered."

"Unfortunately, Kingston's people have proven extremely resistant to outside overtures," Villorisi replied. "We've never been able to get any ears on the inside of his operation. You, on the other hand, were able to walk right into his house."

Sassy thought about it for a moment. While she didn't relish the idea of being allied with Villorisi, she couldn't see a down side in agreeing to provide him with information so long as they didn't double cross Priest in the process.

"All right," she said. "We'll see what we can find out. How do we contact you?"

Villorisi chuckled.

"Don't worry, I'll contact you."

Suddenly the door next to Sassy opened, as though Villorisi had sent a telepathic signal to his driver. Sassy gave it a curious look, then stepped out of the car. Michel slid across the seat toward the door, then extended his right hand to Villorisi. The old man stared at it for a moment, then reached out with surprising speed and gripped it tightly in his own right hand. He locked eyes with Michel, then pressed the nail of his left middle finger into the crook of Michel's hand and ran it slowly across the base of the metacarpal joint of Michel's thumb.

"I'm sure we'll meet again," he said, then suddenly released Michel's hands and began laughing, a wet, demented laugh.

Michel quickly got out of the car.

"That was interesting," Sassy said as they watched the limousine pull away. "How did it feel to be threatened by an old man?"

"Whatever's wrong with him," Michel replied with a shudder, "I hope it kills him quickly."

Sassy took out her cell phone and began searching the list of recent calls.

"Who are you calling?" Michel asked.

"I'm making an appointment," Sassy replied as she located the number she'd found in Deacon's house and hit redial.

"Stop calling me, you crazy bitch," the voice on the other end answered angrily after two rings.

"I want to talk to Kingston," Sassy replied.

"There's no one here by that name," the man said flatly.

"Just tell him it's Sassy Jones and I want to see him."

Sassy could hear muffled voices. She guessed the man had his hand over the receiver.

"Okay," the man replied after a few seconds. "Be here at 11 o'clock tomorrow morning."

"Okay," Sassy said, then hung up.

"You have Kingston's phone number?" Michel asked with a surprised look.

"Oh sure, you know me," Sassy replied breezily. "I'm tight with all the local gangsters."

Michel shook his head with a combination of admiration and amazement.

"Well, I don't know about you," Sassy said, "but I'm ready to call it a night. I'm going to need to get some sleep before I can wrap my brain around all this."

"Yeah," Michel replied, rubbing the base of his right thumb as though trying to get off a stain, "though I'm not sure how well I'm going to sleep."

Chapter 19

Sassy was lying in bed, half-heartedly reading an article about the scandalous downfall of some rich white people in an old issue of "Vanity Fair," when the phone rang. She looked at the clock, then the Caller ID before she answered.

"Why are you calling me at this hour?" she asked with mock irritation.

"I had a feeling you'd still be awake." Michel replied. "I couldn't sleep either."

"Yeah, something's not right," Sassy said. "Priest is a smart man. He had to have known he was being watched and that I'd be followed if I was seen at his office. If he wanted to keep things quiet, why would he risk that? We could have met someplace more discreet."

"I have a theory on that," Michel replied, "but before I say anything, we need to go on a field trip."

"Okay. When?"

"Right now."

"At 2:37 AM?" Sassy asked incredulously.

"It's not the sort of thing we can do in daylight," Michel replied.

"Oh, *that* sort of field trip," Sassy said.

"Exactly. I'll pick you up in ten minutes," Michel replied. "Oh, and wear something black."

"Ooh, how exciting," Sassy replied. "A formal breaking and entering."

Then she hung up.

*****

They parked several blocks past the Bluehawk Terminal, walked down to the edge of the river, and began making their way back along the old docks toward the buildings.

"So what exactly are we looking for?" Sassy asked in a hushed voice.

"I'm not sure, but I'm hoping I'll know it when I see it," Michel replied quietly.

Sassy stopped.

"You mean to tell me we're out here in the middle of the night and you don't even know what we're looking for?"

Michel stopped and looked back at her.

"Is that a problem?" he asked innocently.

"It is if you want me to take another step," Sassy replied adamantly. "You need to explain what's going on."

Michel walked back to her and knelt down, quietly placing his canvas bag on the wood planking. Sassy got onto one knee beside him.

"Okay, I was thinking about the fire," Michel said. "I'm convinced that Patterson and Cornell weren't just trying to scam Chance. I think they were sincere about the project. But if someone else set the fire to send a message, they probably would have burned the whole place down."

"How do you know they weren't trying?" Sassy asked. "Maybe the fire department just got there too quickly."

Michel shook his head.

"If you want to burn a building to the ground, you set the fire on the ground floor, not the top, and not just along the outer walls. Like I said before, I think it was just meant to look spectacular without causing much damage."

Sassy considered it for a moment, then nodded.

"Okay, I'm with you," she said. "We're back to Patterson and Cornell. But why would they set the fire if they weren't scamming Chance or trying to collect insurance money?"

"That's what's been bothering me," Michel replied. "Especially since they told me they were planning to tear the building down now anyway. Why didn't they just burn it to the ground in the first place?"

"And I assume you've thought of a reason?" Sassy replied impatiently, gesturing with her hand for him to cut to the chase.

Michel nodded.

"Suppose they needed an excuse for canceling the project, but couldn't burn the building entirely because there's something there they don't want discovered?"

"That's your big theory?" Sassy asked, arching an eyebrow dubiously.

"That's part of it," Michel replied.

"What's the other part?"

"I'm afraid you're going to have to wait on that," Michel replied, nodding his head in the direction of the terminal.

"All right," Sassy said as she pushed herself wearily to her feet. "But this better be damn good."

*****

Michel cut through the chain link fence using bolt-cutters from his bag. He and Sassy moved quickly into the shadows behind the center building.

"So where do we start?" Sassy asked.

"I'm pretty sure there's nothing in this building," Michel replied, "and the one at that end looks like a warehouse, so I think we should start at the other end. It looks like there's a kitchen on the top floor. I'm guessing the rest of it is offices."

"Lead on," Sassy replied.

They walked to the back of the far left building and Michel took a crowbar from his bag. He began prying a piece of plywood from one of the windows. The nails groaned loudly as they were pulled free.

"Jesus, maybe we should just send up some fireworks, too," Sassy whispered.

"Hey, it's either this or use a power saw," Michel replied as he pulled the last nail free from one end.

He bent the plywood back three feet.

"We're in luck," he said. "The window's already broken."

"Oh joy," Sassy deadpanned.

Michel reached into his bag again and pulled out a thick rubber door mat.

"Do you really think it's necessary to wipe our feet first?" Sassy asked sarcastically as he unrolled it.

"Are you always so funny at this time of night?" Michel asked back, as he laid the mat over the shards of glass still embedded in the bottom of the window frame.

He squatted down and laced his hands together. Sassy just stared at him for a moment.

"What?" Michel asked.

"You didn't have room for a ladder in your magic bag?"

Michel pantomimed heart laughter for a moment.

"You're killing me tonight," he said, as Sassy stepped up on his hands and climbed through the window.

Michel put the crowbar back in his bag and passed the bag to Sassy, then pulled himself up onto the door mat and dropped quietly onto the dusty floor inside.

*****

"You notice anything odd?" Michel asked, as they stood in the middle of the third floor kitchen.

"You mean besides us being here at 3 o'clock in the morning?" Sassy replied. "No."

"The walk-in freezer," Michel said, pointing his flashlight at a large steel door on the far side of the room.

"What about it?" Sassy asked. "Restaurant kitchens always have freezers."

"It's locked," Michel replied.

He focused the flashlight's beam on a long padlock through the door handle.

"So?" Sassy said as they crossed the room. "If I had a big-ass freezer like that, I'd lock it, too. Some damn teenagers are liable to get themselves trapped inside and suffocate."

Michel ran a finger up the seam of the door.

"Would you weld it shut, too?" he asked.

Sassy moved closer and ran her flashlight along the side of the door. There was a thick rope of melted steel in the joint between the door and side panel of the freezer.

"You think Deacon's inside, don't you?" she asked suddenly.

Michel smiled.

"I was thinking about what Villorisi said about Priest taking preemptive action," he said. "Suppose Priest did have Deacon killed, and stashed the body here. Then he finds out about Chance's project. He knows that if anyone sees this they're going to start wondering what's inside, and he can't exactly get it out of here on a dolly cart, so he tells Patterson and Cornell to kill the project."

"So they come up with the idea of setting the fire," Sassy said, following Michel's logic, "only they can't really burn the buildings down because the heat might blow open the door."

"Right," Michel said. "And even if Deacon's body was incinerated, there'd still be evidence. But now that the building's being torn down, Priest can just have the freezer hauled away and buried in a landfill somewhere and no one will think twice about it."

"I like it, though it's pretty convoluted," Sassy replied, "and there are a lot of holes."

"Such as?"

"Such as why hide the body in the first place? And why not just remove it when he found out about the project? And why try to point the finger at Kingston instead of just killing him if he and Deacon were working together? And most of all, why go through the charade of hiring us to look for Deacon? He had to know that was risky."

Michel thought about it for a few moments.

"Okay," he started, "if Deacon's body just showed up, it would be game over for Priest. The other families would just move in and divide up his territory. But so long as Deacon just remains missing, everyone's going to be afraid to make a move, which gives Priest some time to maneuver."

"I'll buy that," Sassy replied. "Next."

"And by leaving Kingston alive, he has a boogeyman, which gives the other families someone to focus on. And if they perceive Kingston as a threat, chances are they'll kill him, so Priest gets what he wants without doing the dirty work."

"That one wasn't quite as convincing," Sassy said, "but go ahead."

"And he hired us because he needed a way to bring attention to Kingston. He knew the other families would be watching us, so he used us. The same way Marchand tried to use me to incriminate Ray."

Sassy considered it. Suddenly she remembered what Priest had said about someone wanting to start a war so they could collect the spoils. Perhaps he'd been right, but he'd neglected to mention that he was the one who might be collecting. With Deacon gone he was vulnerable, but if he could get the other families to go to war against Kingston, they might suffer enough casualties collectively that Priest could survive, or even gain.

"All right," she said, "though you still haven't explained why Priest didn't just move Deacon's body."

Michel frowned.

"I was hoping you'd forget about that one. I've got nothing. I mean, why the fuck would you hide a body in a freezer in the first place when you could just bury it somewhere? But we've obviously got a welded door, so...."

Sassy hesitated a moment, then nodded slowly.

"We certainly do," she said, with a sigh of reluctant acceptance.

"So what do we do next?" Michel asked.

"Well, unless you've got an acetylene torch in that bag," Sassy replied, "I think the next step is to find out exactly what was going on between Deacon and Kingston."

Chapter 20

As Kingston's house came into view, Michel suddenly stopped the car.

"What's in the cage?" he asked, looking out the driver's window.

"Monkeys," Sassy replied.

"I don't see any," Michel said, turning to look at her.

Sassy rolled her eyes and made an exasperated face.

"It's raining out," she said, as though anyone with common sense should know that was the reason.

As Michel eased the car forward again, Sassy turned to her own reflection in the passenger window and smiled.

"Looks like we've got a greeting committee," Michel said a few seconds later.

Sassy looked up. Through the rain-streaked windshield, she could see a line of men standing along the rail of the front porch. They appeared to be on high alert.

"Well, we were invited," she said, "so hopefully they're not going to give us any trouble."

Michel parked the car and they both stepped out.

"We have an appointment to see Mr. Kingston," Sassy called up to the men.

The man nearest the steps waved them forward. He was dressed in the same uniform of cargo pants and a t-shirt as the others, but looked to be a few years older—probably in his mid-thirties—and his manner suggested that he was in charge of the group.

"Are you carrying any weapons?" he asked as they stepped out of the rain onto the porch.

Sassy recognized his voice from the calls she'd made to the number she'd found at Deacon's house.

"So finally we meet," she said, as she handed him her black 9mm Smith & Wesson pistol.

The man gave her a small smile as he took the gun, then looked at Michel.

"I left mine in the car," Michel said.

"That's okay," the man said. "You're not going to see Mr. Kingston, anyway."

"Why not?" Sassy asked.

"Mr. Kingston's only expecting you," the man replied not unkindly. "Your partner can wait with me."

Sassy was about to protest, but Michel gave her a look that indicated he didn't mind.

"Okay," she said, "but when I come back, he better be in the same condition as when I left him with you."

*****

"Why didn't you tell me you had meetings with Deacon Lee?" Sassy asked.

Kingston was seated behind a large oak desk in a back room of the farmhouse. He looked mildly surprised, then impressed.

"You came to me as a representative of a man some might consider my enemy," he replied. "Why would I volunteer information that might make it appear I was in collusion against him with his own son?"

"Maybe because it would look a lot worse if I found out on my own?" Sassy replied caustically.

"One had hoped such information wouldn't be discovered," Kingston said with a sly smile.

"Yes, I'm sure one did," Sassy replied. "So what were you meeting with him about?"

Kingston paused before answering, as though trying to assess his options.

"As I'm sure you've heard by now, Deacon felt it was time for him to take over his father's business," he said finally. "Unfortunately for him, his father disagreed. Deacon came to me to suggest a partnership. He thought that together we could force his father out and take over."

"Force his father out?" Sassy questioned the implication.

"Or remove him," Kingston replied, making it clear that he meant murder.

Sassy thought that Kingston's answer sounded sincere.

"So what did you say?" she asked.

"I told him we should wait," Kingston replied. "I said there was no reason to risk waking a sleeping old lion to kill him when he would die soon enough on his own."

"And you think Priest Lee is going to die soon on his own?"

Kingston turned his hands palms up on the desk.

"Relatively speaking," he replied. "He will be gone soon enough that there will be plenty of time to be king."

"And you think you'll be king?" Sassy asked.

"I was just continuing the metaphor of the lion," Kingston replied with a charming smile.

"So then the plan was that once Priest was gone, you and Deacon would take over," Sassy said.

Kingston frowned slightly.

"Deacon would not have been an appropriate business partner," he said. "He was a soldier, not a general. In the long term, I believe he would have proven himself to be a liability."

"But you didn't tell him that," Sassy said.

It was more a statement than a question.

"No," Kingston replied. "While I did not want him as a partner, I saw no reason to have him as an enemy."

"So what was Deacon's reaction?"

"He was...disappointed."

"Disappointed enough to try and kill you?" Sassy asked.

"No," Kingston replied soberly. "Deacon was smart enough to know that would be a mistake. He couldn't make a move like that without his father's approval, and his father would want to know the reason. Deacon couldn't risk having his father find out about his business proposition to me."

Sassy considered it for a moment.

"And you didn't kill him?" she asked.

"That's not my style, Miss Jones," Kingston replied. "Where I come from, family is sacred. You may kill your enemy, but you don't hurt his family."

"But some people might say that Deacon *was* your enemy," Sassy interjected. "Or might be in the future."

Kingston shook his head slowly.

"No. Deacon and I had no bones between us."

Sassy thought about it. Nothing Kingston had said contradicted what she already knew. Still, she wasn't convinced he was telling her the whole story.

"So who do you think killed him?" she asked.

Kingston shrugged.

"As I told you before, that's old school."

*****

"So where were you?" Sassy asked when Michel finally arrived back at the car ten minutes later.

The rain had just stopped a few minutes earlier and she was standing by the locked passenger door.

"Roland was showing me around the grounds," Michel answered quickly, as he pressed the remote to unlock the doors.

"Roland?" Sassy asked once they were inside. "What, are you buddies now?"

"Something like that," Michel replied opaquely as he started the car.

Sassy studied him as he backed the car up, then started down the driveway.

"You say he was showing you the grounds?" she asked.

"Uh huh," Michel replied with forced casualness.

"Then why aren't you wet?" Sassy asked suspiciously.

Michel turned his head slightly toward the driver's window, but from the shape of his cheek, Sassy could tell he was smiling.

"Well, we only made it as far as the barn," he replied in a barely audible voice.

"You had sex with a Rasta gangster?" Sassy exclaimed.

Michel turned to look at her, his face the epitome of wide-eyed innocence.

"We didn't have sex. We just made out a little. Besides, I didn't have any choice. He had a gun."

"I'll bet," Sassy replied disapprovingly. "When this case is over, you and I are going to have a long discussion about appropriate professional behavior."

Michel gave her a chastened look and turned his attention back to driving. They were silent for a few minutes.

"Okay, so how was it?" Sassy asked finally.

"Really good," Michel replied eagerly, smiling like a teenager. "You should try one of those Rasta gangsters yourself some time."

Sassy had a sudden image of Kingston in his pajama bottoms and tanktop. *If only I were twenty years younger,* she thought.

Chapter 21

"Well, look what we have here," Sassy said, waving an envelope she'd pulled from the stack of mail that was waiting for them inside the office door.

"What is it?" Michel asked.

"Looks like a check to me," Sassy replied. "From our friend Mr. Marchand. You want to do the honors?"

She held the envelope toward Michel, who was already flopped into his desk chair.

"No, you go ahead," he said.

Sassy slit the envelope with a pen knife and took out the check. She stared it at for a moment, then looked at Michel curiously.

"How many hours did you bill him for?" she asked.

"Ten," Michel replied. "Why?"

"Because he paid us for a hundred," Sassy said. "It's a check for $15,000."

"I'll send it back to him," Michel replied with a sigh.

"Like hell you will," Sassy replied quickly. "If some rich fool wants to give us his money, I say we take it."

"I really don't want to be indebted to him...."

"Wait, there's a note," Sassy interrupted.

She unfolded the sheet of paper and began reading.

"Dear Michel, Although you specifically requested that I pay only the amount billed, I feel that the additional gratuity is deserved. This morning I was appointed as a judge for this year's Bourbon Street Awards. Without your professionalism, and the unexpected outpouring of sympathy I've received as a result of your investigation, I'm certain it would never have happened. Please accept this, along with my profound gratitude. Best wishes, Severin."

"Whatever," Michel replied with a roll of his eyes.

"Hey, he's not trying to bribe you," Sassy said. "It's just a really big tip."

She looked at Michel expectantly.

"Please can we keep it? Please, please, please?" she asked, like a child pleading for a puppy.

"Fine," Michel said wearily. "Do whatever you want with it. I don't care."

"What's the matter with you suddenly?" Sassy asked, frowning as she folded the check and slipped it into her purse.

"Nothing," Michel replied. "Just tired."

"And cranky," Sassy added.

"Maybe a little," Michel replied.

"Why?"

"I don't know," Michel replied. "I should be in a great mood. We've only been in business for a few days and we've already got fifteen grand going into the bank, we've got a solid theory that Priest killed Deacon, and I've been getting laid a lot. I should be ecstatic."

"But you're not," Sassy said. "Because of Joel?"

Michel thought about it, then shook his head.

"I don't think so. I think I'm just overly tired. You know how I get when I'm tired. I start seeing the glass as half empty."

"Well, if you're sure that's all it is, why don't you go home and get some sleep?" Sassy offered.

"And what are you going to do?" Michel asked.

"I don't know," Sassy replied with a shrug. "There's nothing else we can do about Deacon right now. I think the next step is to talk to Priest, and I haven't even begun to think about how to approach that. I guess I'll just go to the bank, then maybe catch some lunch and go home. Take a nap."

"All right," Michel said, pushing himself up from his chair, "but if you need me for anything, give me a call. I'll be home. At least for a few hours."

"You have plans tonight?" Sassy asked.

"I was thinking about calling Ray to see if he's free," Michel replied. "I promised him dinner as a thank you for his help with Chance's case."

"Seems to me you've already thanked him at least once," Sassy said, pursing her lips. "Besides, weren't you just locking lips with your friend Roland an hour ago? Maybe if you kept your hormones in check for a while you wouldn't be so tired."

"Can I help it if men suddenly find me irresistible?" Michel asked, with feigned indignity.

"Yeah, irresistible," Sassy said. "More like easy."

*****

Michel arrived at the Bourbon Pub ten minutes early and took a seat at the bar. He felt someone sidle up next to him and turned to look into the flat, smiling face of Severin Marchand.

"Hello, Michel," Marchand said with a little too much familiarity for Michel's taste. "How are you?"

"I'm fine, thank you...Mr. Marchand," Michel replied deliberately. "And you?"

"Oh, I'll be just fine once I have a cocktail," Marchand replied, making eye contact with the bartender to signal that he wanted his usual. "I trust you received my check?"

"Yes, thank you," Michel replied with forced politeness.

Marchand gave him a condescending smile.

"So, are you working on any interesting new cases?" he asked abruptly.

"Mmm, very," Michel mumbled more to himself than in response.

"Oooh, now that sounds exciting," Marchand replied, his usual false enthusiasm increasing another notch. "Do tell."

"Sorry," Michel replied, "but you know how important it is for us to maintain our clients' confidentiality."

He'd hope that Marchand would understand the implied threat and leave him alone, but Marchand seemed totally oblivious.

"It wouldn't have anything to do with Priest Lee, now would it?" he asked.

Michel was taken completely off-guard, but tried to hide his shock.

"Now what would make you think that?" he asked casually.

"I have my sources," Marchand replied, narrowing his eyes in an exaggerated show of mysteriousness.

Then he broke into a wide, relaxed smile and chuckled.

"I have an old friend who works the security desk in the building where Jacard-Lee has their offices," he said breezily. "He told me your partner had an appointment with Mr. Lee a few days ago."

Michel thought to ask how that had happened to come up in conversation, but decided against it. Apparently he and Sassy were the subjects of interest from many people.

"Mr. Lee and I go way back," Marchand continued without pausing a beat.

"Uh huh," Michel replied with genuine disinterest, assuming that they'd met on the charity circuit.

"Why we were practically neighbors in Jamaica," Marchand exclaimed giddily.

"Jamaica?" Michel asked, his interest suddenly piqued though he tried to maintain a neutral tone.

"Oh yes," Marchand replied. "We both had houses on the same beach. He lived with the most beautiful woman back then, and a charming young boy who I assumed was his son, though I never asked. Of course that was a long time ago. I sold that place twenty-five years ago. It was just getting too dirty and touristy down there. I wonder what ever happened to them?"

He waved his hand, as though dismissing old memories.

"What part?" Michel asked in a tone that made it appear no more than a polite question.

"Uh, just outside Kingston," Marchand replied distractedly, his attention having just drifted to two twenty-something boys who'd taken seats at the far end of the bar.

"Oh, I've never been," Michel said.

Marchand didn't respond for a few seconds, then suddenly turned to Michel with a look that suggested he was surprised to find him there. Then he composed himself into his usual superior manner.

"You'll have to excuse, Michel," he said with elaborate politeness, "but I just noticed two old friends I need to speak with."

He began sashaying toward the boys before Michel could say goodbye.

Michel reached for his cell phone to call Sassy, but a hand on his left shoulder stopped him. He turned and saw a smiling Ray Nassir.

"What did he want?" Nassir asked, nodding toward Marchand, who was in the process of buying drinks for his new companions.

"He just wanted to make sure I got his check," Michel replied. "What do you say we go to the restaurant and get a drink there? I'm afraid Severin may find out his new friends aren't for sale and come back over."

*****

Michel had been preoccupied all through dinner. The possibility that Granville Kingston might be Priest Lee's son added a whole new dimension to the case, and he kept wishing he could get home to start checking it out.

"Earth to Michel," Nassir said after their coffee arrived.

"I'm sorry," Michel replied, snapping back into the moment. "Marchand told me something that might be related to another case we're working on, and I was just trying to figure out what it means."

"Oh," Nassir replied with visible disappointment. "Is it something you want to talk about?"

"No, thanks," Michel replied. "It's too complicated a story and I don't want to bore you. Plus it's probably better if you don't know. For your own sake."

"What does that mean?" Nassir asked.

"Just that it involves some pretty dangerous characters," Michel replied.

They were silent for a few moments, then Nassir leaned closer across the table and locked eyes with Michel.

"Look, Michel," he said, "I think it's great that you take your work seriously. I do, too. But when I leave the office, I leave my work there. Based on the limited amount of time we've spent together, it seems like you're always thinking about your work."

Michel stared at him for a moment, then let out a small, self-deprecating laugh.

"Yeah, I suppose that's true," he said. "Kind of an old habit, I guess. When you work homicide, the job is always with you. There's a fear that builds up over time that the longer it takes you to solve a case, the greater the chance someone else might die. That's why the burn-out rate is so high."

"I get that," Nassir said gently, "but you're not a homicide detective anymore. Not to be unkind, but I don't think anyone's going to die if you don't figure out who destroyed a Mardi Gras costume."

Michel felt a sting to his ego.

"So what are you getting at?" he asked.

"I have sort of a three-date rule," Nassir replied. "If I don't feel like something's going to work by the third date, then I move on. I realize that technically this is only our second date, but I'm just not seeing things going any further."

"What?" Michel replied. "Where's all this coming from?"

"I need someone who can be totally in the moment with me," Nassir explained. "The only times I've felt like you were giving me your complete attention was when we were having sex. And then as soon as that was over, your mind went somewhere else completely. I don't think you do it on purpose, but I've got you tell, it hurts. When you left yesterday afternoon, I just felt...empty. Like the whole thing had just been an inconsequential diversion for you. And now you invite me to dinner, and you're still not focused on me."

Michel felt like he'd just been hit by a flurry of quick jabs.

"Don't you think you're overreacting a bit?" he asked. "I mean, we hardly know one another."

"I realize that," Nassir replied evenly, "and because of that, you probably think I'm just some silly, insecure queen. But I'm not. In fact, I'm very secure, which is why I think I have the right to expect the man I'm with to pay attention to me. Especially in the beginning. If we'd been together for ten years, I'd kind of expect you to ignore me half the time, but we were just getting started."

"Were?" Michel repeated, noting the past tense.

Nassir stared at him for a moment, then nodded.

"I'm sorry," he said, "but I just don't think you're right for me."

Michel had a sudden vision of the awkward avoidance dance that he and Nassir would go through in the future.

"Okay," he replied, not sure what else to say.

Nassir stood and walked to Michel's side of the table. He leaned down and gave Michel a kiss on the cheek.

"I'd invite you back to my place for goodbye sex," he whispered, "but I don't think I could handle the letdown afterward."

Chapter 22

"You'll never guess who Granville Kingston's father is," Michel said excitedly as soon as Sassy walked through the office door the next morning.

"Who?" she asked with a look of surprise and confusion.

"Priest Lee," Michel proclaimed, smiling triumphantly.

Sassy shook her head in disbelief.

"What?!"

Michel nodded.

"I ran into Marchand last night," he continued, "and he told me that he and Lee used to be neighbors in Jamaica..."

Sassy held out her hand to stop him.

"I don't even want to know why you were discussing our case with Marchand."

"I wasn't," Michel replied quickly. "He volunteered the information out of the blue. Anyway, he said that Priest lived there with a woman and a young boy he assumed was Priest's son. And you'll never guess where their houses were."

"I'm going to go out on a limb and guess it wasn't Nagrille," Sassy replied.

"Correct," Michel replied. "Kingston!"

"And you have proof that that little boy grew up to be Granville?" Sassy asked.

"Not yet," Michel replied, "but I put in a call to INS, and they have no record of a Granville Kingston emigrating to the States. They do, however, have a record of a Granville Lee, who came here in 1991."

"That's pretty convincing circumstantial evidence," Sassy admitted with a nod. "But why would Priest want to point the finger at his own son?"

"Well, I think our original theory still holds, only Priest would have felt doubly betrayed since it was both of his sons plotting against him."

"So then why didn't he just kill Granville, too?"

"It could still be more useful to have the other families believing there's an outside threat," Michel offered.

"Maybe," Sassy agreed. "Any other theories?"

"Maybe Granville killed Deacon."

"Okay, but why?"

"According to the records I found," Michel replied, "Priest sold his house in Jamaica in 1984, seven years before Granville came here. Suppose Priest ran out on the boy and his mother, and seven years later when Granville came to the States to find him, Priest shunned him?"

"That's a lot of supposition," Sassy interjected.

"I know," Michel replied, "but I'm just laying out a possible scenario. And to make matters worse, Granville found out he had a brother who was the heir-apparent to Priest's empire."

"So you think Granville may have killed Deacon to get back at Priest?" Sassy asked.

Michel shrugged.

"Okay," Sassy said, "but then Priest would know Granville probably did it. So why go through this whole charade? And don't give me the answer about needing a threat to the other families again."

"Why are you asking me all the tough questions?" Michel complained. "You're a detective, too."

"Yeah, but I haven't had my first cup of coffee yet, and you've obviously had all night to think about this."

"Maybe Priest couldn't bring himself to kill his own son," Michel said, "but he could justify setting the wheels in motion for someone else to kill him."

Sassy thought about it for a few moments.

"It's possible," she said. "Either way, it sounds like our next step is still to talk to Priest."

"Agreed," Michel replied.

"You know, I just had a terrible thought," Sassy said. "I wonder how many other crimelord-wannabe bastard children Priest has stashed away."

"You're right," Michel replied. "It could be like 'Buffy the Vampire Slayer,' where there were dozens of potential slayers to take the place of the Chosen One when she was killed."

Sassy stared at him blankly.

"Did you *ever* watch any good TV?" Michel asked, with a deadpan look.

"Apparently not," Sassy replied. "And apparently you are a very lonely person."

Michel just smiled benignly in response.

"And speaking of lonely, how did your date go last night?" Sassy asked.

"Oh, that," Michel replied, then sighed. "I'm done with dating. I just can't seem to get the hang of the whole relationship thing."

"I notice you didn't mention cheap casual sex," Sassy said.

"Oh, no," Michel replied. "I'm pretty good at that, so I'll probably stick with it."

Sassy gave him a comically disapproving look.

"Anyway, when do you want to talk to Lee?" Michel asked, ready to change the subject.

"As soon as possible, I guess," Sassy replied. "I'll give him a call now."

"And do I get to go with you this time?" Michel asked hopefully.

"Oh yeah," Sassy replied, "Because it's much harder to dispose of two bodies than one."

Chapter 23

Priest Lee was seated in a high-backed leather chair in his study, dressed in a maroon silk robe and light blue cotton pajamas. He'd asked Sassy and Michel to come to his house, claiming he was suffering from food poisoning. From the marked change in his appearance since she'd last seen him, Sassy suspected it was more than that. He looked much frailer, and his skin was almost gray and seemed to have aged dramatically.

"I certainly didn't kill Deacon," he said wearily, "and I don't believe that Granville would have killed him either."

"Why not?" Sassy asked.

"Because Granville isn't a killer," Lee replied simply.

"You make it sound like you're close," Michel said.

Lee stared blankly at him, then looked back at Sassy.

"I may not have a relationship with him anymore, but I know my son's heart," he said.

"So then he is your son," Sassy said.

Lee nodded.

"Yes, I had a long relationship with his mother many years ago," he said, "and for the first years of his life, I was very much his father, though I could be in Jamaica only occasionally."

"Then what happened?" Sassy asked.

Lee shrugged.

"Who can say what happens in a relationship? Maybe she tired of me not being there more often. Or maybe she just tired of me. One day I called the house and there was no answer. When I went back, it was empty."

"And you didn't try to track her down or contact Granville?" Michel asked.

Again Lee addressed his response to Sassy.

"I found out where they were and made sure that they were taken care of financially," he said, "but I let them be. I felt it was in Granville's best interest not to be associated with me."

Sassy felt sudden sympathy for Lee, imagining the sacrifice he'd chosen to make for the sake of his son.

"But Granville came looking for you?" Michel asked.

This time Lee looked directly at him, apparently realizing that Michel had no intention of remaining silent.

"Yes," he said.

"And what happened?" Sassy asked.

Lee sighed loudly and stared at the floor for a moment, seemingly lost in thought. Then he looked back up. Sassy noticed his eyes were jaundiced.

"I told him that I thought it best that he return home," he replied.

"Why's that?" Michel asked.

"For his safety," Lee replied. "I thought that if Deacon found out he had a brother he might feel threatened."

"So Deacon never knew that Granville was his brother?" Sassy asked, surprised.

"Not that I'm aware," Lee replied.

"So then it was coincidence that he approached Granville about a partnership?" Sassy asked skeptically.

Lee shrugged.

"Deacon may have lacked judgment, but he wasn't stupid. I suspect he recognized that Granville possessed skills that he himself did not."

"Such as?" Michel asked.

Lee stared at the floor again before responding.

"I failed Deacon," he said sadly. "I never prepared him to lead. But as you've no doubt discovered by now, Granville is quite adept."

Sassy considered it. It made sense that Deacon would seek Granville out as a partner. Their skills were complementary, and both were young and ambitious. She realized it could have been a very fruitful and very dangerous partnership.

"So what happened when you told Granville to go back to Jamaica?" she asked.

"Clearly he made up his mind to disregard my advice," Lee replied with an effort at a smile.

"And you didn't have any contact with him after that?" Michel asked.

Lee shook his head.

"No, but I did my best to protect him by persuading the other families that he wasn't a threat to us."

"You realize that Granville seems like the most likely suspect given your hypothesis about someone wanting to start a war," Sassy said. "He'd have the most to gain, and he seems more than capable of planning something like that."

"He would not kill Deacon," Lee replied adamantly.

Sassy felt a surge of frustration, but tried to remain calm.

"Look Priest, all we can tell you is what the evidence suggests," she said evenly. "If you're not willing to hear that, then I'm not sure how you expect us to help you. We can't just make up another possibility you like better."

"I agree," Lee replied, "which is why I believe your services will no longer be required."

"Just like that?" Sassy asked.

"If you send me a bill, I'll pay you for your time," Lee said, as though he hadn't heard her.

"You realize that this makes you look like the more likely suspect, don't you?" Sassy asked.

"That's not my concern," Lee replied coldly. "And since you no longer have a client, I trust that this matter will no longer be *your* concern."

Sassy stared at him for a moment. Her frustration had turned to anger.

"I wonder what would happen if the police received an anonymous tip that Deacon is in a freezer at the Bluehawk Terminal," she said.

"Indeed, I wonder," Lee replied after a pause, his lips pulling back into his crocodile smile.

Sassy felt a chill run up her spine. She realized she'd pushed too far.

"I think we should go," Michel said quickly. "We'll send you a bill."

He stood up and looked at Sassy expectantly. She stared at Lee for a moment longer, trying to assess whether she'd put her life in danger, then stood up and followed Michel out.

"So, how did it feel be threatened by an old man?" Michel asked as soon as they were outside, hoping to break the tension.

"Fuck you," Sassy growled, then stalked to the car.

Chapter 24

Michel had just finally fallen asleep when the phone began to ring. He rolled over and picked it up without turning on the light.

"Doucette," he said, a reflex from his days on the force.

"Michel, it's Al," the voice on the other end replied.

Michel sat up and turned on the light, wondering if he was dreaming.

"Hey Al," he said. "What's going on?"

"I'm down at the Bluehawk Terminal," Ribodeau replied. "We just found Priest Lee's body. He was shot in the head. Looks like an execution. The captain would like to talk to you."

Michel was fully alert now.

"Down there or at the station?"

"Here," Ribodeau replied.

"All right, let me just call Sassy and I'll be right down."

"I already called her. She's on her way," Ribodeau said.

"Okay," Michel replied. "I'll be there in a few minutes."

*****

As he approached the access road to the terminal, Michel noticed a black Lincoln Town Car limousine parked on the other side of the street. Its light were out, but the engine was running. As he slowed down to get a better look at it, the car suddenly began to move. It traveled slowly down the block, like a shark cruising through dark water, then turned right, away from the river. As it turned the corner, Michel saw its lights finally turn on.

News travels fast, he thought.

He turned onto the access road. The parking lot around the terminal was lit up by flashing blue lights, and two flood lights had been trained on the far right building, where he and Sassy had found the freezer. As he approached the gate, he slowed and opened his window. A young officer approached the car.

"Can I help you, sir?" he asked.

"I'm Michel Doucette," Michel replied. "Captain DeRoche is expecting me."

Michel thought he detected a sudden stiffening in the young man's posture.

"Pull in through the gate and park on the right. The Captain is on the third floor. Miss Jones is already here," the officer replied as though on autopilot.

Michel turned into the parking lot and parked next to Sassy's car, then got out and entered the building. As he made his way to the third floor, he couldn't help but feel a sense of deja vu, though at the same time he felt that he no longer belonged there. By the way the familiar faces with whom he'd worked for years averted their eyes as he passed, he realized they felt the same way.

When he got to the third floor, he was directed down the hall. Sassy was standing with Captain Carl DeRoche and Al Ribodeau in the middle of the kitchen.

"Sassy already filled us in on what you were working on for Lee," DeRoche said, without greeting Michel, "but I'm going to need you both to give a statement down at the station."

Michel nodded, then looked at Sassy. She looked tired and also a little sad.

"Did you tell them about the freezer?" he asked.

Sassy shook her head.

"Not yet."

"What about it?" DeRoche asked.

192

They all turned toward the freezer. Michel hadn't noticed Priest Lee's sheet-covered body when he'd walked in. It was directly in front of the steel door.

"We think Deacon Lee might be inside," he said.

DeRoche looked from Michel to Sassy with disbelief.

"And you didn't think that was something you should tell the police?" he asked.

"It's just speculation," Sassy replied evenly, "based on the fact that the door is locked and welded shut. It wasn't enough to get you a search warrant."

"Especially since we only know about it because we broke in here the other night," Michel added.

"I didn't hear that," DeRoche replied, fixing Michel with a cautionary look.

"But now that there's been a murder here, you should be able to get the warrant," Sassy said.

DeRoche looked at Ribodeau.

"Get the DA working on it," he said.

Ribodeau nodded, then gave Michel and Sassy a combination wave-salute and headed for the door.

"So how did you two get involved with Lee in the first place?" DeRoche asked as soon as they were alone.

Michel had been surprised by DeRoche's initial coldness. He and Sassy had always enjoyed a good relationship with their former boss. Now DeRoche's tone was warmer and more collegial.

"How did you know we were?" Sassy asked. "I have to say I was surprised when Al called."

DeRoche shrugged.

"You know how it is," he said. "It's not that big a city."

"We were investigating a case for another client," Sassy said. "He was involved in a deal with Bulldog Patterson and Double-J Cornell to redevelop the terminal."

"A legitimate deal?" DeRoche asked.

"Seemed that way until the fire," Michel replied. "Anyway,

Sassy went to Lee to ask if he could intervene on our client's behalf, and he asked her to investigate Deacon's disappearance."

DeRoche gave Sassy a curious look.

"What made you think Lee would get involved?"

Sassy looked at the ground for a moment and shifted her weight.

"Priest and I were friends once upon a time," she said. "Back before I was a cop."

"I always knew you had a sordid past," DeRoche replied with a gently teasing smile.

Sassy smiled back, despite the fact that she felt mildly embarrassed by her admission.

"After a while we started to think that maybe the fire and Deacon's disappearance were connected, so we came here and found the freezer," Michel said.

DeRoche nodded.

"And what made you think the two cases were connected?"

"Because the fire was set," Michel replied. "I came up with a theory that Deacon's body was here, and the fire had been set to give Patterson and Cornell a plausible reason to cancel the redevelopment project so that he wouldn't be found."

"It was arson?" DeRoche asked with surprise.

Michel nodded.

"No question."

"So why isn't it being investigated?" DeRoche asked, more to himself than Michel or Sassy.

"For one thing, there was no insurance claim," Sassy replied, "but we suspect that someone also got paid off."

DeRoche thought about it for a moment.

"Well, this entire place is a crime scene now," he said finally. "It shouldn't be a problem to get an arson investigation started."

"Thank you," Michel replied.

DeRoche seemed about to say something else, but then apparently changed his mind.

"What?" Sassy prodded.

DeRoche looked from her to Michel, then back. His expression was suddenly very serious.

"I think you should know that there's been some talk about you since word got out that you've been working for Lee," he said. "Some people are saying that you were on the take."

"That would explain the chill in the air," Sassy replied.

"Oh, you noticed that, too?" Michel asked. "I thought they were just embarrassed for me."

"I know you were clean," DeRoche said quickly, "and I've made a point of conveying that to people, but..."

He shrugged as if to say, "what can you do?"

"Well, we appreciate that, Captain," Michel said. "And thanks for letting us know."

There was an awkward moment of silence.

"So how's Al doing?" Sassy asked finally.

"Great," DeRoche answered enthusiastically, seeming to welcome the change of subject. "His instincts may not be as sharp as some other detectives I've worked with, but at least I don't have to worry about him following procedures."

Sassy and Michel both smiled at the gentle rebuke.

"Well, I've got to get the coroner in here," DeRoche said, "and you've got statements to give."

"All right, Captain," Michel said. "I'm sure we'll be seeing you again soon."

"Oh, are you working on another murder case I should know about?" DeRoche asked, giving Michel a suspicious look.

Michel just smiled in response.

Chapter 25

Michel arrived back at his house just as the sun was casting a pale light across the rooftops. As he walked up to the front porch, he saw something move in the shadows near the door. A jolt of adrenaline shot through him, and he quickly reached into his jacket and pulled out his gun.

"Wait, it's just me!" Joel called out. "Don't shoot."

Michel took a deep breath and exhaled as he reholstered his gun.

"Late night, huh?" Joel asked wearily, his face still hidden in the shadows.

"Sassy and I were at the station," Michel replied quickly, not wanting Joel to think he'd been with another man. "Priest Lee was murdered last night."

There was no reply. Then Joel stepped into the light at the edge of the porch. He was very pale, and his eyes were worried and red-rimmed.

"What's wrong?" Michel asked immediately.

"I've got to go back to Natchez for a while," Joel replied. "My grandfather had a heart attack."

"I'm so sorry," Michel said. "Is he okay?"

Joel nodded, though it was clear he wasn't so sure.

"But he and Mammau are going to need my help."

"How long do you think you'll be gone?" Michel asked.

Joel shrugged.

"Maybe a month. Maybe longer. Chance is going to take care of my place while I'm gone."

Michel nodded, not sure what else to say or do. He wanted to comfort Joel, but wasn't sure what was appropriate given the current state of their relationship.

"But before I go, I wanted to say something to you," Joel said. "I've been thinking a lot about us, and I want you to know that I still love you, and I still want us to be together."

Michel opened his mouth to speak, but stopped when Joel gave him a warning look.

"I'm not done yet," Joel said sternly. "I've been practicing this speech for the past two hours while I've been waiting for you, and I'm going to finish it."

Michel nodded for him to continue.

"But there would have to be conditions. When you were a cop, I was willing to accept the fact that I'd always come second because people's lives were at stake. But since you're not a cop anymore, I would need to come first, or at least tie for first. And I'd need to know that you not only wanted me, but actually needed me to be part of your life."

He paused for a second, seemingly having lost his train of thought, and Michel was struck by the way Joel's words had echoed what Nassir had said. Then Joel looked at Michel with renewed focus, like a stoned person suddenly remembering the point to a rambling story.

"And I know that's all pretty intangible because I'm not even sure how I'd expect you to make me feel that way, but I want you to know that I'm willing to give it another try. A real try."

Michel waited a moment for him to continue, but Joel seemed to have reached his conclusion.

"Are you done?" Michel asked finally.

Joel nodded.

"But I don't want an answer right now. I realize I'm just springing this on you, and you've been up all night, and I don't want your decision colored by sympathy because of Pappy. I want you to really take the time to think about it. "

"Okay," Michel replied.

"But when I come back, I expect an answer," Joel said, "and if the answer's going to be yes, then you better get your ya-yas out of your system while I'm gone. But I don't want to hear about it. Ever. Right now you're still a free man and you can do whatever you want, but if you commit to this relationship, then I expect complete monogamy. Just so you understand."

"I understand," Michel replied.

Joel studied him for a moment, then nodded again in a reflexive way that made him appear almost drunk.

"Okay," he said with finality.

Then he looked at his watch and frowned. He looked back up at Michel and gave a sheepish smile.

"Um, I was kind of expecting you to be home when I got here. Any chance you can give me a ride to the bus station?"

Chapter 26

"Hey, sleepy head," Sassy said when Michel walked into the office just after noon.

"Sorry," he replied. "I had to take Joel to the bus station this morning so I didn't get to sleep until almost eight."

"The bus station?" Sassy asked.

"He's going back home for a while," Michel replied. "His grandfather had a heart attack."

"Is his grandfather all right?" Sassy asked with a look of concern.

"Yeah, looks like he will be, but Joel wants to be there to help out."

Sassy nodded sympathetically.

"Interesting that he came to you for a ride, though," she said, cocking her head slightly.

"Well, there was a little bit more to it than that," Michel replied. "He wanted to tell me that he wants to give things another chance."

Sassy arched her eyebrows with surprise.

"And how did you feel about that?" she asked. "That would severely cut into your slut time."

"Ha ha," Michel replied dryly. "I don't know yet. He didn't want an answer. He just wanted me to know so that I can think about it while he's gone."

"Interesting," Sassy replied with an inscrutable look.

"What?" Michel asked.

"Nothing."

"Don't make me put the coffee maker on a high shelf where you can't reach it," Michel threatened.

Sassy gave him a smile.

"It's just that I think that's nice," she said.

"What is?"

"That the two of you may be getting back together."

"I didn't know you had a feeling about it one way or the other," Michel replied.

"Well, I don't think I did in the past," Sassy replied. "I mean, I always liked Joel, but I tried not to get too attached to him because I wasn't sure how you felt. But now I like the idea of the two of you being together again. Besides, maybe he'll keep you out of trouble."

"Are you being serious?" Michel asked.

It was unusual for Sassy to offer unsolicited opinions on his personal life.

"Yes," she replied without any hint of sarcasm.

Michel studied her for a moment.

"Well, why do you like the idea of us being together again?" he asked.

"What are you? Like twelve?" Sassy asked with exasperation. "It doesn't matter why I like the idea. You have to make up your mind on your own."

"I know, I know," Michel replied defensively. "I'm just curious."

Sassy shook her head and sighed.

"Okay," she said. "I like the idea because I think he's a good kid. I mean, man. He's smart, he's thoughtful, he's got a good heart, and Lord knows he's tolerant if he's put up with you for this long. I just think you could do a lot worse."

Michel thought about it. He knew Sassy was right. Still he questioned his own ability to give Joel what he needed.

"Well, I've got some time to think about it," he said.

"And in the meantime we need to find some more work," Sassy replied. "It's a good thing that Marchand paid us that extra money, because I don't think we'll be getting paid by Priest."

"But we're not done yet," Michel said.

"What are you talking about?" Sassy asked. "Priest is dead. They'll probably be getting Deacon out of the freezer any minute now, and I imagine that Granville is already being questioned. Case closed for us."

"I'm not sure Granville did it," Michel replied.

"Why not?"

"As I was heading to the terminal last night, I saw a car that looked an awful lot like Villorisi's parked on N. Peters, about a block away. When I slowed to take a better look, it pulled away."

"So? I imagine that there were a lot of interested parties around there last night," Sassy said.

"But they weren't all there that quickly," Michel replied. "Either Villorisi has a hotline to the police department, or he already knew Priest was dead."

"And you didn't mention that to DeRoche why?" Sassy asked.

"It didn't occur to me until this morning," Michel replied sincerely.

"Well then I think you should call him now," Sassy said.

Michel started to protest, but Sassy gave him a hard look.

"Michel, we can't fuck around with this," she chastened. "It's a police matter now. In case you've forgotten, withholding evidence is a criminal offense."

Michel gave her the evil eye, but picked up the phone and started dialing.

*****

"Don't you feel better now?" Sassy asked when he hung up.

"Oh yeah, just marvelous," Michel replied with a theatrical sneer. "By the way, you'll be interested to know that there won't be an arson investigation."

"What?" Sassy exclaimed. "Why not?"

"DeRoche says that somebody high up is killing it."

"Motherfuckers," Sassy said, shaking her head angrily.

"Oh, and one other thing," Michel said. "They opened the freezer. It was empty."

Chapter 27

"So'd you see the paper yet?" Al Ribodeau asked.

It had been a week since Priest Lee's killing, and Ribodeau had unexpectedly stopped by Michel's and Sassy's office. He dropped the afternoon newspaper on Michel's desk. On the bottom of the front page was an article about Granville Lee being named the new CEO of Jacard-Lee Development. The article was accompanied by a photo of Lee shaking hands with the head of the company's board of directors. In the photo, Lee was wearing a suit, and his hair had been cropped very close. With the exception of his trim mustache and beard, he looked like a younger version of his father.

"Yeah, we saw it," Michel replied without enthusiasm.

"Looks like your guy is doing pretty well for himself," Ribodeau said.

"For now," Sassy replied. "We'll see what happens when you finish your investigation. Hopefully he'll be running the company from a cell."

"I doubt it," Ribodeau replied. "That's why I stopped by. I wanted to tell you before you heard it on the streets. Granville is no longer a suspect."

Sassy and Michel stared at him with disbelief.

"How is that possible?" Sassy asked.

Ribodeau shrugged.

"He's got ten witnesses putting him at his house that night, and we can't find a single one to contradict them."

"So you're just ruling him out like that?" Michel asked.

"I didn't say we wouldn't keep looking," Ribodeau replied, "but officially he's no longer considered a suspect."

"And what about Villorisi?" Michel asked.

"He was at a private function at Commander's Palace until a little after midnight, then stopped at the Boston Club for a few more hours. He was there when Lee was shot."

Michel and Sassy knew better than to question the credibility of any witnesses at the Boston Club. It was New Orleans' oldest private club, and counted the city's most prominent jurists and businessmen among its members. Villorisi couldn't have chosen a better place to be seen if he wanted an unassailable alibi.

"Of course, he could have had one of his boys kill Lee," Ribodeau offered.

Sassy shook her head.

"That would have been a sign of disrespect," she said. "Villorisi is old school. If he were going to have Priest killed, he would have been there himself."

Ribodeau nodded, knowing it was true. The old guard criminals operated by a code.

"So I guess that means it's all over," Sassy sighed with resignation. "Granville takes Priest's place, Deacon is still among the missing, and things go on as before."

"Seems like," Ribodeau concurred solemnly.

"Well, thanks for letting us know, Al," Michel said.

Ribodeau nodded.

"No problem. So you working on anything of interest?"

"Only if you consider tracking a cheating husband to be interesting," Michel replied.

"Unless it's that bastard who's married to my sister, probably not," Ribodeau replied.

"Afraid not," Michel said with an appreciative smile, "but if we come across him, we'll let you know."

*****

"So any big plans for the night?" Sassy asked after Ribodeau had left.

Michel considered it.

"Well, there is that black tie fundraiser at the mayor's house, but I forgot to drop my tux off to be pressed this morning, so I'll probably just stop by a bar and have a cocktail or twelve. Care to join me?"

"As much as I would like to drown the memory of this whole experience," Sassy replied, "I think I'm just going to go home, fix a nice dinner, and watch some TV."

"Oh, is there a 'Golden Girls' marathon on tonight?" Michel asked, remembering the joke Chance had made at his expense.

"Ooh, I hope so," Sassy replied brightly. "I love that show."

Michel gave her a disappointed look.

"You do?" he asked.

"Oh sure," Sassy replied. "You know how us old folks like to watch shows about other old folks. 'Golden Girls,' 'Murder, She Wrote,' 'Diagnosis Murder,' 'Matlock.' I love them all."

"Oh," Michel replied, feeling completely deflated.

"What's the matter?" Sassy asked with a look of concern.

"Oh, nothing," Michel replied.

"Okay," Sassy said, then paused a beat before continuing. "I just thought maybe you'd found out they won't be doing another season of 'Prime Suspect.'"

Michel stared at her for a moment, trying to get the connection, then narrowed his eyes.

"Oh, that's funny," he said. "A bitter, alcoholic detective who can't maintain a relationship. Nice."

"What?" Sassy replied with a look of shocked innocence. "I just meant because you and Jane Tennison are both such brilliant detectives."

"Uh huh," Michel replied dubiously.

"And because in a wig, you'd look just like Helen Mirren," Sassy muttered under her breath.

*****

Michel had been at the Bourbon Pub for just over an hour and was in the middle of his third Jack Daniels. He was relieved that so far neither Severin Marchand nor Ray Nassir had made an appearance. He was just thinking about stopping by the Clover Grill for some dinner when he felt a tap on his left shoulder. He turned and saw a muscular black man smiling at him. The man was dressed in a dark suit, and his head was shaved. His face looked familiar, but Michel couldn't immediately place him.

"What, you don't recognize me anymore?" the man asked in a thick Jamaican accent.

"Holy shit," Michel exclaimed, suddenly realizing it was Roland. "I'm sorry. The suit and the new haircut threw me."

Roland held his arms out and did a slow turn, showing off his new look for Michel.

"The boss felt it was time to upgrade our images now that we're proper businessmen," he said. " What do you think?"

Michel nodded.

"I like it," he said, "though I have to admit I thought the old look was sexier."

Roland smiled and gave Michel an affectionate kiss.

"Can I buy you a drink?" Michel asked as he pointed to the empty stool next to him.

"Sure," Roland replied as he sat down, "but only one. I'm working tonight."

"Oh?" Michel responded.

"Yeah, the boss has a meeting," Roland replied. "I just slipped away for a few minutes."

He ordered a Red Stripe and downed a third of it in one swallow.

"So what brings you out on a weeknight?" Roland asked, turning his stool to face Michel. "Trying to get lucky?"

"Why, is that an offer?" Michel replied with a smile.

Roland smiled back.

"If I could, you know I would," he replied, "but as I said, I'm working."

"So is this a meeting for Jacard-Lee or the other kind of business?" Michel asked.

Roland shook his head, but continued to smile.

"You know I can't be talking about that," he said.

Michel shrugged.

"Just idle curiosity on my part," he said.

The benignly blank expression on Roland's face made it clear the subject was closed.

"So I take it you're working for Jacard-Lee now?" Michel asked.

Roland reached into his jacket pocket and took out a slim silver case. He opened it and handed Michel a business card.

"Impressive," Michel said, as he read the card. "So what exactly does a Vice President of Operations do?"

Roland let out a hearty chuckle.

"As soon as I find out, I'll let you know," he replied. "So far, I just go from one meeting to another. I don't understand how a company makes money when everyone is in meetings all day. Somewhere there must be people working, but so far I haven't seen them."

He finished another third of his beer.

"Sounds like quite a change," Michel offered.

"Yes," Roland replied, "but it is for the good. The projects we do will help many people."

"Sounds like someone drank the corporate Kool Aid," Michel replied with a gentle smile.

Roland gave him a perplexed look.

"What is this Kool Aid?"

"Long story," Michel replied. "I'll explain it to you some other time."

"Like on a date, perhaps?" Roland asked.

"Perhaps," Michel replied, knowing it was a lie.

As attractive as he found Roland, he knew there would be no future for them given the different worlds in which they traveled.

"Well, I've already been gone too long," Roland said suddenly, then finished the rest of his beer.

He stood up and gave Michel a quick kiss.

"I assume your partner still has my number," he said. "If you were sincere about going on a date, give me a call."

Then he made his way through the sparse crowd and out the side door onto Bourbon Street. He turned left and disappeared from sight. Michel waited thirty seconds, then stood up to follow him.

*****

Roland zig-zagged his way through the French Quarter, first walking three blocks up Bourbon and turning right onto Ursulines, then two blocks and a left onto Royal, then two more blocks and a right onto Barracks. Michel stayed a block behind him, sticking close to the shadows on the opposite side of each street. He got the sense that Roland's route was entirely random, rather than intentionally serpentine.

When he reached Decatur Street, Roland turned left again. Michel stopped and surveyed the intersection. He realized that he couldn't follow without moving into the open. On the immediate right side of Barracks was a brightly lit cafe with a crowd of skinny goth teenagers milling around out front. On the far left side of Decatur was the old Mint building that now housed a branch of the Louisiana State Museum. A wrought iron fence ran around the entire perimeter of the block, offering no concealment.

Michel walked to the corner and peered around it, trying to look casual. He could see Roland a half block up, talking with a group of men in the light from an open door. It was a mixed group, both black and white, all dressed in suits. They all seemed very relaxed with one another. There were several cars parked near the building on the otherwise deserted block. After a moment, Roland nodded to the other men and stepped into the building.

Michel considered his options. He could cross the intersection and walk around the Mint building in order to approach from the opposite side, but he would still have to get past the men who were clearly on guard duty. He decided his best option was to wait, and hope for a glimpse of whoever was meeting with Granville Lee on their way out.

Suddenly he felt an arm drape across his shoulders and a body press up against his right side. Then he felt something hard pressing into his rib cage. He turned his head slowly and saw the ruddy face of Angelo Villorisi's driver.

"Let's take a walk," the driver said.

He nodded up Barracks Street, in the direction from which Michel had come. Michel thought briefly about refusing, not wanting to leave the relative safety of the busy intersection, but decided to go along. He didn't want to risk any of the cafe's patrons getting hurt.

They began walking slowly, with the driver's arm still across Michel's shoulders like they were a couple. When they'd walked a half block, the driver dropped his arm and took a step away from Michel. Now Michel could see the massive black .44 Magnum that had been pressed into his side. The driver held it in his right hand, close against his stomach, where he could hide it under his jacket if someone were to approach.

"Where are we going?" Michel asked.

"Just keep walking," the man said in a low voice.

When they reached the corner of Chartres Street, they turned right. To Michel's disappointment, the street was empty. He knew that in the days before the hurricane the shops would still have been open at that time, but now all their doors and windows were shuttered behind metal gates. Still, he realized that the absence of bystanders might be to his advantage.

He concentrated on his steps, trying to adjust them so that he and the driver would be synchronized, each stepping forward with the same leg at the same time. Then he took a deep breath.

As they stepped with their left legs, Michel swung his right arm up, then suddenly shifted his weight sideways onto his right leg and drove his elbow into the side of the driver's head. The driver fell against the stucco wall to his right, his right arm pinned against his side, and let out a sharp grunt. Michel immediately took a step forward, and as the driver turned toward him he grabbed the man's right wrist with both hands and slammed it back against the wall. The driver's gun dropped to the pavement with a loud clatter, and Michel quickly kicked it ten feet to his left.

"Motherfucker," the driver exclaimed, as he grabbed Michel by the front of his shirt with his left hand and starting pulling him closer.

Michel was shocked by the older man's strength. Despite the fact that he was pushing against the man's chest with both arms, he was being drawn closer, inch by inch.

"I'd kill you now, but I'm sure Mr. Villorisi will want to watch," the driver hissed when their faces were only a few inches apart, spraying Michel's face with spittle.

Michel brought his head back, then snapped it forward, hitting the driver squarely in the forehead with his own forehead. It was like hitting granite. Michel felt a moment of dizziness, while the driver seemed to absorb the blow as if it were nothing. As his head cleared, Michel noticed the man's flat, crooked nose and the web of scars criss-crossing his eyebrows. Shit, he thought, this guy used to be a boxer.

Suddenly the driver buried a right hand into Michel's stomach. Michel gasped for breath and took a feeble swing at the man's chin, but connected only with his left shoulder. The driver looked at his shoulder for a second, then smiled. It was a malevolent, sadistic smile.

"I guess your partner must be the one who knows how to fight," he said.

He pushed Michel back to his arm's length and stared at him appraisingly for a moment. Then his right hand shot out and caught Michel hard on the left cheek. Michel staggered back but managed to keep from falling, mainly because the driver was still holding onto his shirt.

Fuck, Michel thought through the confusion that suddenly clouded his brain. He realized that he was on the verge of losing consciousness. He tried to concentrate and push the blackness away. Then the driver hit him again.

Chapter 28

As he regained consciousness, Michel was aware first of throbbing pain in his head and stomach muscles, then of low voices. He slowly opened his eyes and looked toward the voices without moving his head. Angelo Villorisi and his driver were standing thirty feet to his left. They hadn't noticed he was awake yet.

Keeping his head still, he began to look around. He was in a warehouse loading dock, though from the absence of freight and the thick dust on the floor, it looked like it hadn't been used in a while. There was an old forklift a few feet away from the two men, and a large metal roll-down door at the far end of the room. Otherwise the room appeared to be empty.

He looked down. Both of his wrists had been tied to the arms of a heavy wood chair. With a jolt of anxiety he noticed that his right hand had also been bound, with just the thumb left loose.

"Looks like our guest is awake," a voice said to his left.

Michel looked up and saw Villorisi and the driver walking toward him.

"You treat all your guests like this?" Michel asked, trying to sound unconcerned, despite his mounting fear.

"Still a smart mouth," Villorisi rasped.

He shook his head slowly back and forth as though disappointed.

"Why are you still snooping around?" he asked abruptly. "Unless I'm mistaken, you no longer have a client."

Michel considered making a flip remark about Villorisi's possible role in his client's death, but thought better of it.

"I wasn't snooping," he said instead. "I was just out for a walk."

Villorisi nodded almost imperceptibly at the driver. The driver took a few steps forward, then slapped the back of his right hand hard across Michel's face. Michel's head rocked back, then bounced forward. For a few seconds he didn't feel anything, then pain exploded along the right side of his jaw and in his cheek.

"Shall we try again?" Villorisi asked as the driver moved a few steps to Michel's right. "Why are you still snooping around?"

It was as if the slap had flipped a switch in Michel's head. Now instead of fear, he felt anger.

"Where's Lee?" he asked.

Villorisi looked at his driver and chuckled darkly.

"I think you may have hit him too hard, Carlo," he said. "He seems confused."

He looked back at Michel.

"Priest Lee is dead."

"I'm not talking about Priest," Michel replied firmly. "I'm talking about Granville."

Villorisi arched his eyebrows.

"Ah, the secret son," he said.

"Secret?" Michel replied. "I thought you knew *everything* that goes on in this town."

Michel saw anger flit across across Villorisi's face, then it was replaced by a small smile that Michel wasn't sure how to read.

"So what would make you think that Granville *Lee* is here?" Villorisi asked.

Michel knew that Carlo had seen him following Roland, so Villorisi was obviously fishing to find out how much more he knew. He decided not to respond, in hopes that Villorisi might get talkative. As he saw Villorisi nod at Carlo again, however, he realized that his hope was in vain.

"Perhaps when Carlo cuts off your thumb it'll loosen your tongue," Villorisi said.

Carlo stepped toward Michel and pulled a switchblade from his inside jacket pocket. He pressed the button on the side and a long, narrow blade shot forward. The knife looked very old to Michel. He imagined that Carlo had had a lot of practice with it over the years.

"Okay," he said quickly, "but I think you're going to be disappointed because there's not much to tell."

Villorisi nodded at him to continue.

"I was walking through the Quarter and saw one of Lee's men," Michel said. "I decided to follow him out of curiosity. Then Carlo showed up. End of story."

"You're right," Villorisi said. "I am disappointed. We'll take your thumb and see if your story becomes more interesting."

He nodded at Carlo again. Carlo reached across the arm of the chair and grabbed Michel's thumb with his left hand. His grip felt like a vise. He pulled Michel's thumb back and placed the blade of the knife into the crook of Michel's hand.

Michel locked eyes with Villorisi. As he felt the blade cutting into his skin, he clamped his jaw tightly. He was determined not to give the old man the satisfaction of hearing him cry out.

Suddenly a muffled ringing cut through the tense silence. Villorisi held up his left hand as he reached into his jacket and pulled out a cell phone. Carlo withdrew the knife and took a step back.

Michel stole a nervous look at his hand. There was a cut about three-quarters of an inch long at the base of his thumb. It had begun to well with blood, but didn't look too bad.

Villorisi walked a few yards away toward the cargo bay door and flipped open the phone. He didn't speak, but after a few moments he closed the phone and slowly walked back toward

Michel. His whole demeanor had changed. He suddenly looked very tired.

"Cut him loose," he said flatly.

Carlo stared at him for a moment, then knelt down and began to cut the rope holding Michel's right hand.

"You're letting me go?" Michel asked with cautious surprise.

Villorisi took a deep, ragged breath, then nodded with resignation.

"Go," he said dismissively, as Carlo finished cutting the rope from Michel's left arm.

Michel stood up slowly and rubbed his wrists. He knew he should leave while he had the chance, but his curiosity wouldn't let him.

"So who was that on the phone?" he asked.

Villorisi stared at him for a moment, then chuckled.

"My wife," he replied. "She asked me to pick up some milk on the way home."

"So then it was just coincidence that you decided to let me go after the call?" Michel asked facetiously.

"You're in no position to ask questions," Villorisi replied, a hint of threat returning to his voice.

Michel nodded.

"I realize that, Mr. Villorisi," he replied, "but you've put me in a difficult position."

"How so?" Villorisi asked.

"You and Granville Lee were both suspects in Priest's murder," Michel replied. "I see one of Lee's men going into a building, and the next thing I know Carlo has a gun in my ribs. Then you hold me hostage and threaten to cut off my thumb. You can see how that would appear. If I leave now, it's something I'd have to report to the police."

Michel had been expecting an angry outburst, but instead he could see Villorisi coldly assessing the situation.

"And how much would it take for you to forget?" he asked finally.

"I'm afraid that's not an option," Michel replied.

Villorisi stared at him for a moment, then shrugged.

"You want to go to the police, go to the police," he said. "They've already questioned me about Priest's murder, and I have an alibi. As far as the alleged hostage situation and threat against you goes, five minutes from now I'll have six witnesses saying that Carlo and I were having dinner at Commander's Palace tonight."

He gestured toward Michel with his right hand as if to say "your move." Michel considered his options. He realized that he didn't have any real leverage, but thought he might be able to goad Villorisi into divulging some information.

"It's funny," he said. "I'd always heard that you were the head of your family, but now I find out someone else is pulling your strings."

Carlo took a menacing step toward Michel, but Villorisi held up his right hand to stop him.

"What the hell are you talking about?" Villorisi growled. "I don't answer to anyone."

"If you say so," Michel replied, "but it's pretty obvious that whoever called told you to let me go."

Villorisi's eyes narrowed, but he maintained his composure.

"Let me ask you, Mr. Doucette," he said. "If Carlo had cut off your thumb, would that have discouraged you from continuing your investigation?"

Michel shook his head, though he wasn't sure it was true.

"And if we killed you, would that discourage Miss Jones or the police?" Villorisi asked.

Michel shook his head again, this time certain.

"That's why I'm letting you go," Villorisi said matter-of-factly.

Though it sounded logical, Michel still had his doubts. He couldn't help but wonder who had really called Villorisi.

"I'm a practical man," Villorisi said, as though trying to quell Michel's unspoken suspicions. "There are times when violence serves its purpose, but I don't believe in it for its own sake. In this case, it would serve no purpose. Now if you'll excuse me."

He started to turn away.

"You're dying, aren't you?" Michel asked abruptly.

Villorisi turned back and laughed a wet ragged laugh.

"What gave it away?" he asked mordantly.

"Is that why you killed Priest?" Michel asked. "To settle old scores before it was too late?"

Villorisi cocked his head and regarded Michel curiously.

"Now why would I want to kill Priest?" he asked.

"I don't know," Michel replied, "but I saw your car a block away from the Bluehawk Terminal right after it happened."

Villorisi turned to Carlo.

"Carlo, what was my car doing at the Bluehawk Terminal that night?" he asked in an elaborate play-acting tone.

"I don't know, Mr. Villorisi," Carlo replied in the same tone. "Oh wait, that's right. I told one of the boys to get it washed. He must have taken it for a joyride."

Villorisi turned back to Michel.

"See," he said with exaggerated innocence. "Now you know why my car was there."

Michel smiled for a moment to acknowledge the game that Villorisi and Carlo were playing, then his expression grew serious again.

"As you once said, Mr. Villorisi," he said, "don't treat me like I'm stupid."

Villorisi's expression turned serious, too.

"Again, I ask you, why would I want to kill Priest Lee?"

"Payback," Michel offered.

"Payback for what?" Villorisi asked. "Priest and I were never enemies. I always had great respect for him and the way he ran his business, and he reciprocated those feelings."

"You talk as though you were friends," Michel said, noting the almost nostalgic tone of Villorisi's voice.

217

"Friends," Villorisi repeated, ruminating on the word. "We...shared certain beliefs."

"Such as?"

"The importance of order and honor," Villorisi replied.

He seemed to consider his own words, then nodded, apparently having decided that they were correct.

"Meaning what?" Michel asked, suddenly intrigued.

Villorisi studied Michel for a moment before replying.

"You're very young, Mr. Doucette," he said finally. "You don't know how it was when I was a boy. The families had absolute control back then. Nothing happened without the head of a family approving it, and that kept the city safe. There was violence between the families, but it didn't spill out onto the streets the way it did in other cities."

Michel nodded for him to continue.

"But with our generation, that began to change," Villorisi said. "The other heads of the families didn't honor the old ways. They allowed their people to make decisions on their own, and they let outsiders run the operations in exchange for a piece of the action. They lost control of their territories."

"Except for you and Priest," Michel said.

Villorisi nodded.

"When he first came here, I didn't want it," he said. "I thought he was just another outsider. But over time, I realized I was wrong. He was smart, and he only did as much as was necessary to maintain control. And his people never acted without his consent. He took a territory no one else had been able to control and brought order."

A thousand questions flooded Michel's mind, but he decided to wait to see where Villorisi was headed.

"We developed a bond over our common philosophy," Villorisi continued. "It was something we kept private so that the other families wouldn't get nervous, but we watched out for one another, and worked to keep the other families in check, and we made sure outsiders stayed away from the city."

Michel felt as though he were being given a glimpse into the inner workings of a strange and mystical society. Then a thought occurred to him.

"How did Deacon's arrival affect things between you and Priest?" he asked.

Villorisi shrugged.

"At first it didn't," he replied. "In fact, Priest hoped to groom Deacon to be his successor."

"But it became obvious that that wasn't going to happen," Michel said.

"No," Villorisi agreed solemnly. "Deacon didn't share Priest's vision nor his abilities. He felt the only way to achieve power was by destroying the other families."

"So then what happened with you and Priest?" Michel asked.

"We had a falling out," Villorisi replied. "I understood his loyalty to his son, but I couldn't condone Deacon's actions."

"And that was it?" he asked. "You and Priest never reconciled?"

"We maintained a cordial business relationship," Villorisi replied, "but no, we were never close again."

Michel thought about it for a moment.

"You said that you and Priest kept outsiders out of the city," he said, "but Priest told us that he convinced the other families that Granville wasn't a threat in order to protect him. You didn't find that curious?"

Villorisi smiled. Michel guessed that it was meant to convey embarrassment, but the effect was ghoulish coming from the man's sunken face.

"In retrospect, perhaps it should have raised questions," Villorisi admitted with a dark chuckle. "At the time, I assumed it was because Priest believed Granville's approach was very similar to our own. He would be another stabilizing force."

Michel suddenly wondered if Priest had been honest about his relationship with Granville, whether he'd actually been positioning Granville to take his place. He also wondered if Villorisi had suspected as much. He tucked the thoughts away.

"So why were you meeting with Granville?" he asked.

"I'm afraid you're mistaken about that,' Villorisi replied flatly. "Granville may have been meeting with someone else in the area, but it wasn't with me. I have no business with him."

Michel was sure it was a lie, but decided to let it go. Villorisi would never tell him the truth.

"Who do you think killed Deacon and Priest?" he asked instead.

Villorisi looked at him curiously.

"Who gained the most from their deaths?" he asked.

Michel knew the obvious answer was Granville, but suddenly wondered if all the assumptions he and Sassy had been working under had been wrong. He didn't trust Villorisi.

"Mr. Doucette," Villorisi said abruptly, "I've answered your questions. Now if you'll excuse me, I need to rest."

"Of course," Michel replied distractedly, wanting some time to think anyway.

He watched as Carlo lead Villorisi toward a door at the back of the room. Then another question occurred to him.

"One last question, if you wouldn't mind," he said quickly.

Villorisi turned back and sighed impatiently, but nodded for Michel to continue.

"If Granville did kill Priest, aren't you afraid that he might come after you and the heads of the other families, too?"

Villorisi looked at Michel for a moment, then shrugged.

"For me it would be a blessing," he replied, "but no, I'm not worried. Priest's killing was personal."

Michel considered it for a moment, then nodded.

"I trust we won't be receiving any visits from the police tonight?" Villorisi asked.

"No," Michel agreed.

Villorisi started to turn away again, then stopped. He fixed Michel with a look that seemed almost paternal.

"A word of advice," he said. "What's done is done. If I were you, I would let sleeping dogs lie."

Chapter 29

"So what's bothering you?" Sassy asked, after Michel had finished telling her about his encounter with Villorisi.

"One minute he's about to cut my thumb off, then he gets a phone call and decides to let me go, then suddenly he's Chatty Cathy," Michel replied. "I mean, I'm pretty good at getting people to talk, but in retrospect, it just seemed contrived."

"Are you sure you're not just being a little paranoid because of the Marchand case?"

"I'm being plenty paranoid, and not just because of Marchand," Michel replied. "With this case, too, every time we think we know what's going on, we find out something different. Priest played us, Granville played us. I can't help but wonder if Villorisi is playing us, too."

"But what does he have to gain?" Sassy asked.

"Well, I've got a theory on that," Michel replied with a slight hesitation.

Sassy raised her eyebrows expectantly.

"What if Priest lied about his relationship with Granville?" Michel said. "What if he was actually setting Granville up to take his place all along? And what if Villorisi knew, and was helping him?"

Sassy sat back hard in her chair.

"And you're basing that on what?" she asked, shooting Michel a skeptical look.

"We know from what Priest told you that he was concerned about what would happen once he was gone," Michel replied.

"And Villorisi told me that at one time Priest had hoped that Deacon would take his place, but that it became clear that couldn't happen. I would think that someone like Priest would have a backup plan."

"Okay," Sassy said. "And?"

"And Priest himself admitted that he was protecting Granville from the other families."

"And?"

"And the only thing that would stand in the way of Granville taking over from Priest would be Deacon. Deacon goes missing and suddenly Granville's in charge."

"Okay," Sassy said, "but if Priest was grooming Granville to take his place, and killed Deacon to clear the way, why would he hire us to look for Deacon?"

"To throw off suspicion," Michel replied. "Just like Marchand. But when we came back and told him we thought Granville was responsible, he fired us because we were getting too close to the truth."

Sassy considered it for a moment, then nodded slightly.

"Maybe," she conceded. "But I'm still not seeing why you think Villorisi is connected."

"Well, we know he was meeting with Granville last night," Michel started.

"That's supposition," Sassy corrected. "We know Granville had a meeting, and we know Carlo was in the area. But we don't know that Granville was meeting with Villorisi."

"True," Michel agreed, "but Carlo took me to a warehouse in Lee's territory, and when I left I checked and there were no signs of a break in. That means someone *let* them in."

"Oh, come on, that's circumstantial evidence at best," Sassy exclaimed. "Besides, if Villorisi was working with Priest, why would he lead us to Granville in the first place? If he hadn't talked to us at Harrahs, we might never have circled back to Granville as a suspect."

Michel pursed his lips in contemplation.

"Okay, maybe they wanted the other families to think Granville did it," he replied finally.

"Have you been drinking?" Sassy asked with a look of bewilderment. "That makes no sense at all. Priest fired us when we pointed the finger at Granville, but at the same time he wanted to throw suspicion on him?"

"Maybe he didn't want us to find any evidence that could convict Granville...or himself...but he could still have wanted to plant the *idea* that Granville was responsible."

"Why?" Sassy asked.

"To create fear, for one thing," Michel replied. "I would imagine that the other families would show a lot more respect for Granville if they thought he was capable of taking out the legendary Deacon Lee."

"Maybe," Sassy agreed, "but it seems like a lot of work just for that. What else have you got?"

Michel slouched back in his chair and frowned in concentration. He was silent for almost a minute, then suddenly rocked forward.

"Maybe Priest was telling the truth about someone wanting to provoke a war," he said. "But maybe that someone was him."

Although she'd considered the possibility herself before Priest's death, Sassy made a sour face.

"Hear me out," Michel replied quickly. "Suppose that Priest and Villorisi weren't just grooming Granville to take over Priest's family. Suppose they had bigger plans, like positioning him to take over all the families."

"And how would they manage that?" Sassy asked.

"By convincing the other families that he was a threat they all needed to deal with together."

Sassy studied Michel for a few seconds, then began nodding slowly.

"So they make the other families think they all have a common enemy, and convince them to go to war against Granville, then Priest and Villorisi gut them from the inside?"

"Exactly," Michel replied enthusiastically. "Granville would have known everything that was coming, and Priest's and Villorisi's men could have picked off the families' soldiers and made it look like Granville did it. By the time it was over, the remaining members of the other families would have had no choice but to accept Granville as their new boss."

Sassy thought about it for a moment.

"Wow, that's quite a theory," she said finally, "but it doesn't explain everything."

"Such as?"

"Who killed Priest?"

"I still haven't figured that one out," Michel admitted.

"Okay, and what happened to the war?"

"Maybe Priest and Villorisi overestimated the heads of the other families," Michel offered. "Maybe they'd just prefer to live out their lives in peace."

"Maybe," Sassy replied, "but I still feel like we don't have the whole story."

"So what do you want to do about that?" Michel asked.

"I'm not sure what we can do," Sassy replied. "If you're right, the only definite crime was Priest's murder, and the police are already investigating that. We assume that Deacon was killed, but there's no body, and if Priest killed him then there's no killer. I think we may be at the end of the line."

Michel nodded.

"Do you think I should call the Captain and tell him my theory?"

Sassy thought about it then shrugged.

"I suppose it couldn't hurt," she said, "and I'll call Ken Lauer. He's coming to town in two weeks. Maybe he can dig up something else."

"Well, I guess it's better than nothing," Michel said.

Chapter 30

"Looks like you've got a new kingpin in town," Ken Lauer said after the waitress had brought them their drinks.

He and Sassy were seated along the back wall of the patio at the Court of Two Sisters on Royal Street. It was an unseasonably warm night and the patio was nearly full.

The previous day's paper had carried an article about Jacard-Lee's acquisition of Villorisi Construction. The article had been accompanied by a photo of Granville Lee and a smiling Angelo Villorisi.

"Yeah," Sassy replied, "and I can't help but think we're partially responsible for it."

"I think it was inevitable," Lauer replied in a consoling tone.

"I suppose," Sassy replied half-heartedly.

They sipped their drinks quietly for a moment, then Lauer handed Sassy a manilla folder he'd brought with him.

"What's this?" she asked without opening it.

"It's the coroner's report on Priest," Lauer replied.

"Don't tell me the gunshot was post-mortem," Sassy said.

"Oh no, it was definitely the bullet that killed him," Lauer replied, "but he didn't have long anyway. He had cancer."

Sassy remembered the way Priest had looked the last time she'd seen him.

"What kind of cancer?" she asked.

"I tracked down his oncologist," Lauer replied. "He said it started in the stomach, but by the time Priest came to see him it had already spread to the lymph system. The coroner says his body was riddled with it. Priest underwent some chemo to try to slow the spread, but it wasn't working."

"Did the oncologist say how long he had?"

"A few weeks at best," Lauer replied. "His kidneys were failing and he was refusing any further treatment."

"Doesn't sound like the way a man like Priest would want to go out," Sassy said.

"That's what I thought."

Sassy studied Lauer for a moment.

"So why are you telling me this?" she asked finally.

Lauer shrugged.

"I just thought you'd want to know."

"I'll bet," Sassy replied.

They were quiet again while they sipped their drinks, then Sassy fixed Lauer with a probing look.

"I have a question for you, and I hope you won't take it the wrong way," she said.

"Shoot."

"If Priest and Villorisi were really working together for years, how is it that your guys didn't know about it?"

"I've been wondering the same thing," Lauer replied, "but so far I don't have an answer."

"You're not hiding anything from me, are you?" Sassy asked.

"Of course not," Lauer replied with a hurt look.

Sassy gave him an apologetic smile.

"I'm sorry. I guess I'm just a little oversensitive. We've been played on this case from the very beginning."

"I understand," Lauer replied, "but you know I wouldn't do that to you."

"Yeah, I know," Sassy replied.

There was a moment of awkward silence.

"So what's next for you?" Lauer asked finally.

"I guess I'll just stick with this private investigation gig for a while and see where it goes. Why?"

"Well, because we're looking for some senior people in the Bureau," Lauer replied. "I think you'd be a great addition."

Sassy almost laughed, then realized he was being serious.

"I appreciate that, Ken," she said, "but I think I'm good here. I'm not sure I could work in that kind of structure anymore. Plus my partner is here."

"I'm sure we could find something for him, too," Lauer offered.

Sassy gave him a doubtful look.

"Now I know you're joking," she said. "Michel would never survive in that kind of environment."

"Why not?" Lauer asked.

"Well, because he's gay for one thing," Sassy replied. "I don't exactly get the impression that the FBI, or any place in the federal government, is the best place for gay folks these days. Plus he has a slight problem with authority."

Lauer nodded.

"That's probably true," he said.

Again there was a moment of awkward silence. This time Sassy broke it.

"So what's next for *you?*"

"Only seven more years until I can retire with a full pension," Lauer replied.

Sassy narrowed her eyes at him.

"That's not what I meant and you know it."

"Ah, you mean with Linda," Lauer replied, trying to sound as though he really hadn't understood.

Sassy stared at him expectantly in reply.

"I don't know," Lauer said.

Sassy leaned forward and touched his right hand.

"You know I normally don't pry into your personal life," she said. "When you've wanted to talk about it, I've listened, but I've never brought it up because I've always figured that was your own business."

Lauer nodded.

"But that doesn't mean I don't worry about you," Sassy continued. "I mean, this thing between us has been going on for a long time now, and I have to wonder if it would be if you were really happy with Linda. And you know I'm not asking because I'm looking for more of a relationship with you. I'm asking as a friend."

Lauer stared at the table for a moment before replying.

"It's not that simple," he said without looking up. "I still love her. It's not the same love we had when we were first married, but it's still love. And we've built a life together."

"But don't you worry that you're missing out on something more?" Sassy asked. "And again, I don't mean with me. I just mean in general."

Lauer looked Sassy in the eyes.

"Passion is great," he said, "but it doesn't last. I think the only reason it's lasted so long for us is because we only see one another a few times a year. Maybe you're right. Maybe I am missing out on something, but I'm not unhappy with what I have. Sometimes I just want a little more, and I've gotten that from you."

Sassy had always understood that she fulfilled a need for Lauer, in the same way that he fulfilled her need for occasional companionship and romance.

"There's something else," Lauer said. "Linda had a breast cancer scare."

"I'm sorry," Sassy said, truly meaning it. "Is she all right?"

"The tumor was benign," Lauer replied, "but it was tense there for a while."

"Why didn't you tell me?" Sassy asked. "I would have sent her a card."

Lauer gave her an amused smile.

"As far as she knows, Sassy Jones is just the name of someone I knew back in college," he said.

Sassy shook her head and smiled back.

"Oh yeah. I don't know what I was thinking there."

"Anyway," Lauer said, his tone suddenly more serious, "the whole cancer thing got me thinking, and I realized that..."

"You don't even need to say it," Sassy interrupted. "I know where this is going, and it's fine."

Lauer gave her a wistful smile.

"I'm going to miss this," he said.

"And I'll miss it, too, but I understand."

"Are you sure?" Lauer asked, searching Sassy's face.

"I'm sure," she replied. "I always knew it would end something like this. Either you'd leave Linda and want to start something more serious with me and I'd have to break it off, or you'd decide you couldn't do it anymore and you'd break it off. That's the way these things go. Besides, I'm getting a little long in the tooth to be the other woman."

"But you're still beautiful," Lauer said.

"Of course, I am," Sassy replied with a regal smile. "I'm a beautiful nubian queen."

*****

After Lauer dropped her off, Sassy went into the house and poured herself a Jack Daniels. Then she took out her cell phone, searched the list of recent calls, and hit redial. Roland answered on the second ring.

"What can I do for you, Miss Jones?"

"Hi Roland. I need to see Mr. Lee," Sassy replied. "Would you please ask him to meet me tomorrow night at my house?"

Chapter 31

Granville Lee arrived at Sassy's house promptly at 7:30 PM. Though he came to the door alone, Sassy could see Roland in the driver's seat of the dark blue Jaguar parked by the curb.

"Good evening, Miss Jones," Lee said with a courtly bow.

"Good evening, Mr. Lee," Sassy replied with a smile. "Please, come in."

She led Lee into the living room and he took a seat on the sofa.

"Can I get you a drink?" Sassy asked.

"Just some water, please," Lee replied. "I don't drink alcohol. But I'm not morally opposed to it, so please don't hesitate on my behalf."

Sassy gave him a deadpan look.

"I wouldn't hesitate even if you were opposed," she replied. "This is my house."

She went into the kitchen for a minute, then returned carrying two glasses. She handed one to Lee, then settled on the opposite end of the sofa.

"Your home is very beautiful," Lee said, looking around. "I think it reflects its owner quite well."

"Don't be trying to flatter me," Sassy replied with mock reproach. "I'm *almost* old enough to be your mother. In fact, I could have been your stepmother if I'd taken your father up on his offers to marry me."

"You and my father were involved?" Lee replied with genuine surprise.

"No, we were just friends," Sassy replied, "but that didn't stop him from asking me. He kept telling me that a woman like me should have more than she could get by becoming a cop."

"I suppose that would depend on what one wanted out of life," Lee replied.

"That's what I kept telling him," Sassy replied, "but Priest could never quite understand that."

Lee smiled in response.

"I have something for you," he said, reaching into the inside jacket pocket of his Hugo Boss suit.

He handed Sassy an envelope. She opened it and took out a check made out to Chance LeDuc, in the amount of $350,000.

"If you send me an invoice, I'll see to it that you are paid, as well," Lee said.

"I'm sure Chance will be glad to see this," Sassy said, "but how did you know about this?"

"I'm aware of the various dealings you had with my father," Lee replied.

"Well, that answers my first question," Sassy replied. "So you and Priest did have a relationship?"

Lee nodded.

"And he was grooming you to be his successor?"

Lee shrugged noncommittally.

Sassy stared at the check for a moment, then looked back up at Lee.

"Why do I feel like this is a payoff to make me go away?" she asked.

Lee smiled.

"I assure you, that is not the intention, Miss Jones," he said. "If it were, the check would be in your name, would it not?"

Sassy returned the smile.

"I suppose," she said, though she realized that the check effectively removed any legitimate excuse she and Michel might have to continue investigating Lee's business dealings.

"I am simply buying out Mr. LeDuc's interest in the Bluehawk project," Lee said, "though if he chooses to reinvest, he is welcome. I fear, however, that the project will be far less profitable than what he'd envisioned."

"Why's that?" Sassy asked.

"Because we've decided to move ahead with a more modest venture. It will be primarily residential, but will also include a community center and sports center for the children. The project will be called Priest's Place."

"I think your father would have liked that," Sassy said with a warm smile.

"I believe he would," Lee replied, smiling back and nodding his head slowly.

He took a sip of water, then his expression grew serious.

"So why did you want to see me, Miss Jones?" he asked.

Sassy studied him for a moment.

"I know that your father was dying," she said evenly.

She watched Lee's face for a reaction, but didn't see any.

"I see that you've not yet abandoned your investigation," he said.

"Actually we have," Sassy replied. "That information just sort of came to my attention."

Lee seemed to consider Sassy's answer, then nodded as though accepting it.

"So what would you like to know?" he asked.

"Well, I've got a theory I want to run by you," Sassy replied.

Lee nodded for her to continue.

"I think you killed your father," Sassy replied evenly. "And I think it was a mercy killing at his request. But I also think that in his mind it was a symbolic gesture."

"How so?" Lee asked, tilting his head with curiosity.

"I'm pretty sure your father was responsible for Deacon's disappearance. And for some reason, he thought that Deacon's body was in that freezer, though I still haven't figured out why. I'm guessing that he was worried that without some level of

233

fear, the other families would be reluctant to accept you as the new head of your family. But if Priest's and Deacon's bodies were found together, it would make a pretty definitive statement that you weren't to be fucked with. I think that was his final gift to you."

Lee stared at her for a moment, then he began to smile in a way that was eerily reminiscent of his father's crocodile smile, though less menacing.

"Do you know the first thing my father told me about you?" he asked.

Sassy shook her head.

"That you would never betray your principles," Lee said.

As he placed his glass on the coffee table and stood, Sassy realized he had no intention of answering her implied question.

"It is a very interesting theory," he said. "And given the pain that my father was experiencing, it certainly would have been merciful to end his life."

"But you're not going to tell me whether you did it?"

"As I said, it is a very interesting theory," Lee repeated. "Now if you'll excuse me, I have other business this evening."

"Of course," Sassy said, rising.

She walked with him to the door, then out onto the front porch. The night air was still and humid.

"Thank you for coming," she said.

"Not at all," Lee replied, as he stepped onto the top step of the stairs and turned to face her.

He shook her hand, then turned toward the car. Sassy looked over his right shoulder and raised her hand to wave to Roland. A shock of adrenaline surged through her as she saw him slumped over the steering wheel.

Suddenly an engine roared and Sassy saw a flash of light through the hydrangeas that bordered the left side of her yard.

"Get down," she screamed as a black SUV shot in front of the house and screeched to a halt alongside the front hood of the Jaguar.

As Sassy dropped to the porch, the air exploded with the sound of automatic gunfire. She could feel shards of wood and glass raining down on her head and back.

She looked toward the stairs and saw Lee slumped against the railing post, clutching the right side of his chest. Keeping her head down, she crawled toward him and grabbed his left sleeve. She leaned toward him, then rolled hard onto her right shoulder, pulling Lee onto his side and away from the edge of the porch.

Suddenly Sassy heard three deafening gun reports directly behind her. She looked back and saw Michel crouched inside the right jamb of the front door, his gun extended.

"Get down," she yelled at him.

He responded by firing two more times.

Sassy heard squealing tires and looked back toward the street, just in time to see the tail lights of the SUV move out of sight. Everything was suddenly quiet and still again. Though the whole experience had lasted less than ten seconds, to Sassy it had felt like hours.

"Help me get him inside in case they come back," she said, as she sat up and looked at Michel.

He was down on his knees, breathing heavily, and his skin was pale and clammy looking.

"Are you all right?" Sassy asked.

"Oh yeah," he replied. "I just need to change my underwear."

He took several more quick deep breaths.

"Who the fuck was that?" Sassy asked rhetorically.

Michel held up the index finger of his right hand to indicate he needed a minute. Then he leaned forward and dry heaved over Sassy's door mat.

Chapter 32

"And you thought that was a good idea to invite him into your home and ask him if he killed his father?" Carl DeRoche asked, after Sassy finished explaining why Granville Lee had been at her house.

Sassy was seated on the couch nursing a Jack Daniels. Michel was on the floor beside her, resting against the arm of the couch. Some of his color had returned, but he was still clearly recovering from the adrenaline rush and subsequent bout of nausea.

"Michel was in my bedroom in case there was any trouble. Besides, how was I supposed to know a death squad was going to show up?" Sassy replied.

DeRoche turned to Michel.

"Are you sure it was Deacon in the passenger seat?"

"I can't swear to it," Michel replied. "It all happened pretty quickly, and I was kind of busy dodging bullets, but it sure as hell looked like him."

"If it was Deacon, he owes me a new house," Sassy interjected, "because he shot the fuck out of this one."

She looked at the holes in the ceiling and hallway walls, and shook her head. She was afraid to see what had happened to her bedroom.

"I'll be sure to mention that as soon as we catch him," DeRoche replied.

There was a sudden wail of a siren out front, then it quickly faded into the distance.

"Lee's on his way to the hospital," Al Ribodeau said as he walked through the front door.

"How is he?" Sassy asked.

"The paramedics said he should be fine. One slug in the right side of his chest and one in his left thigh. No apparent organ or nerve damage."

"He's lucky," Sassy said. "We were all lucky. They must have fired five-hundred rounds at us."

"Well, his man wasn't so lucky," Ribodeau replied.

Sassy reached down and rested her right hand on Michel's left shoulder.

"Single gunshot to the left side of his head," Ribodeau continued. "He must have had the window open. Someone walked up and shot him at close range."

Sassy felt a pang of guilt for insisting that Michel stay in the house and wait for the police rather than checking on Roland, though she knew there was nothing either of them could have done for him.

"I'm sorry, Michel," she said.

Michel reached across his body with his right hand and laid it over Sassy's hand.

"Was this the same man you followed from the Bourbon Pub?" DeRoche asked curiously.

Michel nodded slowly.

"Were you...friends?" DeRoche asked.

By the tone, Michel knew that "friends" had been meant euphemistically.

"We were acquainted," he replied. "Roland kept an eye on me when Sassy and I went to Lee's farmhouse."

DeRoche gave him a skeptical look but didn't press.

"Well, I'm sorry," he said.

"So now what?" Sassy asked.

"You know the drill as well as I do," DeRoche replied. "We put out an APB on a black SUV that may have bullet holes in the side, and we've got someone watching Deacon's house."

Sassy nodded.

"That is unless you've got some other ideas?" DeRoche added.

Sassy knew he was asking whether she and Michel had some information that they hadn't shared.

"No," she said.

DeRoche nodded.

"I'm afraid you're going to have to move out of here for a few days while we process the scene," he said.

"That's okay," Sassy replied. "The whole broken glass and bullet hole motif isn't really my style anyway."

"You can stay with me," Michel offered.

Sassy nodded and looked around the room.

"I sure as hell hope my insurance covers this," she said.

Chapter 33

"Hey, I tried calling you last night but I kept getting a busy signal," Ken Lauer said. "Haven't you ever heard of call waiting?"

Sassy smiled at the phone receiver.

"Well, we had a little shoot out at my place last night," she replied. "The phone may have taken a bullet."

"A shoot out?" Lauer replied with alarm. "Are you okay?"

"I'm fine," Sassy replied, "but my house is going to need some serious help."

"What happened?"

"It looks like Deacon Lee tried to make a hit on his half-brother. Granville was leaving my house, and an SUV pulled up and opened fire. Michel thought he saw Deacon in the passenger seat."

"Is Lee okay?" Lauer asked.

"He will be," Sassy replied. "He took two bullets, but nothing too serious."

"And what was he doing at your house?" Lauer asked. "Or do I even want to know?"

Sassy laughed.

"I was following up on what you told me about Priest being sick," Sassy replied. "Basically I asked him if he killed Priest as an act of mercy."

"And what did he say?"

"He said it was an interesting theory," Sassy replied.

This time Lauer laughed.

"So since you didn't know about the shooting, you must have another reason for calling," Sassy said.

"Yeah," Lauer replied. "I did some follow-up regarding your question on how our guys didn't know about the relationship between Priest and Villorisi. Apparently we did know. I spoke with the head of the local task force. He said that Villorisi is an informant for them."

"You're kidding?"

"No. For almost forty years."

"That's hard to believe," Sassy replied. "He's so old school. I can't believe he'd break the code like that."

"According to our guy, Villorisi mostly feeds them information on outsiders trying to move into the territory," Lauer said. "Seems like he wants to make sure things stay under control of the families."

Sassy thought about what Priest had said about he and his "friends" being better than those waiting to take their places. If Villorisi and Priest were allies, it would make sense that they'd shared the same sentiment.

"Interesting," Sassy said.

"Well, I've got something even more interesting," Lauer replied. "Villorisi isn't the only informant. We have someone in Granville's camp."

"Who?" Sassy asked.

"A guy by the name of Roland Tate," Lauer replied. "He's been giving us info for about a year. He met with his handler a few days ago and said he knew who killed Deacon. Said he had evidence and would be willing to testify if we'd put him into witness protection. Of course, if Deacon's still alive, then he's obviously not credible."

There was a long pause while Lauer waited for Sassy to respond.

"What's wrong?" he asked finally.

"Roland's dead," Sassy replied.

Chapter 34

"Look, it's still an NOPD case," Sassy said. "We just want to help."

She and Michel were seated beside Al Ribodeau on one side of Captain DeRoche's desk.

"I understand that," DeRoche said, "but you have to admit it's kind of an awkward situation."

"I know," Sassy said, "but we've got a big head start on your people."

DeRoche scratched the back of his head and sighed.

"All right," he said, "but you've got to play it by the book. No improvisation on the fly."

He looked from Sassy to Michel.

"Fine," they both answered simultaneously, as though the thought of deviating from procedure would never cross their minds.

"Okay," DeRoche said. "So what are we looking for?"

"Roland told his contact at the FBI that he had evidence on who killed Deacon," Sassy said. "I'm hoping we can find it."

"Apparently he lived at Lee's farmhouse," Ribodeau said, "but without having some evidence, first we won't be able to get a search warrant."

"He probably wouldn't leave it there, anyway," Sassy said. "It would be too dangerous. It might have been something he was carrying with him."

"Okay," DeRoche replied. "So let's go down to the coroner's office and see what they have."

*****

"This is everything?" DeRoche asked as they looked down at Roland's belongings.

There was a bloodstained white shirt and gray suit jacket, a pair of gray suit pants, a pale blue tie, a pair of boxer shorts, two black dress socks, a pair of black Cole Haan shoes, a silver Rolex watch, and a battered leather wallet laid out on the steel table.

"That's everything," the coroner's assistant replied.

"Okay, we'll let you know when we're finished," DeRoche said, making it clear that the assistant's presence wasn't wanted.

"Let's start with his wallet," Sassy said, after the young woman had left the room.

DeRoche nodded at Ribodeau, who picked up the wallet and methodically emptied the contents onto the table. When he was done, he began double checking the various slots and compartments.

"Here's something," he said after half a minute, pulling a small folded piece of yellow paper from deep in one of the credit card slots.

He unfolded it, looked at it for a moment, then handed it to Sassy. Michel and DeRoche moved to her sides to look at it.

It was a hand-drawn floorplan of a rectangular room. There were two openings in the walls, one at the bottom and one on the right side. The top wall had a row of eight small horizontal rectangles stretched across it. Along the left wall, was a large vertical rectangle, with a smaller horizontal rectangle inside it, near the top. There was an X drawn on the smaller rectangle.

"That mean anything to either of you?" DeRoche asked.

Michel shook his head immediately.

Sassy studied the paper for a moment longer, then looked up and smiled.

"Looks like an insurance policy to me," she said.

"Come again?" DeRoche asked.

"We need to take a field trip," Sassy replied.

"What? Where?" DeRoche asked.

"To Deacon Lee's house," Sassy replied. "But first we have to stop at my house to pick something up."

Chapter 35

As soon as they'd entered the front door of Deacon's house, it had been obvious that someone had been there after Sassy. The doors to the downstairs closet and bathroom were both open, and there was a cigarette butt crushed out on the foyer's marble floor. When they entered Deacon's bedroom, it was clear that whoever it was had been searching for something.

"Jesus," Al Ribodeau said. "This place has been turned pretty good."

Deacon's pillows, sheets, and quilt were lying in the middle of the floor, and the mattress was on its side next to the bed. The armoire was open, with a pile of DVDs scattered in front of it, and all of the drawers in the nightstand were open. Clothes spilled from the side hallway into the room.

"What were they were looking for?" DeRoche asked.

"This," Sassy said, as she pulled the remote controller from her jacket pocket.

"You think they really wanted to watch TV that badly?" Michel asked.

Sassy knew that normally she would have found the joke funny, but for some reason, seeing the mess in Deacon's room made her feel sad.

"Come on, smart ass," she said, as she lead the group to the open doorway behind the bookcase.

As she reached the bottom of the stairs, Sassy let out a small sigh of relief. The door to Deacon's safe room was closed. She pressed the On Demand button, and the door whooshed open.

"Damn, this guy was ready to hole up in here for a month," Ribodeau said, as he walked into the center of the room and looked around.

"And to fight his way out," DeRoche added, pointing at the shelves of guns and ammunition.

Sassy walked to the bed and knelt down. She patted the top of the pillow, then flipped it over and felt the other side. She slipped her hand into the pillowcase and pulled out two DAT cassettes.

If only I'd decided to take a nap last time, she thought, as she stood up and walked to the bank of recorders. She pushed the tapes into the first two recorders on the top row and hit the Play buttons. The two upper left video monitors came on, one showing Deacon's bedroom and the other his bathroom. Both indicated the same date and time: 12-28-05; 10:33:05 PM.

After a moment, Deacon Lee walked into the bedroom, followed by Kimora Tucker, though Sassy had never seen Tucker looking so glamorous. They were both dressed as though they'd been out for dinner at an upscale restaurant. Deacon took off his jacket and laid it carefully over the back of one of the chairs along the right wall of the room, while Tucker sat on the foot of the bed and took off her high heels.

Deacon walked over to Tucker and gave her a kiss, then crossed the room to the hallway leading to the bathroom. A second later, he appeared on the other video monitor.

"Why would he have a video camera in his bathroom?" Michel asked.

"I suppose so he could make sure no one went in there and planted a bomb or something while he was gone," Sassy replied.

"But it would take forever to review the tapes," Michel said.

"He probably just watched everything on fast forward and looked for anything unusual," Sassy said.

She reached down and hit the Fast Forward buttons on both recorders. The images on the screens moved at quadruple speed, though it was still possible to see what was happening.

They watched as Deacon undressed and stepped into the shower. Michel wished for a second that he and Sassy were alone so they could slow the tape to normal speed. Deacon was very well built, and appeared to be quite well endowed.

"What's she doing?" DeRoche asked, pointing up at the first monitor.

Kimora Tucker had gotten up from the bed, and picked up Deacon's jacket.

Sassy reached down and hit the Play button on the first recorder. The image returned to normal speed.

They watched as Tucker carried the jacket to the bed. She laid it down, then picked up her purse and took something from it. At that point, her body blocked the camera's view for a few seconds as she leaned over the jacket. Then she picked it up and carefully placed it back over the chair, just as it had been. She walked back to the bed, opened her purse again, and put something inside. Then she sat back down.

"I wish this thing had a zoom on it," Sassy said.

"It looked like she pulled a switch," Michel said.

"We need to synch these things back up," Sassy said.

She hit the Pause on the second recorder, then the Fast Forward on the first. When the times matched again, she restarted the second recorder.

They watched in fast forward as Deacon finished his shower, dried off, and left the bathroom. Sassy hit both Play buttons, and the action returned to normal speed.

After a few seconds, Deacon walked into the bedroom, wearing a paisley print bathrobe. Tucker stood and said something to him. He walked over to her and put the back of his hand against her forehead. They talked for a few seconds, then Deacon nodded and gave Tucker a kiss on the cheek.

"I recognize that move from my ex-wife," Ribodeau interjected. "She's pretending she has a headache."

While Tucker sat on the bed and began putting her shoes back on, Deacon walked over to his jacket. He reached into the inner pocket and took out what looked like a cigarette case, and put it in the right pocket of his robe. Tucker watched him carefully, but looked down as soon as he turned back to her.

She finished buckling the straps on her shoes, then stood up. Deacon said something to her, but she shook her head. She walked over and gave him a hug. The two of them walked toward the camera arm in arm, then Tucker disappeared from view. Deacon stood directly under the camera for a moment, then walked to the hall leading to the bathroom. A second later he was back on the second monitor.

He walked to the bathroom sink and took the case out of his pocket. He laid it on the slate countertop, then walked into the toilet enclosure and closed the door.

"At least we don't have to watch whatever he's doing in there," Ribodeau commented dryly.

A minute later Deacon reappeared and walked back to the sink. Though his back was to the camera, they could see his face and upper body in the mirror.

"It looks like he's checking his blood sugar," Michel said, as they saw him jab at the index finger of his left hand with something about half the size of a pen.

"There's definitely a hereditary link with some types of diabetes," Sassy said, "and now that I think about it, Priest was never much of a drinker, and when Granville was at my house he said he didn't drink at all. Maybe they all had it."

"Doubtful unless Priest met both mothers at a diabetes support group," Ribodeau said.

The other three turned to look at him curiously.

"What, I'm not allowed to have any arcane knowledge of my own?" he asked. "Genetics is sort of a hobby of mine. There are only a handful of hereditary conditions that are passed on through the Y chromosome, and so far as researchers have been able to tell, diabetes isn't one of them."

Everyone stared at him a moment longer, then nodded and turned their attention back to the monitors.

Deacon checked the reading on his lancet, then reached down again. When his hands came back into view, he was holding a small glass bottle in his left hand and a narrow syringe in his right. He poked the syringe into the bottle and drew out some fluid, then put the bottle down and tapped the syringe to release any trapped air.

"I have a bad feeling about this," Sassy said.

Deacon opened the front of his robe and injected the fluid into his stomach. Then he put the syringe down and refastened the belt on his robe. He started to reach back down when a convulsion went through his entire body. They could see a look of panic on his reflected face. He reached for the edge of the sink to steady himself, but his legs buckled and he dropped down onto his knees.

"Jesus, the girl killed him," Ribodeau exclaimed, as they watched Deacon's eyes roll upward and his body fall sideways onto the floor.

He lay there convulsing for another minute, then was still.

*****

"Okay, I'm definitely confused," Sassy said a few minutes later, sitting on the safe room's bed. "If Deacon's dead, then who shot Granville?"

"And why did Roland hide the tapes?" Michel added. "What's his connection to Tucker?"

"Maybe we haven't seen everything yet," Ribodeau offered.

Sassy got up and walked back to the DAT recorders. She crouched down and hit the Fast Forward buttons, as everyone turned their attention back to the video monitors. A few minutes of time elapsed on the video time codes, then there was motion at the bottom of the screen showing Deacon's bedroom.

"Here we go," Sassy said, as she hit the Play buttons.

Two men dressed in black, long-sleeved jerseys and black pants crossed the bedroom to the bathroom hall, their backs to the camera. They disappeared from the first monitor, then reappeared a moment later on the second. One was carrying a large black duffle bag over his shoulder.

The first man walked directly to Deacon, knelt down, and checked his pulse. He looked up and said something.

"Either of you recognize him?" DeRoche asked.

The man looked to be in his late twenties. He had very dark skin and close-cropped hair.

Sassy and Michel shook their heads.

Then the second man stepped forward and placed his bag on the floor. It was Roland Tate.

"Holy shit," Michel exclaimed. "That means Granville paid Kimora Tucker to kill Deacon."

"I don't think he's dead yet," Sassy replied. "I think his right leg just twitched."

They watched as Roland opened the canvas bag and removed several rolls of silver duct tape.

"He was definitely still alive or they wouldn't need those," Ribodeau agreed.

The younger man lifted Deacon into a sitting position, supporting him from behind with his knee, then picked up a roll of tape and wrapped it several times around Deacon's head, covering his mouth. At the same time, Roland used another roll to secure Deacon's ankles.

The younger man removed his knee and Deacon flopped back hard onto the floor, his head literally bouncing off the tile. The man smiled and said something to Roland. Roland stood and rolled Deacon onto his stomach, then crossed Deacon's arms behind his back and wrapped them with tape. Then he and the other man lifted Deacon to his feet, and leaned him against the sink. While Roland held Deacon up, the other man used an entire roll of tape to wrap Deacon from his shoulders to his ankles.

Then the man grabbed Deacon by the ankles while Roland held Deacon's shoulders. They lifted him and carried him out of the bathroom, through the bedroom, and out of view.

Sassy hit Fast Forward again. Almost five minutes passed on the time display, then Roland reappeared in Deacon's bedroom. Sassy hit the Play button.

They watched as Roland straightened up the room, smoothing the bed where Kimora Tucker had sat, and picking up Deacon's jacket from the chair. Then he walked to the bathroom hallway. He was out of sight for a half minute, then appeared on the bathroom monitor carrying what appeared to be the clothes Deacon had been wearing that night. He put them in the canvas bag, along with the duct tape and Deacon's insulin kit.

Then Roland looked directly at the camera. His expression was hard to read, but seemed almost pleading. He walked to the shower, then leaned very close to the door and began visibly breathing very quickly. He lifted his right hand and wrote something on the glass.

"That's pretty fucking genius," Michel said.

Roland turned and looked at the camera again, then picked up the bag and walked into the bedroom. He crossed the room to the night stand on the near side of the bed and picked up the remote controller, then approached the camera. He paused there for a minute, facing to the left, then disappeared. A minute later, the video monitors both went blank.

*****

"Here goes," Sassy said with a hopeful look as she brought her mouth close to the shower door.

She let out a long, slow exhale. Barely visible letters began to appear in the vapor on the glass. She exhaled again, moving her mouth a few inches to the right.

"Can you read it?" she asked quickly.

Michel leaned close to the shower door and looked at the letters from the side.

"It says, 'Bluehawk'," he replied with disappointment.

"And that's it?" Sassy asked.

"That's it," Michel nodded. "The plans must have changed after they left."

Sassy looked at the fading letters.

"Maybe not," she said. "Maybe they took Deacon there to kill him, but didn't leave his body."

"And then sealed the freezer so no one would find the evidence?" Michel asked skeptically.

"Or Priest told Granville to leave Deacon there, but Granville had other ideas, and just sealed the door so Priest wouldn't know," Sassy replied.

Michel considered it for a moment.

"I suppose that would explain why Priest was killed there," he admitted. "Whether Granville did it or it was somebody else, there's obviously some symbolism to that freezer."

Sassy looked at DeRoche and Ribodeau.

"Did you process the inside of the freezer as part of the crime scene, or just the rest of the room?"

"Just the rest of it," Ribodeau replied. "We figured the freezer was already sealed when Priest was killed."

"Then there might be blood in there," Sassy said.

"Could be," Ribodeau replied. "I'll get a team over there right away."

He started toward the door, but Michel stopped him.

"There's just one thing," Michel said, looking at the others. "Now that we know that Deacon really is dead, or at least we're pretty damn sure, who shot Granville?"

Sassy looked at Ribodeau.

"You wouldn't happen to know what caliber slugs they took out of him, would you?" she asked.

"Yeah, they were 9mm," Ribodeau replied. "Why?"

"Because I've got about five-hundred 39mm rounds in the front of my house."

Chapter 36

"Miss Jones," Granville Lee said. "What a nice surprise."

"I just wanted to see how you're doing," Sassy replied as she walked up to the side of the hospital bed.

"Thanks to you and your partner, I'm fine," Lee said. "The doctors said I should be able to go home in a few days."

"That's good to hear," Sassy replied.

"I want to thank you for saving my life," Lee said, his voice filled with sincerity. "If you hadn't pulled me out of the way, I might not have been so lucky."

"You're welcome," Sassy replied. "I'm very sorry about Roland."

Lee frowned and nodded.

"Yes, he was a very good friend and a good man. I miss him very much."

They were quiet for a moment.

"I do have one question for you, though," Lee said finally, cocking his head to the side and regarding Sassy curiously.

Sassy nodded for him to continue.

"How is it that your partner happened to be there that night?"

Sassy gave an embarrassed smile.

"Well, some people get kind of testy when you accuse them of killing their father," she replied. "He was just there in case of emergency."

"I see," Lee replied with an understanding smile. "And it was fortunate for me that he was."

"For us both," Sassy replied.

"So what is next for you both?" Lee asked.

"Oh, I'm sure something a lot less exciting," Sassy replied with a small laugh. "We'll probably just stick to cheating husbands and missing kittens."

Lee laughed in reply.

"Perhaps I'll be able to find some work for you," he said. "Related to my more public business, of course."

"That would be fine," Sassy replied.

She looked at him for a moment, then her expression grew contrite.

"I owe you an apology," she said.

"For what?" Lee asked.

"For thinking that you killed Priest," Sassy replied. "It was just that Deacon hadn't been seen in so long, and..."

"There's no need," Lee replied. "I understand. In your position, I would have believed the same."

"Well, thank you," Sassy said.

"Not at all," Lee replied.

"Anyway," Sassy said more brightly, "I should probably let you get some rest. As I said, I just wanted to see how you were doing."

Lee reached out and squeezed her hand.

"Thank you, Miss Jones. I appreciate it very much. And I'm sure I shall see you again."

"No doubt," Sassy replied.

She walked to the door and opened it, then turned back.

"I almost forgot," she said. "I ran into a friend of yours."

"A friend?" Lee replied with curiosity.

"Yeah," Sassy replied with a smile. "Kimora Tucker. She told me to say hello."

Then she moved aside as Al Ribodeau and two uniformed officers stepped into the room.

"Granville Lee, you're under arrest for the murders of Deacon Lee and Roland Tate," Ribodeau said.

Sassy turned and walked out of the room. She could hear Granville calling her name as the door closed.

*****

"So do you think you've got enough to make it stick?" Sassy asked, standing outside the hospital with Michel and Captain DeRoche.

"I think so," DeRoche replied confidently. "Kimora Tucker is willing to testify that Lee paid her to switch Deacon's insulin, we've got the tapes showing Roland taking Deacon from the house, and we found blood in the freezer. I think it's a pretty solid chain of evidence."

"You're not worried that the tapes will be thrown out because they were acquired without a search warrant?" Sassy asked.

DeRoche shook his head.

"No. You had permission to be in Deacon's house. The fact that you had the key and the alarm code proves that, plus you were seen meeting with Priest by several employees at Jacard-Lee. It'll hold up."

Sassy nodded.

"The only thing we're missing is Deacon's body, and based on the amount of blood in the freezer, I'd guess that's in little pieces all over the state," DeRoche continued. "But our guys and the Feds are on their way to Lee's farmhouse now, so we're hoping we'll find some blood in one of the vehicles, or maybe even the murder weapon."

"The Feds?" Michel asked.

"Yeah," DeRoche replied. "We got an unexpected offer of assistance from them."

He gave Sassy a curious look.

"You wouldn't happen to know anything about that, would you?"

"Not a thing," Sassy replied with a smile.

"Anyway, I spoke to the Chief a little while ago," DeRoche said. "We're prepared to offer you protection until the trial's over."

Sassy thought about it, then shook her head.

"I don't think it'll be necessary," she said. "I figure the other families will be grateful to have Granville gone, and at this point, Priest's people are probably wondering whether Granville had anything to do with his murder, so I doubt they'll get involved. So that only leaves Granville's gang, and with him gone, they're going to be in disarray for quite a while."

"I don't think we have to worry about them, anyway," Michel said. "When the cops find all the dope stored in the barn, everyone at the farm house will be going to jail."

DeRoche gave Michel a curious look.

"And how do you know the barn is filled with dope?"

Michel gave an embarrassed smile.

"I kind of got a tour a few weeks ago."

"I'll bet," DeRoche replied, shaking his head tolerantly. "But what about Villorisi? You don't think he'll be out for revenge? If he helped put Granville in position, I imagine he'd be pretty angry about now."

"I think he's probably more concerned with erasing anything that might link him to Granville," Sassy replied. "He's an old man and he's sick. I'm sure the last thing he wants is to spend his final days behind bars."

"You're probably right," DeRoche agreed, "but if you change your mind, let me know."

"So I guess that's it," Sassy said. "I just hope we did the right thing."

"Meaning?" DeRoche asked.

"I keep thinking about what Priest and Villorisi said about the old way being better because it kept the crime under control," Sassy replied. "What if they were right? What if whatever's coming next is much worse?"

"Fortunately it's not our job to worry about that," DeRoche

replied. "Our job is to investigate and prosecute crimes that have already happened. There's no situational ethics involved."

Sassy and Michel both knew that DeRoche was being intentionally simplistic. He was too intelligent to see things as only either black or white.

"All due respect, Captain," Sassy replied, "we all know there's a little more wiggle room than that. Besides, that's *your* job. It's not ours anymore."

DeRoche smiled.

"That's true," he said, "though given the manpower shortage we're having these days, I could probably get you reinstated. If you're interested, that is."

Although his tone had been casual, Sassy and Michel both realized he was being serious.

"I don't know about Sas," Michel replied, "but I think I'm better where I am. But thank you."

DeRoche looked at Sassy.

"Sorry," she said, "but wherever he goes, I go."

"Okay," DeRoche said with a resigned sigh, "but don't say I didn't offer."

Chapter 37

"He said he'll talk, but only to you," DeRoche said.

He, Sassy, Michel, and Al Ribodeau were standing in the hallway outside an interrogation room. It had been three days since Granville Lee's arrest, and one day since his release from the hospital.

"But he has to know you'll be watching and recording what he says," Sassy said.

DeRoche shrugged.

"And you're sure you're okay with this?" Sassy asked.

"So long as you don't start slapping him around," DeRoche teased.

Sassy nodded.

"All right, I'll try."

She turned to the door and composed herself for a moment, then opened it and stepped inside. She could feel her former identity settle back onto her immediately. It was like putting on a comfortable old sweater.

"Hello, Granville," she said.

"Hello, Miss Jones," Lee replied. "Thank you for coming."

"So why am I here?" Sassy asked, without emotion.

"Because you were a friend of my father," Lee replied. "He said you could be trusted."

"Okay," Sassy said.

She crossed the room and took a seat on the opposite side of the small table, facing Lee.

"So what did you want to tell me?"

"That I'm innocent," Lee replied.

Sassy smiled.

"That's not what Kimora Tucker told the police," she replied. "She said you paid her to switch Deacon's insulin."

"Who is this Kimora Tucker?" Lee asked.

"Deacon's girlfriend," Sassy replied. "Or should I say, ex-girlfriend."

"I don't know this woman," Lee said, his tone growing more agitated.

"And I suppose you don't know anything about Roland kidnapping Deacon either?" Sassy asked sarcastically.

"Roland?"

"We have the tapes showing the whole thing," Sassy said.

"I don't understand," Lee replied. "Why would Roland kidnap Deacon?"

"I imagine because you or your father or Angelo Villorisi told him to," Sassy replied matter-of-factly.

Lee gave her a confused look.

"What does Angelo Villorisi have to do with this?" he asked.

"Come on, stop playing games, Granville," Sassy replied impatiently. "We know that Villorisi and Priest were working together to position you to take over."

Lee sat back in his chair and stared at Sassy for a moment.

"My father and Villorisi despised one another," he said with conviction.

"That's not what our contact in the FBI tells us," Sassy replied. "And if Villorisi and Priest despised one another, doesn't it seem odd that you'd buy Villorisi's business right after your father died?"

Lee sighed and shook his head with frustration.

"Villorisi came to me and offered me his company," he said slowly. "He said it was a peace offering. He wanted to put any old animosity between our two families to rest. I accepted because it was a good business proposition."

"Is that why you were meeting with him on Decatur Street a week after your father died?" Sassy asked.

"You are mistaken," Lee replied. "I didn't meet with Villorisi until a few days before we announced the acquisition. And we met in my office."

Sassy shook her head.

"My partner followed Roland to your meeting," she said, "then Villorisi's man Carlo took him hostage."

Lee shook his head back at Sassy.

"The only meeting I've had on Decatur Street was with the owner of the building opposite the old Mint," he said adamantly. "We're in the early stages of planning to redevelop that entire block."

"And I suppose the owner of the building will confirm that?" Sassy asked.

"Yes," Lee replied. "His name is Mr. Mitchell Page. If you contact my secretary, she will give you his phone number."

Sassy studied Lee for a moment.

"So you're saying that you and Villorisi had no relationship before your father's death?" she asked doubtfully.

"Prior to his offer, I had met him only once, many years ago when I first came to New Orleans. My father suggested that I reach out to the heads of the other families to assure them that I had no intention of infringing on their territories."

Sassy thought the answer sounded sincere.

"But you didn't tell them that you were Priest's son, is that correct?" she asked.

"No, my father thought it best that that remain secret," Lee replied.

"Why?" Sassy asked.

"Because he feared that Deacon would see me as a threat and it would endanger my life," Lee replied.

It was the same thing Priest had told Sassy and Michel.

"Okay," Sassy said, "so let's talk about Deacon. What was your relationship with him?"

"As I told you before, he approached me about a partnership and I turned him down," Lee replied.

"And then what happened?"

"Nothing," Lee replied.

"He didn't contact you again?"

Lee shook his head.

"Did you tell Priest about Deacon's offer?" Sassy asked.

"Yes, of course."

"And what was his reaction?"

"He was not surprised," Lee replied. "He'd known for a long time that Deacon coveted his position."

"What did he plan to do about it?" Sassy asked.

"There were some things my father wouldn't discuss with me," Lee replied. "He merely said that when the time came for me to take over his interests, Deacon would not be a concern."

"And you were never curious about what that meant?" Sassy asked skeptically.

"I believe we both know what was meant," Lee replied.

"How much contact did Priest have with your people?" Sassy asked.

Lee gave her a curious look.

"None," he said. "My people were unaware of my relationship with my father."

"Even Roland?"

"No. Roland was certainly aware," Lee replied. "Roland was aware of everything."

"Is that why you killed him?" Sassy asked.

Lee shook his head in bewilderment.

"How could I have killed Roland?" he exclaimed. "I was in your home. Deacon killed Roland, and your partner saw him try to kill me, did he not?"

Sassy shrugged.

"He saw someone who looked like Deacon," she replied, "but the funny thing is that you were shot with 9mm rounds. Every other slug that's been recovered came from an AK-47."

260

Lee gave Sassy a blank look.

"So what does that mean?" he asked.

"It means it was a set up to make it look like Deacon was still alive, and that he tried to kill you," Sassy replied. "While the gunmen with the AK-47s were shooting high, someone else wounded you with a more precise handgun."

Lee stared hard at her for a moment.

"You believe I would have myself shot?" he asked.

Sassy shrugged.

"I think that perhaps my father thought too highly of you," Lee said with a bitter laugh.

Sassy realized that she was hitting a dead end. She decided to change her tack.

"Okay," she said in a quieter, more reasonable tone. "You want me to believe you? Tell me the truth about Priest's killing."

Lee stared at her for a moment, his pale green eyes searching her face. Then he looked down at the table.

"You were correct," he said, with a sigh. "I killed my father, at his request."

He looked back up and steadily met Sassy's gaze.

"Do you have any proof of that?" Sassy asked. "Did anyone else know about it?"

"Roland," Lee replied with a touch of sadness. "But my father also left me a letter detailing his request, in case I were to be prosecuted. It is notarized by one of his attorneys, though I don't know if he was aware of the contents."

Sassy felt an odd sense of relief knowing that Priest's killing had been merciful.

"And you can produce that letter?" she asked.

Lee nodded.

"Why in front of the freezer?" Sassy asked. "What was the significance?"

"I don't know," Lee replied. "I asked him, but he wouldn't say. He also said that the building should be preserved."

"Preserved?" Sassy questioned.

Lee nodded.

"In the plans for Priest Place, the other two buildings are to be torn down, but that building will be saved and renovated."

Sassy stared at the table for a moment, trying to figure out how this latest information fit with everything else she knew.

"All right," she said finally, looking up at Lee. "I think we're done here."

*****

"So do you believe him?" DeRoche asked, as Sassy walked back into the observation room.

"He's either the most practiced liar I've ever met, or he was telling the truth," she replied, then gave Michel a questioning look.

"I agree," Michel said.

"What about you, Al?" Sassy asked.

"Well, I don't have as much experience with this stuff," Ribodeau replied, "but I buy it. The only time he averted his eyes was when he admitted to killing Priest, and I think that was a show of remorse."

Sassy smiled at him like a proud teacher.

"What about you, Captain?" she asked.

DeRoche shrugged.

"I'm with the rest of you," he said. "Any suggestions on what we do next?"

"I have a feeling that the key to this whole thing is the significance of the freezer to Priest," Sassy replied. "Something must have happened there."

"I think so, too," Michel said. "We assumed that the weld on that door was recent, but we never really got a good look at it. It might have been sealed years ago."

Sassy looked at Ribodeau.

"When the lab processed the freezer, did they just check for the presence of blood, or did they type it?"

"They just checked for it," Ribodeau replied. "We didn't know Deacon's blood type."

"But you kept samples?" Sassy asked.

Ribodeau nodded.

"Okay," Sassy said. "We know that Deacon was taking insulin, which means he probably has a standing prescription at a local pharmacy. If you can track it down, you can find out who his doctor is and get his medical records. Then check the blood in the freezer against Deacon's blood type. If it's not a match, then you should date the samples."

Ribodeau nodded. Sassy noted that he looked slightly embarrassed.

"Don't worry, Al," she said sympathetically. "This is the sort of stuff you can only learn over time."

Ribodeau gave her a grateful smile.

"Anything else?" he asked.

"Yeah, see if there's anything in the database on Angelo Villorisi's medical history," Sassy replied.

"Villorisi?" DeRoche questioned.

Sassy shrugged.

"Hey, you never know," she said.

*****

"So what do we do?" Michel asked, as they left the station.

"I have a feeling that Villorisi knew that Granville was Priest's son before everyone else found out," Sassy replied.

"How?" Michel asked.

"That's what I'm going to find out," Sassy replied.

"And what about me?" Michel asked.

"You can answer the phones," Sassy replied.

Chapter 38

"Ken, it's me," Sassy said.

"Hey," Lauer replied. "Decided you can't live without me after all?"

"Well, I can't live without your help," Sassy replied dryly.

She could hear Lauer chuckling through the receiver.

"Okay, so what do you need?" he asked.

"Have you ever met Villorisi's handler?" Sassy asked.

"No."

"Know anything about him?"

"He was with the bureau for forty years," Lauer replied.

"Was?" Sassy asked.

"Yeah, I heard he just retired," Lauer replied. "Why?"

"Doesn't the timing seem kind of odd?" Sassy asked. "He retires right when there's so much activity in his contact's territory?"

"Actually, it's odder that he stuck around as long as he did," Lauer replied. "He could have retired seven years ago. Why, what's going on?"

"I'm not entirely sure," Sassy replied, "but we suspect that someone may have been feeding Villorisi information."

"And you think it was our guy?" Lauer asked with disbelief. "Based on what?"

"Villorisi told us that he and Priest were buddies," Sassy replied. "Your guy confirmed that. But Granville swears that his father and Villorisi despised one another."

"What does that prove?" Lauer asked with a hint of

annoyance. "Granville could be lying. And our guy's information was just based on what Villorisi told him."

"Well, that's true," Sassy replied calmly, "but doesn't it seem strange that no one else knew about a connection between Priest and Villorisi until you started asking questions? And Villorisi had to be getting his information from somewhere."

Lauer was silent for a moment.

"What kind of information?" he asked finally, his tone more even.

"That Granville was Priest's son for starters," Sassy replied.

"But we didn't know that," Lauer replied.

"Roland Tate knew," Sassy replied, "and he was one of your informants, too."

Lauer was silent again for moment, then Sassy heard a sigh of resignation.

"Okay, I'll check it out," Lauer said. "Anything else?"

"Yeah," Sassy replied. "See if Villorisi's handler knew about Roland."

Chapter 39

"Okay, Mr. Geneticist, is that possible?" Sassy asked.

She and Michel were seated with Al Ribodeau in Captain DeRoche's office.

"No way," Ribodeau replied. "Priest was A-positive, so his offspring would have to be A or AB, depending on the mother's blood type. O-negative isn't a possibility."

"So then Deacon wasn't his son?" Michel asked.

"No," Ribodeau replied emphatically.

"And what about the blood in the freezer?" Sassy asked.

"The lab isolated two samples, both type A. One came from a female and the other from a male," Ribodeau replied.

"So they could both be related to Priest?" Michel asked.

Ribodeau nodded.

"Did you date them?" Sassy asked.

"They were approximately fifty years old," Ribodeau replied.

"That was before Deacon was even born," Sassy said.

"Yeah," Ribodeau agreed, "which means that this whole thing started a long time ago."

"Does the Captain know yet?" Michel asked.

"Yeah, he went down to talk to the Chief as soon as I told him," Ribodeau replied.

"About what?" Sassy asked.

"I'm not sure," Ribodeau replied, "but he said he wanted you to wait here."

Chapter 40

"So you actually do eat here sometimes," Michel said.

Angelo Villorisi looked up from his newspaper. He was seated alone in a corner booth at Commander's Palace.

"Mr. Doucette. Miss Jones," he said without emotion.

"This is Detective Sergeant Al Ribodeau," Sassy said. "Do you mind if we join you?"

"Actually I do," Villorisi replied in a low rasp.

"Well, I'm afraid we're going to anyway," Michel said, as he slid into the booth to Villorisi's right, followed by Ribodeau.

Sassy sat on Villorisi's left.

"This is harassment," Villorisi said.

"If you'd prefer, we could cuff you, march you out in front of all these people, and take you down to the station for questioning," Ribodeau said.

Villorisi stared at him for a moment, then shook his head.

"That won't be necessary," he said.

"Good," Sassy said.

"So does this mean you're back on the police force?" Villorisi asked, trying to sound nonchalant.

"No, we're just here to assist Detective Ribodeau," Michel replied. "We thought you might be more willing to talk if we were here, since we're old friends and all."

Villorisi smiled his usual ghoulish smile.

"I have nothing to say," he said.

"That's fine," Sassy replied. "How about if we talk and you listen? Then if you have anything to add, feel free."

"So have you spoken to Bob Hughes lately?" Michel asked.

"Who?" Villorisi replied.

"You know, your handler at the FBI," Ribodeau replied. "Surely you couldn't have forgotten his name that quickly. We understand you were in touch with him just a few weeks ago."

"I have no idea who you're talking about," Villorisi replied evenly.

"Well, don't bother trying to contact him now anyway," Michel said. "He's in protective custody."

"I bet when he goes into witness protection, they'll put him in a nice house right down the block from Kimora Tucker," Sassy added.

Villorisi narrowed his eyes and looked from Sassy to Michel to Ribodeau, as though trying to gauge whether they were bluffing. Then his eyes darted quickly to the door.

"It's amazing how easy it is to get people to talk when it's pointed out that it's not in your best interest to keep them alive anymore," Michel said.

"Oh, and you can stop looking at the door," Sassy said. "Carlo won't be joining us. He's being detained outside."

Villorisi glared angrily at Sassy for a moment, then appeared to regain his composure.

"So, we already know that Deacon wasn't Priest's son," Sassy began. "We're guessing he was yours."

Villorisi's expression didn't change.

"And we also found out that Priest was married in 1957, and his wife gave birth to a son in 1958." Sassy continued. "The records say they both died in 1959, though there's no indication what happened to them. And we know that the blood found in the freezer at the Bluehawk Terminal dates from around that time, and came from a male and female. The blood type of the male was consistent with the woman being his mother and Priest being his father."

For a split second, Sassy thought she saw a flicker of emotion cross Villorisi's face, though she couldn't identify it.

"So here's what we think," Sassy said. "You killed Priest's wife and son and put the bodies in the freezer. Instead of killing you right away, Priest decided to wait, and when he found out your mistress was pregnant, he paid her off to disappear. Fifteen years later, he brought her boy back and claimed him as his own. You couldn't do anything about it because you were already married when Deacon was conceived, and by the time he came back you had your social standing to consider."

"So then you waited for your chance," Michel said, "and when you found out that Priest had a son, you made your move."

Villorisi's expression remained blank.

"You found out that Roland Tate was also an FBI informant and blackmailed him into kidnapping Deacon," Michel continued. "Then you killed Deacon and tried to frame Granville for it."

"But then you started to get scared that Granville wasn't going to be charged, so you tried to have him killed," Sassy added.

"And had Roland killed at the same time, since he could tie you to Deacon's killing," Michel said.

"Does that sound about right?" Sassy asked, though she didn't really expect a response.

Villorisi's gaze dropped to the table for a moment. When he looked back up, his eyes had gotten red and glassy.

"All except for two things," he said in a slow, ragged voice. "The boy in the freezer was *my* son, and Deacon isn't dead."

Sassy felt as though she'd had the breath sucked out of her lungs.

"What?" she stammered.

She gave Ribodeau a questioning look. He nodded to confirm that it was possible, given the boy's blood type.

"I met Cecilia in 1955," Villorisi said in a quiet, dreamlike voice. "I fell in love with her and asked her to marry me. But Priest told her he'd kill me if she didn't marry him instead."

"Why?" Michel asked.

Villorisi shrugged.

"Priest always hated me. I think he saw me as a threat. The truth is that we were probably too similar. Both young and ambitious. Both convinced we were smarter than everyone else. I also think he didn't like the idea of a black woman marrying a white man."

"So what happened?" Ribodeau asked.

"They married," Villorisi replied, "but that didn't stop us from seeing one another, and Cecilia got pregnant."

"And Priest figured out the baby was yours and killed them?" Sassy asked.

Villorisi closed his eyes and his frail body began to shake. Sassy reached out and put her right hand on his shoulder as she gave Michel and Ribodeau a helpless look.

They sat in silence for a minute, listening to Villorisi's muted sobs. Finally Villorisi's tears began to subside. He wiped his eyes with his napkin and took a sip of the water Sassy handed him.

"Thank you," he said.

"Mr. Villorisi," Sassy said gently, "We're sorry to put you through this, but we need to understand what's been going on."

"I understand," Villorisi replied.

He took a deep breath, then nodded at Sassy to continue.

"So what happened then?" she asked. "Why didn't you kill Priest?"

"I couldn't," Villorisi replied. "Priest never admitted to the killings. He painted himself as the victim. If I'd done anything, the other families would have killed me. I didn't have any power then. I was just another soldier. So I tried to move on. I met another woman and we were married."

"But you had a mistress," Sassy said. "Deacon's mother."

"Yes," Villorisi replied. "My wife couldn't conceive, and I wanted another son, even if I could never acknowledge him publicly."

"And then Priest stole him away, as well," Michel said.

Villorisi nodded.

"And the rest is as you thought," he said, his voice shaking. "Eventually Priest brought Deacon back as his own son, and I couldn't do anything about it without hurting my wife."

Sassy remembered how odd it had always seemed to her that Priest had so readily embraced his illegitimate son. Now it made sense.

"So Priest was taunting you," she said. "First he took your son from you, then he brought him back, knowing that you couldn't reach out to him."

She felt a rush of sympathy as Villorisi nodded.

"So what were you planning to do?" Michel asked.

"Nothing at first," Villorisi replied. "So long as Deacon was treated well and had a good life, I was willing to let things be."

"Then you found out that Granville was Priest's son," Michel said.

"Yes, and I realized that Priest never intended for Deacon to take over his family," Villorisi replied. "It was just another game to hurt me."

"Do you think Priest intended to kill Deacon?" Sassy asked.

Villorisi shrugged. "It seemed likely."

"So then what?" Michel asked.

"My wife was gone by then, so I reached out to Deacon," Villorisi replied, "and I told him the truth."

"Where's Deacon now?" Michel asked.

"I don't know," Villorisi replied. "I told him I thought it would be safer if he disappeared for a while. I haven't heard from him since."

Sassy tried to fit the rest of the pieces into the puzzle.

"So Deacon's kidnapping was a fake to frame Granville?" she asked.

Villorisi nodded.

"But Roland didn't know that? He thought he was bringing Deacon to the Bluehawk to be killed?" Sassy asked.

Villorisi nodded again.

"What about Kimora Tucker?" Michel asked. "Did she know it was a fake?"

"She has a relationship with Deacon," Villorisi replied circumspectly.

Sassy sat back against the booth and looked at Michel and Ribodeau. They looked as confused and surprised as she felt. She looked back at Villorisi. He'd regained his composure, but he seemed smaller, as though the unburdening of his story had left him deflated.

"Who killed Priest?" she asked suddenly.

Villorisi's eyes grew cold.

"I did," he replied. "I only wish I'd done it fifty years earlier."

They were all silent for almost a full minute. Sassy felt conflicting emotions. She felt genuine pity for Villorisi as she imagined the emotional torment he'd had to endure for most of his life. At the same time, she knew he had to pay for his crimes.

"You realize that you just admitted to two murders and an attempted murder," she said quietly, leaning closer to Villorisi.

Villorisi's expression became suddenly calm.

"I'm aware of that," he replied, his voice steady and stronger than before. "I'm also aware that given my health, I'll never stand trial."

"Given the circumstances, Mr. Villorisi," Ribodeau said, "we'd be willing to wait outside while you finish your meal."

"I would appreciate that, Detective," Villorisi replied, nodding toward a waiter who was hovering nearby.

Sassy slid out of the booth. Ribodeau got up and moved beside her. Michel started to follow, then stopped.

"Who really called you at the warehouse?" he asked.

Villorisi looked at him for a moment, then did his best impression of a gentle smile.

"There was no call," he said. "That was just an alarm to remind me to take my medication."

*****

"So do you think we finally have the complete truth?" Ribodeau asked when they were outside.

"Given that we have two people confessing to killing Priest, I imagine not," Sassy replied, "but I think we know everything we need to know. Two old men never got over something that happened fifty years ago, Deacon and Granville were pawns in their game, and Villorisi will be gone soon and none of it will matter."

Michel gave her a hard look.

"That's uncharacteristically cynical," he said.

Sassy shrugged.

"Yeah, well you see enough of the horrible things that people do to one another and that happens."

"You sure that's all it is?" Michel asked.

Sassy's first impulse was to say yes, but she stopped herself.

"No, that's not all it is," she admitted. "I'm pissed."

"At who?" Michel asked.

"At Priest," Sassy replied. "I feel like he betrayed me."

"How so?" Michel asked. "It's not like you didn't know who he was."

"I knew what he was *about*," Sassy corrected, "but obviously I didn't know who he really was. I didn't think he'd be capable of doing what he did to Villorisi. It was...inhuman. I thought that maybe he was right about the next generation being more dangerous, but I don't know how anyone could be more dangerous than that."

Michel nodded sympathetically.

"Do you think Granville knows the truth about Priest?" he asked.

"I hope to God not," Sassy replied, "and I hope he rips that fucking terminal right out of the ground."

Chapter 41

"Hello, Miss Jones, Mr. Doucette," Granville Lee said, as Sassy and Michel entered the interrogation room.

"Hello, Granville," Sassy replied.

She and Michel sat on the opposite side of the table.

"So I've got good news and bad news for you," Sassy said.

Lee gave her a wary look, but nodded for her to continue.

"The good news is that we know you didn't kill Deacon and Roland," Sassy said. "In fact, Deacon is apparently still alive, though we don't know where."

"Who was responsible for Roland's death?" Lee asked immediately, his voice rising slightly.

"Angelo Villorisi confessed to it," Michel replied. "He also confessed to trying to kill you."

"But why?" Lee asked. "Why would he kill Roland?"

"Roland was an informant with the FBI," Sassy replied. "Villorisi found out and blackmailed him into kidnapping Deacon. He was trying to frame you for it. He killed Roland to tie up loose ends."

Lee stared at the table, lost in thought for a moment.

"Roland was an informant?" he asked finally, his voice conveying disappointment and sadness rather than anger.

"I'm afraid so," Sassy replied kindly.

Lee continued staring at the table for another few seconds, then looked up at Sassy.

"He was a good man and a good friend, anyway," he said with conviction.

"Yes, I think he was," Michel replied reassuringly.

"So what now?" Lee asked.

"Well, we have a little problem," Sassy replied. "You confessed to killing your father."

"Yes, I did," Lee agreed, nodding, "and I'm willing to accept the consequences."

Sassy studied his face for a few moments before speaking.

"The problem," she said finally, "is that Villorisi confessed to killing Priest, too. And we can't convict two men for the same crime, especially if they weren't working together."

Lee met Sassy's gaze steadily, then sighed resignedly.

"So why did you tell us you killed him?" Sassy asked.

"Because I didn't want it known that he died that way," Lee replied. "I would rather people believe his death was merciful."

"Why?" Michel asked.

"To protect his legacy," Lee replied. "My father was a good man. He did a lot for this city. I didn't want him to be remembered for his association with the other part of his life."

Sassy looked at her hands for a moment, trying to decide how to phrase her next question.

"Do you know why Priest and Villorisi hated one another?" she asked finally.

"I know only that it had to do with a woman, many years ago," Lee replied.

"Well, that's true," Sassy replied, "but that's not the whole story. Your father was married once."

"To whom?" Lee asked with obvious surprise.

"Her name was Cecilia," Sassy replied. "She was Villorisi's girlfriend, but she married your father because he threatened to kill Villorisi if she didn't."

Lee started to speak, but Sassy held up her hand.

"She and Villorisi continued to see one another, and she became pregnant with his child. When Priest found out, he killed Cecilia and the child in the freezer at the Bluehawk Terminal."

"That's impossible," Lee exclaimed loudly. "My father would never do such a thing. He was not that kind of man."

"I'm afraid he was," Sassy replied not unkindly.

"And you have proof?" Lee asked with angry skepticism.

"The police are doing DNA tests to prove that Villorisi was the child's father," Sassy replied.

"But that won't prove that my father had anything to do with their deaths," Lee said.

"That's true," Sassy replied. "We only have Villorisi's word for that."

"And you would trust the word of a man who hated my father?" Lee asked accusatorily. "I thought you were his friend."

He stared at Sassy with cold eyes.

"I thought I was, too," Sassy replied evenly, "but apparently I wasn't. Apparently I didn't know him well at all."

"What about Deacon?" Michel interjected abruptly, realizing that Sassy was at an impasse. "Did you know that he wasn't actually your brother?"

Lee stared at Sassy for a moment longer, then shifted his gaze to Michel.

"Yes, I knew," he said. "He was the son of a friend of my father. When the woman died, my father took him in and later adopted him."

"He's Villorisi's son," Michel said. "Priest knew his mother, and paid her to disappear when he found out she was pregnant. He wanted to hide Deacon from Villorisi. And when Deacon came looking for him, Priest claimed him as his own son."

"Why would he do that?" Lee asked contemptuously. "You seem to believe my father was a monster."

"Look, Granville," Sassy said, her tone conveying frustration, "you told us yourself that Priest was planning to kill Deacon, so why is it so hard for you to believe the rest? He took Deacon in and raised him as his own son, yet he was willing to kill him so that you could take over. Does that sound like the act of a moral, righteous man?"

Lee didn't respond. He lowered his eyes and stared at the table. Sassy could read the hurt on his face.

"I understand that you loved Priest," she said in a gentler tone, "and you're right, he did a lot of good for the city. He helped a lot of people. We're not trying to change that. So far as the rest of the world is concerned, they never need to know what happened. But I think you need to know the truth."

"Why?" Lee replied, without looking up.

His voice sounded small, almost pleading.

"So that you don't carry on his private legacy," Sassy replied. "I think that's why he sheltered you from it. I think that he genuinely wanted things to change, and you were his chance for that to happen."

Lee lifted his eyes toward Sassy and gave a slight nod.

"But I think he was wrong to not tell you the truth," she continued. "I don't think we can change things if we don't understand what happened in the past. In a few minutes, you're going to be a free man. I just hope that you'll learn from Priest's mistakes, and carry on only the better part of his legacy."

"I understand," Lee said. "And thank you for telling me the truth. I'll keep what you said in mind."

"Good," Sassy replied. "And just remember, we *will* be keeping an eye on you."

Lee gave her a small smile.

"Just two last things," Sassy said. "The first is that Deacon is apparently still out there somewhere, so you should be careful. But let the police handle it if he tries anything. Okay?"

Lee nodded.

"And the second thing?" he asked.

"I'd like you to reconsider your father's wishes about preserving the terminal building," Sassy replied. "Given what happened there, regardless of whether Priest was responsible, it would be a monument to a horrendous crime."

She looked at Lee expectantly.

"I will see what can be done," he replied.

*****

"So did you believe what you told him?" Michel asked after Lee had been escorted from the room. "About Priest genuinely wanting change?"

"I want to," Sassy replied, looking at the ground thoughtfully. "I'd like to think that in his old age, he finally realized there was a better way."

"But you're not sure it's true?"

Sassy looked up and shook her head.

"No. Not given the fact that he planned to kill Deacon."

"So why did you say it?"

Sassy sighed.

"Maybe I'm just getting soft in my old age," she replied. "I wanted him to know the truth, but I didn't want to completely destroy his image of his father. I think he should have something good to hold onto."

"I understand that," Michel replied. "And I think it was the right thing to do."

"I hope so," Sassy said. "And I hope to God he's a better man than Priest."

Chapter 42

"What's going on here?" Sassy asked, when she walked into the office and saw Michel and Chance sullenly staring at one another across the room.

It had been three days since Granville Lee had been released from jail.

"Chance wants a job with us, but he's too pigheaded to ask," Michel replied.

"I don't *want* a job," Chance replied. "I just said that if there were a company that needed my help, I'd consider working for them. But he won't admit that you guys need my help."

"So you've decided to stick around?" Sassy asked, surprised.

"I may as well," Chance replied. "It's not like there are tons of opportunities waiting for me back home."

"And you're not worried about slipping back into old habits?" Sassy asked.

"No," Chance replied with certainty. "When I came here the first time, it was all about being gay. I wasn't thinking about what I was going to do or anything like that. I was just trying to escape. All I knew was that I wanted to be the most fabulous gay boy ever."

"Wow, way to set the bar high," Michel replied sarcastically.

"I know," Chance replied, embarrassed. "But I didn't know any better. I was just an ignorant hick. I thought that being gay was all about hanging out in bars, doing drugs, dressing in drag, and whoring around, because that's what I'd seen in movies. In fact, you were probably the first sort of normal gay person I ever met, and I couldn't figure you out at all. I thought you were a closet case."

'Thanks a lot," Michel replied.

"You know what I mean," Chance said with exasperation. "Anyway, now I realize that doesn't have to be my life."

"That's great," Sassy replied sincerely, "and I'm really happy for you, but I'm not sure what we'd need your help with."

"Answering phones, billing clients, ordering lunch, doing research for you," Chance replied.

"Well, I'm sure you could do those things, but we can't afford to pay an assistant yet," Sassy replied.

"You wouldn't need to pay me," Chance replied. "At least not right away. I make enough from my properties to get by. I just need something to keep me busy during the day. Besides, I'm going to be living right upstairs."

"You're what?" Michel exclaimed.

"Oh, didn't I tell you?" Chance replied. "I'm buying the building and converting the upstairs into a condo. So actually, I'm going to be your new landlord."

"You're buying the building?" Sassy asked with disbelief.

"Yeah," Chance replied. "In fact, I'm surprised you guys didn't. It was really cheap. Your rent will more than cover the mortgage. Which is actually another reason why you need me. You guys suck at finance. Look at all the money you put into fixing this place up, and you don't even own it."

"We need to move," Michel said.

"So you used the money Lee gave back to you to buy this building?" Sassy asked. "I thought your great grandfather wanted you to do great things with it."

"I'm only spending part of it for the building," Chance replied quickly. "I'm using the rest to go to school to get an MBA. But first, I've got to take some night classes to get my GED, so I'll be free all day."

Sassy found Chance's enthusiasm charming. She looked at Michel. His expression was noncommittal.

"Okay, it's fine with me if Michel agrees," Sassy said, "but there would have to be rules. You'd need to show up on time, which shouldn't be a problem since you'll be living upstairs, you'd need to be properly dressed, and you'd need to behave in a professional manner, both with our clients and with us."

"Yes, ma'am," Chance replied, sitting up straighter.

"Oh, and I don't care if you do own the building," Sassy added. "This is a place of business. I don't want to see strangers parading out of your place every morning. If you want to do that, then you need to add a separate entrance out back."

"Not a problem," Chance replied.

Then he looked at Michel with an impish smile.

"Unless you consider Ray to be a stranger," he added.

Michel stared at Chance without reacting for a moment, then realized what Chance had said.

"Ray Nassir?" he asked. "You're dating Ray Nassir?"

Chance shrugged.

"Well, I don't know if I'd call it dating yet. So far we've pretty much spent all of our time in bed."

Michel knew that Chance was goading him, and was determined not to let Chance get the best of him this time.

"That's fine," he replied with a smile, then paused a beat. "You're welcome to all my rejects."

"That's funny," Chance replied immediately, as though he'd been expecting the comment, "I could have sworn you were the one who got dumped."

"All right, enough," Sassy interrupted loudly. "Remember the part about acting professionally? That goes for both of you."

"Yes, mom," Chance and Michel replied simultaneously, then broke into conspiratorial laughter.

"Good Lord," Sassy said, shaking her head, "what the hell have I done?"

"By the way," Chance said, "Ray gave me the names of a couple of contractors who could fix up your house. If you'd like, I can set up appointments with them so you can get estimates.

Oh, and you should call your insurance company to get an adjustor out to your place, if you haven't already."

"Okay, that seals the deal," Sassy declared. "As far as I'm concerned, he's hired."

Chance smiled broadly in reply, then looked at Michel.

"Okay," Michel said, "You've got a job. And I think it's cool that you and Ray are dating. He's a great guy."

"Well, thanks," Chance replied. "Maybe we can go on a double date sometime, assuming you and Joel get back together, which I think you should if you have any brains."

Michel thought about it for a moment.

"Yeah, let me get back to you on that one," he said.

Chapter 43

"So far this private eye stuff isn't so bad," Sassy said, as she filled her glass with more chardonnay. "Neither of us got shot or stabbed this time."

She watched a hummingbird make its way from one hibiscus flower to another along the back wall of Michel's patio.

"Excuse me, but I almost had my thumb cut off," Michel replied, holding up his hand so she could see the Bandaid.

"What you got was a paper cut," Sassy replied. "And if you took better care of yourself, an 80-year-old chauffeur wouldn't have been able to beat you up like that."

Michel gave her a mock sneer.

"But you came through when it counted," Sassy continued. "If you hadn't started shooting back at Villorisi's men, they probably would have killed me."

She waited a second, then added, "Of course, if you'd actually hit something, we might have been able to solve the case a lot more quickly."

"Gee, why do I feel like you just complimented me and bitch-slapped me at the same time?" Michel asked.

"I don't know," Sassy replied innocently. "I certainly didn't intend to do both."

She took a sip of wine.

"I have to admit, it wasn't my finest moment," Michel said with a laugh. "I'm pretty sure Dirty Harry never almost puked after he shot at someone."

"Probably not," Sassy replied dryly.

She took another sip of wine, then looked at Michel.

"You know, there's just one thing I still can't figure out," she said, her tone suddenly more serious.

"What's that?"

"When Deacon disappeared, Priest had to have suspected that Villorisi was behind it, and that he'd go after Granville in some way. So why didn't he do something to stop him?"

"Maybe he did," Michel said. "He hired us."

"Oh great, so we were Priest's last big 'fuck you' to Villorisi," Sassy replied with a bitter laugh.

"Well, that's one way to look at it," Michel said.

"What's the other?"

"We kept Granville from going to jail for a crime he didn't commit. Regardless of what Priest did to Villorisi, Granville didn't deserve to be punished for it."

"I suppose," Sassy replied.

"Actually there's one thing I can't figure out either," Michel said, leaning forward in his chair.

"What?"

"Why Roland hid the tape showing him kidnapping Deacon," Michel replied. "When we found the map, you said it was an insurance policy. But it wasn't. If he'd written 'Villorisi' on the glass, that would have made sense, but 'Bluehawk' just told us where he thought they were taking Deacon."

"That's true," Sassy said, sitting forward as well. "Unless Villorisi saw the tape and changed what he'd written on the glass."

"But if Roland had hidden the tapes, he couldn't have seen it," Michel replied.

Sassy frowned and looked down at her glass for a long moment, then her eyes suddenly narrowed and she looked back up at Michel.

"If Roland hid them," she said.

Michel raised his eyebrows quizzically.

"Well, we know that Roland *took* them because we saw him pick up the remote and open the bookcase, then they went blank," Sassy said. "But what if he didn't actually *hide* them? What if he just gave them to Villorisi?"

"And Villorisi planted them?" Michel asked.

"Right," Sassy replied. "Then had whoever shot Roland put the map in his wallet."

Michel considered it for a moment.

"Then it was probably Roland who trashed Deacon's place," he said. "He must have realized what Villorisi was doing and gone after the tapes."

Sassy nodded, though her expression was still troubled.

"But why would Roland bother to write a message on the shower if he knew Villorisi was going to have the tapes?" she asked.

"Maybe Villorisi told him to do it," Michel replied.

"Why?" Sassy asked.

"Because when this whole thing started, Villorisi couldn't have known that Priest was going to hire us," Michel replied. "And he sure as hell didn't know that I was going to go snooping around the Bluehawk because of Chance. He had to make sure that whoever found the tapes was going to connect Granville to the Bluehawk."

Sassy began tapping her fingers absently on the left arm of her chair, and her gaze grew distant for a few moments. Then she sat up straighter.

"Suppose you weren't wrong about Deacon being in that SUV?" she asked. "What if he really was there, and he actually killed Priest?"

"And Villorisi's trying to take the rap?" Michel asked.

"Yeah," Sassy replied. "Didn't it seem a little odd how easily Kimora Tucker turned against Villorisi?"

"No odder than the way Villorisi suddenly decided to admit to everything," Michel replied in a tone that made it clear they were both on the same page.

"Exactly," Sassy said. "Suppose Villorisi was trying to set Granville up, but Deacon got impatient and decided to take matters into his own hands."

"Then Villorisi decided to take the fall. He told Tucker, and maybe even his FBI contact, to come clean."

"Right," Sassy agreed. "Granville didn't end up in jail, but neither did Deacon, and Villorisi knows he's going to die soon, so he won't serve time. It's like a last gift to Deacon. And in a way, he finally got the best of Priest."

"Okay," Michel said, "so then where's Deacon now?"

"Well, if you were in hiding, when would you come out?"

"When I thought I was safe."

"I'm thinking that Deacon's probably feeling pretty safe right now," Sassy said.

"You think he's back home?" Michel asked.

"Well, I've still got the key," Sassy replied.

Chapter 44

There appeared to be a dim, shimmering glow coming through the stone railing that surrounded the third floor patio of Deacon Lee's house.

"Looks like we might be in luck," Sassy said.

"If you consider breaking into the house of a killer while he's home to be luck," Michel replied dryly.

"I mean the security cameras," Sassy said. "They're not on. See. No glowing red lights."

"That's odd, don't you think?" Michel asked.

"Not if he doesn't think he needs them anymore."

They watched the house in silence for another minute.

"You ready?" Sassy asked finally.

"You're sure you don't want to call the Captain about this?" Michel asked. "I mean, you're one who said we shouldn't be fucking around with police business."

Sassy looked at him for a moment, then shook her head.

"This is just a social call," she replied with exaggerated innocence.

"Uh huh," Michel replied. "Whatever helps you sleep."

"So are you ready, or what?" Sassy asked impatiently.

Michel took one last look at the house and sighed.

"Yeah, I'm ready," he said.

They crossed the street quickly and Sassy unlocked the gate. As they slipped inside, they noticed the black Cadillac Escalade parked by the right side of the house.

"That wasn't here before," Sassy whispered.

"Hmmm, looks sort of familiar," Michel replied sarcastically. "Oh wait, that's right, but the last time we saw it there were people shooting at us from the windows."

They crossed to the door and Sassy pulled her gun.

"Just a social call, huh?" Michel deadpanned.

"Be quiet and get your gun out," Sassy whispered, giving him a chastening look.

She unlocked the front door and stepped to the left side, while Michel took up a position on the right. Sassy pushed the door with her left hand and it swung silently open. They waited three beats, then simultaneously stepped into the doorway, their guns held out in front of them. In the dim light from the street, they could see a dozen suitcases stacked near the base of the stairs.

"Looks like someone's going on a trip," Michel whispered.

"No surprise there," Sassy replied.

They stepped into the foyer. Sassy immediately moved to check the room on the left, while Michel crossed to check the one on the right. Then Sassy motioned Michel down the hall to the kitchen. While she waited for him to return, she quietly closed the front door and walked to the stairs. She leaned in and looked up toward the third floor. She could see what looked like candlelight dancing on the walls and railing.

After a few seconds Michel came back and gave her a thumbs up. Sassy nodded and started up the stairs.

*****

The door to Deacon's bedroom was open, and they could hear someone moving around inside. Sassy took a deep breath, then slowly peered around the door frame. The room had been returned to the state in which she'd first seen it, though now it was lit by a dozen squat white candles set on the nightstands and top of the armoire. In the flickering light, she could see a large black suitcase open on the neatly made bed.

288

Suddenly Kimora Tucker walked into the room from the side hallway, carrying an armload of sweaters. She walked to the bed and began placing them neatly in the suitcase.

"Hi, Kimora," Sassy said in a low voice, as she stepped into the room, her gun in front of her. "You're looking much better than the last time I saw you."

Tucker started, and turned slowly toward her.

"Did you say something, honey?" a deep male voice asked from the hallway.

Sassy held the index finger of her left hand to her lips as she took another step into the room, followed by Michel. Tucker took a quick, nervous look toward the bathroom, then looked back at Sassy and Michel. Her expression conveyed a mixture of fear and lost hope.

"What's wrong, honey?" the male voice said, closer and clearer now.

"Deacon, it's Sassy Jones and Michel Doucette," Sassy said. "We just want to talk with you."

Tucker looked back toward the hallway for a moment, then Deacon Lee stepped stiffly into the room, his hands held up in front of him with the fingers spread.

He was dressed in the same paisley robe he'd been wearing in the video of his "kidnapping." He was smaller than Sassy had remembered, and she was struck by how gentle his eyes looked.

"Just want to talk, eh?" he said, nodding toward Sassy's gun.

"I'll make a deal with you," Sassy replied. "You put the gun you've got behind your back on the nightstand, and we'll put our guns down."

Deacon gave her an appreciative smile.

"How'd you know I had a gun?" he asked, as he reached slowly behind his back with his left hand and pulled a silver handgun from the belt of his robe.

"The way you were walking like you had a stick up your ass," Sassy replied, as Deacon walked to the nightstand and placed the gun down gently.

Then he walked to Tucker and wrapped his left arm around her protectively. Sassy and Michel lowered their guns.

"So what's this all about?" Deacon asked.

His tone was smooth and reasonable.

"Like I said, we just want to talk," Sassy replied.

"What's with all the candles?" Michel asked. "A little romantic packing?"

"I had the electricity turned off," Deacon replied. "We're going out of town for a while."

"Obviously," Sassy replied. "Where to?"

Deacon smiled in a way that made it clear he had no intention of answering.

"So what did you want to talk to me about?" he asked instead.

"Well, for one thing, that 9mm on the nightstand," Michel said. "I'm betting if we ran it through ballistics, we'd find out it's a match to the gun that shot Granville Lee."

Deacon smiled again and shook his head.

"You're talking like you're still cops," he said.

"Old habit," Michel replied.

"Well, I think you're mistaken," Deacon said.

"Maybe," Sassy replied. "But I bet we could find one in your safe room that's a match."

She took the remote controller out of her jacket pocket and held it up.

"You think that's the only one of those I've got?" Deacon asked with an amused smile.

Sassy and Michel both understood the implication. The gun that had been used to shoot Granville Lee was long gone.

"Besides," Deacon said, "my father already admitted to shooting Granville."

"And killing Priest," Michel added.

Deacon nodded.

"And you're going to let him take the fall?" Sassy asked.

Deacon stared at her appraisingly for a moment.

"Why would I have wanted to kill Granville?" he asked finally.

"You wouldn't, if you knew the truth," Sassy replied.

Deacon gave her a curious look.

"What truth?"

"The truth that Granville never knew about what happened between your father and Priest," Sassy replied. "He didn't know that Priest killed his wife and your father's son. He didn't know that you were Villorisi's son."

Deacon didn't say anything, but it was clear from the look in his eyes that he was surprised.

"We just thought you'd want to know that in case you had any ideas about finishing what you started," Michel said.

Deacon took a deep breath and sighed wearily.

"Would it be all right if we sat down?" he asked, gesturing toward the bed. "We've been packing all day. I promise there are no guns hidden under the pillows."

"Okay," Sassy replied.

Tucker scooted up onto the bed in a way that reminded Sassy of a little girl. Deacon sat on the edge next to her, his left arm resting on her knees.

"I noticed that you didn't ask us why you'd want to kill Priest," Michel said.

For a moment, anger flared in Deacon's eyes, then he regained his composure.

"I'd have plenty of reasons to kill Priest," he said.

"Any we don't already know about?" Sassy asked.

Deacon stared at her for a moment.

"I'm not the monster you think I am," he said in a quiet voice. "Priest Lee was the monster. Deacon Lee was just his creation."

"Meaning what?" Sassy asked.

"Do you know why I had to live like this?" Deacon asked. "Because Priest made me a target."

"How so?" Michel asked.

"I never did the things that people think I did," Deacon said with a hint of helplessness. "Priest did them. But he made people believe it was me."

"Why?" Michel asked.

"At first, I thought he wanted people to fear me so that I'd have respect when I took over," Deacon replied sadly. "Then I realized he was using me."

"Using you how?" Sassy asked.

"So long as the fearsome Deacon Lee was around, no one would dare touch Priest," Deacon replied. "And since everyone thought I was responsible for all the killings, he could keep his precious reputation relatively clean. I also think he was hoping that eventually someone would kill me."

"So you're saying that Priest used you as his boogeyman?" Michel asked skeptically.

Deacon nodded.

"There never was a Deacon Lee," he said. "I had his name, but the rest was a fictional character Priest created to take responsibility for all the things that *he* did. But now Deacon Lee is dead. I'm Deacon Villorisi."

Sassy and Michel exchanged surprised looks.

"Look, Deacon, I'm not saying I don't believe you," Sassy said, "because if we've learned anything over the last few weeks, it's that Priest was capable of some horrible things. But how did he pull it off? Witnesses said they saw you commit some of the murders."

"And then they also said they didn't," Deacon replied. "I imagine he paid them to say they saw me, then paid them some more to change their minds. He couldn't afford to have me ever stand trial."

"Because you might tell the truth?" Michel asked.

Deacon shrugged as though the answer were obvious.

"And none of Priest's people knew the truth?" Sassy asked.

"Maybe some did," Deacon replied. "I don't know. Priest kept me isolated from them."

"And what about Villorisi?" Michel asked. "Did he realize what was happening?"

"He had his suspicions," Deacon replied, looking down at the floor.

"So why didn't he reach out to you earlier?" Sassy asked. "If he suspected, he had to have been worried about you."

Deacon looked at the floor for a moment longer, then looked up at Sassy. His eyes were glassy.

"Because he was afraid," he said finally.

"Afraid of what?" Michel asked.

"Priest Lee took almost everything from my father," Deacon replied. "I think he was afraid that if he contacted me or tried to take any action, Priest would take the rest. But now my father has nothing left to lose. His wife is gone, and he'll be gone soon, too."

"But he still had you to lose," Sassy said.

Deacon nodded.

"So that's what finally made him take action," Sassy said. "He realized that Priest was planning to kill you."

Deacon nodded again.

"So then you really didn't kill Priest?"Michel asked.

Deacon seemed to consider how to respond for a moment, then he shook his head slowly.

"No, of course not," he replied. "My father killed him."

He looked at Kimora Tucker and smiled gently. She returned the smile, and laced the fingers of her right hand over Deacon's left.

"So now that Deacon Lee is gone, what's next for Deacon Villorisi?" Sassy asked.

Deacon looked back at her.

"I'm not sure," he said. "We're going to get married, then travel for a while. Maybe we'll settle down someplace in a few months and start a family."

"Congratulations," Sassy said. "So you won't be coming back here?"

"I'll be back to see my father," Deacon replied, "but there's nothing here for us anymore. It's time to move on."

Sassy nodded.

"And what about Granville Lee?" she asked.

Deacon met her gaze evenly.

"I have no issues with Granville," he replied. "He's not responsible for his father's actions."

"That's good to hear," Sassy replied. "I'll be sure to let him know."

They were silent for a few moments, then Deacon stood up.

"If you wouldn't mind," he said, "we need to finish packing. We're leaving early tomorrow morning."

"Of course," Sassy replied.

She walked to the bed and leaned down to give Tucker a quick hug.

"You take care of him," she said, nodding toward Deacon. "I think you've got yourself a good man."

"I do," Tucker replied with a smile.

Sassy and Michel shook Deacon's hand, then started for the door. Suddenly Sassy stopped and turned back.

"I do have one other question for you," she said.

"What's that?" Deacon replied.

"What are you planning to do with this house?"

Deacon shrugged.

"I'm not sure yet. Why?"

"Well, because my house has a lot of bullet holes in it," Sassy replied, "and right now I'm staying with my partner here until it's fixed. But I wouldn't mind a little more space. Especially space with a jacuzzi and a big walk-in closet."

Deacon smiled at her.

"Seeing as you already have the key," he said, "I suppose you may as well."

*****

"You don't see a conflict of interest in living in Deacon's house?" Michel asked when they were back in the car.

"What conflict?" Sassy asked with mock affront. "Deacon is innocent. Besides, I'm just housesitting for him."

"Uh huh," Michel replied dubiously.

"You're just jealous because I'm going to have a big old house all to myself," Sassy said.

"Yeah, a big old empty house with no furniture," Michel replied.

"Oh, don't worry about that," Sassy said. "We'll move some of my stuff over there. Make it nice and comfortable."

"*We?*" Michel asked.

"Yeah, me and Chance," Sassy replied. "Now that he's working for us, we've got to keep him busy."

"I thought he was supposed to be doing work related to our *business*," Michel said, shooting Sassy a sideways glance.

"It *is* related to our business," Sassy replied.

"How's that?" Michel asked.

Sassy crossed her arms and gave him an imperious look.

"Well, you can't expect me to do my best work sleeping on that tiny little bed in your guest room, can you?" she asked. "After all, I'm a queen. I need to sleep in the bed of a king."

"I thought I was the queen," Michel replied.

"Well, you are," Sassy replied, "but you're the kind of queen who'll sleep in pretty much anyone's bed."

Chapter 45

"So you feeling okay with everything?" Michel asked an hour later, back on his patio.

Sassy thought about it for a moment.

"On balance, yes," she said finally. "I still think Deacon may killed Priest and tried to kill Granville, but if Villorisi wants to take the fall, I guess I'm all right with that."

"You realize that if we were still cops you wouldn't be saying that," Michel said.

"Maybe," Sassy agreed, "but fortunately we're not. I don't think Deacon's going to be a danger to anyone else, and I guess I feel like Villorisi's suffered enough. He doesn't need to see his son dragged off to prison, too. And this way, with people thinking he killed Priest, maybe he finally gets a little dignity."

Michel nodded thoughtfully and took a long, slow drag on his cigarette. They both watched the smoke swirl upward into the warm evening air.

"You hear from Joel?" Sassy asked after a minute.

"Yeah, he's going to be there at least another month," Michel replied. "His grandfather's out of the hospital, but it's going to be a while before he's back on his feet."

"You give any thought to what you're going to tell him when he gets back?"

"Some. But I still haven't made up my mind yet."

"Why not?" Sassy asked.

"Because I've been too busy sleeping around, of course," Michel replied, rolling his eyes like an exasperated teenager.

Sassy leaned forward and gave him a castigating look.

"Just kidding," he said quickly. "I haven't been with anyone since Ray."

"But you're still not sure about Joel?"

"Yes and no," Michel replied. "I'm sure it's something I want to do, but I have no idea how I can make him feel like I need him."

"*Do* you need him?" Sassy asked.

Michel leaned back in his chair and took a sip of Jack Daniels as he considered it.

"How about this?" he offered. "I want to need him, but I'm not sure if I actually do yet."

"Well, it sounds honest," Sassy said, "but I think you're going to have to figure out the last part before he gets back."

"Yeah, I know," Michel replied.

They sat in comfortable silence for another few minutes, then Sassy leaned forward in her chair and turned to Michel. Her brow was knitted with concern.

"There's one other thing I'm wondering about," she said in a troubled tone.

"What now?" Michel replied, his tone suddenly serious, too.

Sassy frowned for a moment, then broke into a sly smile.

"Okay, kill, marry, or fuck..."

"No way," Michel interrupted. "I'm not playing that game with you anymore."

"Why not?" Sassy asked imploringly.

"Because last time you made me choose between Dom DeLuise, Paul Prudhomme, and Sergeant Schultz from 'Hogan's Heroes'."

"So?" Sassy replied. "They're all nice guys."

"Yeah, but would you want to see any of them naked?" Michel asked.

"Okay," Sassy replied. "How about if I promise to give you at least one decent choice each time?"

Michel thought about it for a second, then nodded.

"Okay, go ahead."

"All right," Sassy said eagerly. "This one is a classic. Dracula, the Wolfman, and the Mummy."

Michel gave it a moment of serious consideration.

"Okay, I'd definitely kill the Mummy, because he'd smell bad and he'd be leaving dust and little pieces of bandage all over the house, plus he's not much of a conversationalist. Then I'd fuck Dracula because he's hot, and marry the Wolfman."

"Why the Wolfman?" Sassy asked.

"Mainly because I'd get the bed to myself every time there was a full moon."

Sassy nodded.

"Good point, and I agree with you about the Mummy, but I think I'd fuck the Wolfman and marry Dracula," she said. "Of course, that would depend on what happens with Wolfie's private parts when he transforms. If he gets one of those little pink Rover dicks, then I'm not having it."

"And why marry Dracula?"

"Because he could turn me into a vampire and we could spend eternity together," Sassy replied.

"And you think that would be a good thing?"

"You don't?" Sassy replied.

Michel fixed her with a deadpan look.

"Neither one of us can commit to a relationship for this lifetime. Do you really think we'd be ready for an eternity?"

Sassy smiled.

"No, I suppose not. Okay, your turn."

Michel put his drink down and rubbed his hands together theatrically, like a villain hatching a plot in an old movie.

"Okay, Mama Cass, Janis Joplin, Dusty Springfield."

Sassy gave him an arch look.

"You know I already got rid of those Birkenstocks, don't you?" she asked.

"I know," Michel replied. "It's just theoretical. Come on, you just asked me about three fictional monsters."

Sassy stared at him for a moment, then sighed. "Fine," she said, "but just you wait."

Available Fall 2011
from

BLUE'S BAYOU

A New Michel Doucette
& Sassy Jones Novel

DAVID LENNON

Chapter 1

Verle Doucette knew he was being stalked. Though he hadn't seen anything moving in almost ten minutes, he could hear the occasional snap of a twig or rustling of leaves through the dense cypress and tupelo forest on his right. The creature was keeping its distance, but always staying abreast of him.

He could see a clearing ahead in the moonlight and stopped. He knew that was where it would strike, once he was in the open. He closed his eyes and listened. There was a faint rustling just ahead on his right, much closer than before. He took a deep breath and slowly began moving forward again, his senses fully alert.

As he reached the edge of the clearing, he stopped again, his eyes searching the tangle of vegetation along the right perimeter. He couldn't see anything moving. He cocked his head and listened. He couldn't hear anything except the steady buzzing of mosquitos and chirping of grasshoppers. He realized he was just going to have to trust his instincts.

He paused another second to ready himself, then jumped into the clearing, landing in a sumo wrestler's crouch in the muddy water, facing to the right.

"Ha," he yelled, ready for the creature to bound out of the darkness at him.

Nothing happened. He slowly straightened up and stared curiously into the forest. A mosquito hovered close to his nose and he absently swatted it away with his left hand.

Suddenly he heard a low growl behind him. He slowly

turned and saw the dog, its head and chest close to the water and its hind quarters raised, ready to pounce. Before he could react, it lunged forward and jumped up, its muddy front paws hitting him hard in the chest and causing him to stagger back a foot. Then the dog's face moved closer and its long tongue shot out and began to bathe his face.

Verle began to laugh.

"Okay, you got me," he said. "You're the best hunter in the whole wide swamp, Blue."

The dog continued enthusiastically licking his face for another few seconds, her long, bushy tail furiously brushing the surface of the water as Verle rubbed the thick damp scruff of her neck. Then suddenly she stopped and dropped her front legs almost silently into the dark water. Her nose began to pulsate quickly as she stared into the blackness farther up the trail. Then she bounded away.

"Wait," Verle called as he saw the dog disappear into the night.

Despite the fact that Blue had lived almost her entire life in the Atchafalaya Basin and was naturally cautious, Verle still worried about her. Though she'd proven herself more than capable of handling herself with the smaller predators that lived in the swamps and bayous, at forty-five pounds she was no match for the Florida Panthers and Louisiana Black Bears that were occasionally spotted there.

He unshouldered his shotgun and started after her, his heavy rubber boots slogging through the muddy water. Up ahead, he heard Blue begin to bark and broke into an ungainly run.

"Come here, girl," he called, trying to sound authoritative despite his anxiety and the immediate raggedness of his breathing. "Come on back."

In response, the urgency of the dog's barking increased. Verle stopped for a moment and concentrated. He knew from years of experience that the still, thick waters of the swamp could play tricks with sound. He turned to his left and began running again.

Twenty yards ahead, a thick curtain of Spanish moss hung from the branches of a massive live oak, its lowest tendrils nearly touching the water. Blue's barking was clearer and sharper now.

Verle quickened his pace, despite the stabbing pain that had begun along the lower right side of his rib cage.

"I'm coming, girl," he managed to call through heavy, labored breaths.

As he reached the moss, he ducked below it, then froze, still in a crouching position. Fifteen feet away, a nude woman lay on a moss-covered hummock at the base of a tree. Blue stood beside her, now silently staring at him.

Verle slowly straightened up and took a few hesitant steps. He could hear his heart beating quickly and loudly in his ears.

"Hello?" he said reflexively, although he already knew the woman wouldn't respond.

If Blue's barking hadn't stirred her, his own timid greeting certainly wouldn't.

He stopped again, suddenly unsure that he wasn't dreaming. He'd seen this woman before, lying in that exact position: on her back with her pelvis and legs twisted toward him, her right arm out to her side with the hand resting just above the water, and her left arm draped languidly over her eyes and forehead. It was all so familiar.

Then he remembered where he had seen her before. It was in a painting called "Repos" by Wojciech Gerson that he'd seen at the National Museum in Warsaw many years ago.

"Okay," he said, taking a calming breath. "I'm not losing my mind."

Blue stared at him quizzically.

"It's all right, girl," he said reassuringly as he waded forward.

As he reached the hummock, he scratched Blue behind her right ear for a moment, then placed the back of his right hand

3

against the side of the woman's neck. Her skin was cool and damp. Verle slowly withdrew his hand and searched the shadows around them. He couldn't see anyone else.

"I'm sorry," he said to the woman's body.

He stood staring at her for a few minutes as he considered what to do. He knew that if the woman had been killed, he should leave her there and hike the mile back to his truck to radio the police so that they could investigate the scene, but he also knew that before very long the inhabitants of the swamp would find her and there might be nothing left to investigate. Though the alligators had all moved into deeper water for the winter, there were still plenty of carnivores left who would welcome a free meal.

"Looks like we're going to have to carry her out of here," he said to Blue. "But I want you to stay close by me. You can't go running off, okay?"

Blue tilted her head and began to wag her tail. Then she began trotting further into the woods to their right.

"No, not that way," Verle called.

Blue stopped and cocked her head at him.

"This way," Verle said, pointing to his left.

Blue hesitated for a moment, then came back and started in the direction he'd indicated.

"Good girl," Verle said.

*****

Verle was slick with perspiration and his heart was thumping wildly in his chest. He'd kept his focus by counting the number of mosquitos who'd bitten him over the last hour.

He'd had to stop four times to rest, and each time the exertion of lifting the woman back onto his shoulders had become more difficult. He hoped he could make it back to the road without having to stop again, because he wasn't sure he could manage it one more time.

In the distance he thought he saw a brief flash of light through the trees. He stared at the spot and waited. The light flashed again.

"Hey! Over here!" he called out. "I need some help."

The light turned in his direction and began to move closer.

Verle let out a deep sigh and dropped to his knees. He lowered his right shoulder and gently placed the woman's body on the ground.

"It's going to be okay," he said in a hoarse whisper.

The light was moving quickly toward them now. Verle could see it bouncing up and down with each step of the person carrying it.

"Right here," Verle called out.

Suddenly the fur on Blue's back rose into a pointed tuft, and her tail lifted into the air. She let out a deep, low growl.

"It's okay, girl," Verle said. "They're going to help us."

Then the light was on Verle's face, momentarily blinding him. He moved his right hand in front of his eyes to shield them, and looked between the fingers. He could just make out the shape of a man wearing a wide, flat-brimmed hat. The man had a pistol pointed at him.

"Don't move!" the man called out.

"Okay, officer," Verle replied quickly, his weariness suddenly gone as adrenaline coursed through his body.

"Now I want you to slowly take that shotgun off your shoulder and place it on the ground in front of you," the state trooper said.

From the tone of his voice, Verle could tell that trooper was both young and nervous. He heard Blue emit another growl.

"Lay down," he said tersely.

Out of the corner of his eye, he could see the dog settle on the ground next to the woman's body.

He reached over his right shoulder with his left hand and grabbed the muzzle of the shotgun, then slowly slid the strap off his shoulder and brought the rifle out in front of his body. He

5

lowered it until the butt was resting on the ground, then gently laid it down. Then he straightened up and clasped his hands behind his head.

"Okay," he said in a calm voice. "Now just do me a favor and lower your gun. My dog gets very protective of me, and I don't want either of you getting hurt."

Made in the USA
Lexington, KY
07 September 2011